BELOW THE RIM

A NOVEL

DAWSON RIVERA

Ebook ISBN: 979-8-9857306-3-0
Paperback ISBN: 979-8-9857306-4-7
Hardcover ISBN: 979-8-9857306-5-4

"Don't aim to be the best. Aim to be the only."

—Kevin Kelly

CHAPTER 1

The ball rolls off the rim. Arms compete for the first touch of it. The tallest girl wins and throws a textbook outlet pass to her point guard who charges up the floor like she's on fire. She dishes it to her teammate on the wing who nearly takes off for the hoop before the ball reaches her hands. Once there, she changes directions in the air to avoid contact and lays the ball in the hoop with a finger roll. On the sideline, a coach has his arms crossed and thinks to himself, *This is as easy as taking candy from Grandma.* No cheers ring out. There's no crowd on hand. It's quiet except for the sounds of squeaky shoes and a basketball bouncing.

The three girls are the returning starters for the Hoover High School girls' basketball team. They play quickly. Not fast, but in a hurry, like they are getting away with something good and they need to get in enough trips up and down the court before the ball is taken away from them. Bentley Kramer is the tough-nosed, fiery point guard, best known by her teammates for not taking any crap. She'll usually be the shortest one on the court and the one who is the first to stand up against or for someone. Being a senior she is well aware this is her last go of it. Zoey "Zo" Jones, a junior, is their smooth shooting guard. Those who watch her will tell you there isn't a shot she doesn't like, and she often chooses the one where the degree-of-difficulty meter disappears. Sasha Hudson, a junior, is the tall one. She made her presence felt in the lane last year intimidating teams with her size; this year she has primed herself to be more productive.

The head coach is Mack. This is year number nineteen at the helm. Mack knows his three returning starters are the types of players who don't come around very often, if ever, let alone all at once. This is the best chance he'll have at winning a state championship, and he is feeling elated even if he doesn't look like it. He's a serious man because he likes order and getting things done. Mack is a middle school teacher and most students fear him. To his family, the perception of him isn't quite accurate. They know him differently. So do many of his peers who see him as personable. Mack has never cared much about what other people think of him. His focus is on doing his job. Giving his all to his team and the game of basketball. However you feel about the varsity girls' coach, and it's varied, you can't say he isn't dedicated to his position. Mack puts his whole heart into coaching basketball.

Their team is the Hoover Knights. They are coming into the season with unfinished business on their minds. After losing in the state championship game the previous season, the Knights are focused on another shot at the Iowa class 2A title. Expectations are sky high in Hoover after the team went from unranked to taking the state tournament by storm—knocking off the #1 team and making it all the way to the championship game where their magical run ended with a lopsided loss.

The town they live in is Hoover, Iowa. There is nothing mystical about living in Hoover. You know what you're getting. Four seasons. It's green, flat, and farm fields are everywhere. As early as October you can feel winter coming. These three girls could feel the basketball season approaching even earlier. Now that it's November and both have arrived it feels like the town's heart is finally beating again. Hoover is a small town, and small towns are predictable. One thing that isn't this year is what their girls' basketball team will do for an encore. Can they reach the state tournament again? Do they have what it takes to win the title? It's a debate that will rage all the way to March. That's what sports will do to a small community. It will bring people together, tear them apart, and bring them back together again. It can give a town purpose. Hope. At the very least something to talk about.

The Knights are only scrimmaging teams today. It's a way for them to get a taste of real competition while they await their first game of the season. Practice officially started a week ago, and Mack is happy with how they look. The three returners are oozing with confidence and restless energy wanting to get to the first official game of the year. Their mood is rubbing off on their teammates. A second senior will start for the Knights, Krista Hanson, who was the first player off the bench a year ago in limited action. Becoming a starter has her feeling herself, and she is ready to be on stage. Front and center. Krista's favorite phrase has become "I'm eighteen years old" and that is her go-to answer for most things these days, be it about basketball, schoolwork, or life in general. The fifth starter will be sophomore guard Hayley Bell. She sat on the varsity bench her freshman year only seeing the floor for the end-of-game garbage minutes. Her experience on the JV team is enough to secure a spot in the starting lineup. Hayley is a smaller guard who is a scrappy defender with a decent outside shot.

The Knight's take the floor for the last scrimmage of the day. They are unfamiliar with the team they match up to face. The girls don't think much of the group that doesn't live around here. The team wears maroon, and soon the Knights will be sick of seeing that color. When the game starts they notice how tall, strong, and fast they are. They press the Knights as soon as the ball is inbounded. Bentley and Zo never flinch at a full-court press. It's welcomed. They like the challenge. Today makes them rethink that stance. They get frustrated. It doesn't help that Hayley has little experience playing against this kind of pressure. The other team can tell and zone in on forcing her to give them the ball. The Knights look puzzled by the situation they are in. Who is this team?

Mack bobs his head up and down as he watches his team get outplayed. While he wanted his team to fare a little better, he is still pleased by the outcome. The maroon team traveled two and half hours from Nebraska to participate in the day of scrimmages. They are ranked in the top ten in the largest class in their state. Mack knows how good they are because his cousin coaches their boys' team. Mack knows *his* players too; they need a little dose of reality and a reason to keep a chip on their shoulders. They have areas to improve, and just because they made it to state a season ago doesn't mean anything. Mack doesn't want them getting too comfortable and overconfident. He needs to see the same determined drive he saw in their eyes last year.

The players look winded and frustrated when they walk to the sidelines after a break in the action. They catch their breath. They blame their play on already exerting their energy in the previous games that day. It isn't fair; they played right before this and the girls in maroon didn't. Mack lets them stew. All day he has stood back like a spectator.

Observing. He wanted to see how his team would act and let them have space to play their way. Mack watches intently as the Knights take the court and try to charge back at their opponent. His big three are noticeably sharper, and the team starts playing with an edge. The way they did during their fantastic run that led them through a tough playoff stretch all the way to the state championship a season ago.

While the Knights play better, there is no catching up to the girls in maroon and they get outplayed. The starters make their way to the side of the court. They grab water bottles and slide themselves down the wall to a sitting position. Nobody speaks. You can hear huffs and puffs in between sucks of water. Knowing this is the last scrimmage of the day, Bentley hastily gets up, grabs her slides and keys off the ground, then exits the gym without looking back.

Mack walks over to Monty, his assistant coach, who has sat the bench next to him all but two of his previous eighteen seasons. Monty is busy scribbling notes on his clipboard. When he looks up he lets out a whistle and says, "Brutal."

Mack presses his lips together. "Well, they just went up against a really outstanding team."

"I will say we played better at the end," Monty says. "But by golly, we have a lot to work on."

Mack nods and says, "Well, the good news is we won't face that team this season, and I think they just gave our girls a much needed kick in the pants."

Both coaches know everyone wants a championship around here. Anything less? Well, the team has already experienced that. The fans have already seen it. There is *one* goal. Anything less will be a disappointment. One coach has already booked the team's hotel for state. One thinks this is all a little too much to put on the shoulders of high school kids.

This season is going to be something. Fans won't soon forget it. The players will remember it for the rest of their lives. However you feel about expectations, winning and losing, one thing can't be denied: this game these girls play matters.

CHAPTER 2

It's not a secret the three returning starters are a little more eager than the rest of their teammates for the season to start. Bentley has a countdown running on her phone that keeps track of the number of days until their first game. She set it up five months ago. Pinned to the door of her bedroom is the score from their championship defeat. Both reminders to not forget what they lost and to keep focused on where they are going. For Zo, a true gym rat, the wait to get back on the court after their season ended last March has been excruciating. Zo's desire ever since she first touched a basketball is a chance to play. Anytime. Always. Last Saturday when Mack brought in the four teams for a day of scrimmaging, Zo was up at 4:00 a.m., too hyped up to sleep. Sasha is happy the season is here too; even so, she has waited more patiently for basketball to approach. Unlike her two teammates, who are guards, and always seem to be in continuous motion, Sasha is low-key. She never gets too high or too low. Sasha learned a lot from their state appearance last year. Most noticeably was a need to get stronger and more mobile. She spent hours practicing her post moves and improving her footwork. Over and over. Sasha doesn't need reminders flashing in her face and isn't losing sleep excited. She is simply prepared. Ready.

On Friday when the bell rings to end the school day, every Hoover girls' basketball player makes their way to the locker room to get ready for practice with more enthusiasm than usual. It's loud and celebratory. After the beat-down Hoover received at the scrimmage, the team had a productive week of practice. Everyone is excited that after today hard practices will ease up and the fun of games will begin.

For the players, the locker room is their tree house. A place that is all their own. A place they are free to be themselves. None of the girls chose each other. They chose basketball, and this game banded this group together. School is required; everyone must put in their time before they are released into the wild. For this group, the basketball season gives them something meaningful to do. They get to be basketball players while they walk through four years of high school. Maybe that's not much in other schools, but they made it so here at Hoover High. Together they rose to this position faster than people thought they could. The players razz each other freely because they remember when not one of them had made any kind of mark at all on the world around them. They know what they earned is real and where they want to get can't be reached without one another. Winning can automatically give a team swag and a clear purpose. Hoover has it.

Jemma Reeves, the freshman coach, looks around the locker room. She tolerates the loudness of their voices and the thumping bass of their favorite songs blaring through the small speaker in the middle of the floor. Her team isn't even in here; they are getting ready to practice in the junior high gym. Jemma, a middle school teacher and Zo's aunt, is counted upon to read the temperature of the team. To manage sensitive matters, Mack either doesn't want to attempt to handle or knows better than to think he can.

Jemma walks over to Krista who is still getting her practice gear on. "Hey, Mack needs me to talk to you about something."

The girls next to Krista playfully tease her as if she's in big trouble.

"What now?"

Jemma lowers her voice to be discreet. "Do you want to do this in the office?"

"Whatever Mack has to say these guys can hear it." Krista waves her hand out toward her teammates, a wicked grin on her face. "You know you can tell Mack if he has something to say he can just say it to my face."

The girls giggle.

"Yeah, why don't you go tell him that, Jemmers," Sasha says. "Tell us how that goes over."

Jemma gives Sasha an eye roll before directing her attention back to Krista. "Okay. So Mack is sick of 'everyone and their mom' talking to him about you flying around town on your 'darn' scooter. He said if he hears it one more time he doesn't know what he'll do."

Krista smiles and spreads her hands and fingers out, shaking them toward Jemma, pretending to be scared while her teammates explode into laughter. The bunch talks loudly over each other discussing the famous scooter Krista bought this past summer. She would cruise into Hoover from her house out in the country, visiting friends and giving out rides even with no real space for a passenger while beeping the high-pitched horn everywhere she went.

Krista slips her reversible practice jersey over her T-shirt and turns to Bentley, Sasha, and Zo who are near and says, "I'll pop a wheelie coming into Hoover with my *swimsuit* on *tomorrow* if I want. I'm eighteen years old yo."

Jemma knows Krista is playing to her audience so she walks back over to the office doorway and waits for them to calm down. When there is an opening she says, "I'll let Mack know you received the message, or do you want to discuss it directly with him?"

Krista throws her hands up because it's always like this in her eyes. Every little thing is scrutinized. "Look, it was crazy nice out, that's why I brought my rocket out last weekend. A little throwback to summer. One last ride. A blizzard is coming. There will be snow on the ground, probably for months. You really think I am going to ride it in that weather? Have Big John throw some snow tires on that bad boy. You can tell Mack the scooter is done. For now. The only thing people will see Krista driving for a while is my hooptie, The Slick Ick."

Jemma rolls her eyes again. Krista drives a red beat-up Buick station wagon, and on the back a couple letters are missing displaying only the letters **i-c-k**. Two deep dips on separate roads in town provide Krista with a way to get The Slick Ick airborne. Jemma knows this because Zo has mentioned how much air they get and how it's the greatest thing ever. When you live in a small town you have to create your own adventure. While most kids in Hoover have never been on a big time roller coaster before, a select few have been passengers in Krista's car and that's as close as they will get to a thrill ride.

"Mack will be pleased to know the scooter isn't being winterized." Jemma turns to go into the office. Because she knows both Mack and Krista well, she pauses. "Seriously though, don't be funny, Krista, and bring that thing into town again during the season. Mack will have a conniption fit."

Krista bounces two fingers off her eyebrow giving Jemma a salute. "You got it, Jemmers. Glad I could be of service."

Jemma holds back a laugh. She gets an inside look into the team that Mack and Monty don't get because of her access to the locker room. The girls like her and know if it was any other teacher than her coming in here they wouldn't act the same. It helps that she is twenty-seven years old and Zo's aunt. When Jemma became a coach last season they saw how Zo was able to act around her. If Zo, the one who can clown around with her teammates but never in front of adults, could be that free around Jemma, they could too. The players found out quickly it was easy. Jemma isn't shy like her niece; she's outgoing and blunt and has a louder laugh than all of them.

Jemma enjoys her role with the varsity girls. She knows how special of a thing they have going and how special it is that she gets to play a part. This year Jemma will have a partner in crime. The school board approved of Monty strictly serving as the assistant varsity coach. All these years he has coached both as the assistant varsity coach and the head JV coach. Monty is glad to be able to dedicate all his time to the varsity team and not have to juggle both roles. Miss Easton, who is the school's German language teacher and varsity volleyball coach, accepted the JV position. Jemma coaches eighth-grade volleyball too, and the pair have become good friends. The students like Miss Easton. She is tough but fair and fun. Her personality is welcomed in the Hoover halls.

Out on the basketball court players loft up shots, warming up before Coach Mack blows his whistle to start practice. Coach Monty is rebounding and glancing at the practice itinerary at the same time. If Mack is the serious one, Monty is the soft one. The high school shop teacher has a good-natured personality with an "ah shucks" attitude. Where Mack raises his voice, Monty scratches his head and wants to try to understand the why of what you are attempting. Mack and Monty, who the girls call M&M, both share the same commitment to the team and get along well. They spend their summers going to coaching clinics, golfing, and painting houses together. While they are different from each other, they share the same coaching philosophy and complement each other well. With three returning starters coming back, Mack and Monty know what kind of opportunity is in front of them. Of course they have concerns coming into the year because what coach doesn't. The two new starters are not the same caliber players the Knights lost to graduation last year. They are unsure about what they can expect out of their reserves as well. The coaches are hoping Ellie Jacobsma, a junior, will be able to give both Krista and Sasha breathers. Who else will step up off the bench is a mystery to them at this point.

Mack blows his whistle and calls out the name of the first drill. Practice is officially underway. The girls go through drills looking much like their head coach, all business. Once practice starts they are on Mack's time, and the girls for the most part stay silent and attentive. When Coach Mack yells out, "Scrum ball," the players finally crack smiles. This is the team's favorite drill. A ball is thrown out to a random spot on the floor, and it's a fight between a group of four players to see who can get to it and hang on to it long enough to take it to the hoop and score. With no fouls and no rules, it gets wild. It's a free-for-all that borders on a wrestling match, and that's precisely why the players love it. Mack usually breaks the game up after a few minutes because it gets too feisty. Today, being the last preseason practice, he ends the day with the drill and lets them play for a long time. He will give them what they want. They earned it—a prize for getting through preseason practices.

After a while, Mack blows his whistle. The game continues, and a mad intense scrum forms so he blows his whistle in rapid bursts. Finally the players relent and gather around him with smiles on their faces. Mack, who rarely hands out praise, tells the team he is pleased with their effort. He instructs them to enjoy their weekend but get some rest and "stay off your feet"; he wants fresh legs for Tuesday when they tip off the season. The team breaks the huddle with a loud "together" shout. The girls scatter, jogging to a hoop to make twenty free throws, a ritual that ends every practice. They start putting up shots fast, all wanting to get out of there.

After a few minutes, in his stern, even voice, Mack calls out: "Bentley Kramer and Zoey Jones." All the players freeze and lock eyes on the pair. The sound of Mack's voice makes Bentley and Zo flinch. Mack uses last names when he feels something he is saying should be taken seriously. He uses last names often.

With everyone's attention, Mack continues talking, "I need to see the two of you in my office before you leave."

After a short pause to see if there is going to be any additional comments from Coach Mack, the sound of basketballs and shoes squeaking on the court resumes. Bentley and Zo shoot their free throws wondering what Mack wants. Bentley scans her mind thinking of any red flags. Zo is hoping it isn't to tell them they can't wear their game jerseys like they prefer—loose with the top barely tucked in—or that he doesn't want them wearing the headbands or long socks they have been experimenting with in practice. Bentley starts to get nervous thinking it could be something serious. What rumor did someone eagerly share with Mack that has the two of them visiting his office?

Neither one can think of anything they have done. While they hadn't got into any trouble over the summer, they did flirt with it, even if it was only good trouble, at least in their eyes. The kind that comes from being a typical teenager in a small town. Regardless, they know Hoover; in their hometown anything can be blown out of proportion.

Bentley and Zo follow their coach into the boys' locker room when the last player finishes their free throws. With the boys' practice just getting underway, the place is deserted. The two girls grin and take in the surroundings. Nobody to their knowledge has ever been back to Mack's locker room office. In fact, they didn't even know their coach had one until now. Zo and Bentley are surprised by how big the boys' locker room is. They pass a few offices before Mack turns into one and flips the light on. The girls follow him in, and he closes the door. Bentley gives Zo an "uh oh" glance as if to say, "If the door being closed is really necessary we're screwed."

Mack sits behind a standard desk that doesn't have much on it besides a few yellow notepads and Manila folders. "Well ladies, with the season starting I just want to take a moment and address a few things." Mack folds his hands on the top of the desk.

Zo fidgets in her seat while Bentley crosses her arms tightly against her stomach. She quickly puts one fist to her teeth and bites down. They've gotten to know Mack over the years. They're not as scared of him as they used to be. They can even joke with him now and then, but that doesn't make this meeting any easier. Both are glad they have each other.

"You know what really burns me up?" Mack takes his gaze back and forth between the two girls while keeping his teeth clenched.

Bentley looks at Zo then at Mack. She shoots Mack a smile and says, "Krista riding around town on her scooter?"

Mack forces a fake chuckle. "Yes, that is one of the things, but hopefully that has been addressed and I won't hear about that darn thing again."

The girls flash more smiles then wipe them off and brace for what they are in trouble for. "The other thing is you two doing that jumping in the air nonsense. Bumping into each other at full force like you just scored a touchdown." The girls smirk while Mack holds his glare and pauses for effect. "I know it only happened in a few games last year, but I don't want to see it at all this season. After the game when you go into the locker room if you want to twirl, spin, do handstands, cartwheels, or perform one of those five-minute handshakes you've spent hours perfecting, do all that nonsense in there, not on the court."

The girls are amused by Mack's use of hand gestures. They sit silently knowing what he is telling them isn't up for discussion.

"Are we clear?"

"Yeah," Bentley says.

Zo nods. "Crystal."

Mack eyes Zo.

Zo clears her throat. "Got it, Coach."

Mack waits a few moments and looks back and forth at his two guards. "While I have you ladies here I have a few more things." He directs his eyes at Zo. "You, I don't want to hear that you're playing any pickup basketball games during the season or that you're dunking in driveways around town." He pauses and keeps his eyes focused on Zo. "I know you sprained your ankle this summer playing basketball with the young kids at the Harrison house."

Zo doesn't say a word.

Mack raises his hands up. "I hear it all, ladies." He interlaces his hands on the desk and fixes his glare on Bentley. "And you, young lady, I know you have been riding four-wheelers and snowmobiles since you could walk, but I ask you to consider shelving that for the season."

Bentley grimaces and nods at the same time.

Mack starts shaking his head back and forth. "And no skirmishes with any opponents if you happen to run into them in town."

Zo puts her hand over her mouth to hide a smile. Mack is referencing this summer when a few Mason Valley players were in the

Pizza Barn at the same time Bentley and her friends were. Rumors flew around that an altercation between the two groups occurred. Bentley swears the Mason Valley players made all of it up to get her in trouble. She claims she never even saw them this summer.

Bentley rolls her eyes and starts to plead her case, but Mack darts his hand up letting her know he doesn't want to hear it.

"We have a great chance to put together a fantastic season, and you two are a big part of the reason. I need you two on the court. Any extracurricular activity going on outside the lines is hogwash. Do you two understand?"

Bentley shakes her head back and forth still wanting to defend herself. She changes direction and nods in agreement along with Zo, knowing it's a lost cause. The girls brace for the next item on the list.

"Okay then." Mack scoots his chair back and rises up.

The two girls jump out of their seats feeling lucky.

Zo flashes a smile. "Hey, since Krista's not going to be using it, can we ride around town on her scooter?" With the meeting over, Zo wants to see if she can get a rise out of Mack.

Mack's frown attempts to take a break for a moment then returns. "Absolutely not. That thing needs to be burned." He holds the door open. "You guys know your way back. I have to finish up a few things before I can get out of here. Have a great weekend. Let's be ready to kick off the season with a win on Tuesday."

The girls are relieved the meeting with Mack is over and that it wasn't anything too serious. They inspect the boys' locker room as they take their time leaving. They want real lockers like the boys have with the option to keep their gear in them overnight. Their shoebox-size locker room only has hooks to hang their belongings on. They approach a closed door, and Bentley turns the knob. The two girls peek in. Their eyes grow big. They are amazed to see there is a small ice bath container and first-aid supplies lining the shelves. They wonder how they didn't know about this. Bentley and Zo consider setting up a prank before they exit the locker room because it would be so easy. After their talk with Mack, they know they have to pass up the urge. Nothing is going to keep them off the basketball court. This is their year, and the start of the season is so close they can feel it.

Four more days and it's game on.

CHAPTER 3

Game day is finally here. Tuesday, November 28. The moment the girls on the Hoover basketball team have been waiting for. Once and for all, the Knights can start their return-to-state tour. They can get back to playing basketball, not just talking and dreaming about it. Snow is on the ground from the first blizzard of the year that hit the area over the weekend. Bentley walks into school earlier than normal with a wide smile on her face. The Mustangs of Mason Valley are going to get lit up tonight, and Bentley is counting down the final hours until she gets back in the ring with that team. It has all the makings of a drama-filled season opener; neither team likes each other, and emotions and bad blood will be coursing through the game. It's the perfect way to open up the season, and to be playing at home makes it even better.

Zo walks into school as late as she can. She hates having to sit through classes all day. It's game day though so she has a bright sunshiny look on her face too and is eager to get to class so the clock can tick closer to tip-off.

When Bentley spots Zo, she stops talking to her friends and races toward her. "Hey, Zoey, did you hear?"

Zo is stuffing her book bag inside her locker. She raises her eyebrows seeing Bentley lit up like a Christmas tree. "Hear what?"

"We're #1, baby!" Bentley throws her index finger in the air pointing to the sky then whips it down across her body.

Zo doesn't comprehend. Bentley lets out a shriek. "Dude us, the Knights, they ranked us #1 in the state! The poll came out this morning."

Zo's mouth dropped open, and her eyes became saucers. "Dude!"

"I know." Bentley bites down on her fist not knowing what else to do to contain her excitement. "This season is about to be lit, and everyone put some respect on our name, finally." Zo starts to beam as bright as Bentley. "Hey, let's throw down some beats this week, put together a #1 Knights rap song. We can work on it before practices."

The two give each other fist bumps then snap their fingers. Down the hall walking toward them with speed is Krista, Sasha, and Ellie. Krista breezes by them with a big grin on her face and yells, "Yo, Monty needs everyone in his classroom."

Bentley and Zo follow them.

"Why a team meeting now?" Bentley asks. "School is starting."

"No idea," Krista says. "But Ellie saw Jemma and Mr. Williams come through the middle school doors a while ago, so it must be something important if every coach is in there."

Bentley breaks out in a smile. "Oh it's probably to tell us the big news."

"What news?" Ellie and Sasha ask in unison.

"Nothing. I'll let the coaches tell you guys."

Bentley and Zo exchange high fives, causing the three other girls to pry to no avail. Bentley and Zo keep the #1 ranking to themselves; if the coaches want to gather and surprise them with the news, they feel it is only right to give them the honor. The girls walk across the commons area being loud and proud; they are getting to be tardy while everyone else is scattering to make it to first period. When the girls walk into Monty's classroom they are met with looks of gloom and doom. Reading the room, they immediately shut their mouths and go sit down with the rest of their teammates. Jemma looks away after making eye contact with Zo. She is leaned up against the wall with her hands behind her back. Next to Jemma is Gordy Williams the junior high coach and Miss Easton the new JV coach. Monty has his arms crossed in front of his desk.

A shiver goes down Sasha's back. *What is going on?* Her guess was a surprise breakfast to celebrate the season starting. There are no donuts or bagels anywhere in sight, and nobody looks in the mood to celebrate. Now her guess is one of her teammates has done something incredibly stupid.

Zo and Bentley's giddiness disappears instantly. The coaches have definitely not gathered everyone here to unveil their #1 ranking.

Monty leans off his desk and stands up straight. "Okay, I believe everyone is here." He puts his fingers together and taps them. "Listen, I don't know any other way to say this, so I'm just going to say it." Monty pauses a moment and looks at the girls. "Coach Mack had some chest pains when he got home from practice last night. It got bad enough that his wife took him to the local hospital, and upon arriving they immediately rushed him up to the Sioux Falls hospital."

Every player is stunned. Some eyes get watery as Monty continues, "We don't know much more at the moment. They are still running some tests and monitoring him."

The room is quiet. The girls can't believe what Monty just said. Every one of them has been locked in on the excitement of getting to play the first basketball game of the season. "I know you are all concerned and this is a big shock. I will keep everyone informed when I get more information."

Krista is biting her lip. Bentley has her hands covering her head, looking down. Sasha has her fingers covering her mouth, and Zo looks like she is about to burst into tears. The rest of their teammates share similar demeanors. They can't believe what they are hearing. Their season is hours from tipping off, and their head coach is in the hospital. They have been so optimistic and joyful anticipating the season opener. Now it really doesn't matter much.

"You guys know how excited Coach Mack was for the season to start," Monty says, a lump building in his throat. "You know how much he loves this game and loves being your coach. He would want you guys to keep your heads up and stay strong."

Monty dismisses the players, not knowing what else he can say. The girls trickle out of the room and slowly go to their classrooms. No small talk is shared, only somber glances. Monty exhales and thinks about Mack. His phone rang at 7:52 p.m. last night. Mack was calling. Monty assumed he wanted to go over the details of the home opener with him for the umpteenth time. Monty was confused when it wasn't Mack's voice on the other line. It was a gentleman saying he was a doctor and Mack was in his emergency room. It took Monty by surprise, and he wasn't able to process what the doctor said after that. The next thing he knew Mack was on the phone asking if knew the starting lineup for the game. They ended practice earlier that night debating having Ellie start in place of Krista to "light a fire under her pants" as Mack put it. They ultimately decided against it. Monty wanted to tell Mack to forget about the game, but instead he assured him he knew the starting lineup. Mack asked Monty to drive up and see him. Bring a notebook. He had so much he needed to tell him. Monty left right away.

Once Monty walked into his hospital room, Mack started talking. Monty jotted down notes even for the things he already knew. If it was important to Mack, he wanted him to be assured he was absorbing it. Mack kept thinking of little things for Monty to be aware of. It wasn't a long meeting because visiting hours were ending for the night. Mack told Monty he wasn't sure what was going to happen to him and he needed him to know he'd have to take over the team. The two coaches have always looked at coaching their team as a partnership. Mack's forte is offense, Monty's is defense; they share duties fairly evenly with Mack signing off on final decisions. Monty let Mack know he would handle the reins while he was gone. He felt helpless leaving the hospital. It was like a punch in the gut, and all he wanted was for his buddy to make it through okay. It took Monty awhile to shake off the shock of what was happening. As he drove the long hour back from the Sioux Falls hospital to his home in Hoover, his thoughts went to the players. They would be devastated, and he knew he would be the one who would have to deliver the blow in the morning.

After the players leave his classroom, Monty lets the other coaches know the obvious. He will need their help. He won't speculate and only says Mack could be out for an extended period of time. Monty asks Gordy Williams, the junior high coach, if he will sit the bench for the games while Mack is out. Gordy doesn't hesitate telling him he will and that he can attend the varsity practices when it doesn't conflict with his own team's schedule. It's an all-hands-on-deck situation. Miss Easton is heaven sent. Monty can't imagine what kind of juggling would have been needed if they hadn't approved of him solely being the varsity assistant coach. The coaches part ways knowing they have a challenging day ahead of them.

Chapter 4

The moment they have been waiting for is finally here, but their head coach isn't, and for the girls it's not the same. The locker room is quiet as they prepare to take the court. They don't even play music. Their normal routine is a loud-as-it-can-get jam session before the coaches come in for their pregame speech. Tonight a pregame party doesn't seem appropriate.

Word of Coach Mack being hospitalized with heart problems spread fast through the town of Hoover. Of course that set off an array of speculation with many different rumors circulating through the community. The story gaining the most traction and being spread like wildfire is that Mack suffered a massive heart attack in his driveway while shoveling snow and is in the ICU.

Word of the team's #1 ranking spread at a slower rate. Most of the girls hadn't even thought about the rankings coming out, and it caught them off guard. It was neat to be given the #1 ranking, but they knew this much from last year: rankings don't mean everything. And at the moment they are trying their best to focus on beating the Mason Valley Mustangs under difficult circumstances. Even though the Mustangs are a class 1A team, they are a tough, experienced team and received their own ranking that day of #13 in their class. Last season the Knights started their season at Mason Valley and suffered a painful loss. The Mustangs have some feisty, physical players who enjoy challenging the Knights. Hoover being tabbed #1 will have them motivated to try to pull off another upset.

Monty sits in his classroom going over the notes he took last night. He has been Mack's assistant, his right-hand man, for many years. Monty likes being the assistant coach. It's a big commitment but not as strenuous as being the head coach. Final decisions and outcomes fall on

Mack, so he is able to be more laid back. He can already feel a shift in pressure and wonders how the girls will accept him being the one in charge. He doesn't worry about the kids causing him problems; they're good kids. He just hopes he can be a good leader for them during this trying time, one they will follow and trust.

Monty gathers his notes and finds Gordy Williams in the hallway outside the locker room. They discuss the game plan. Jemma appears and slips into the locker room to check on the players. She returns a few minutes later.

Monty looks at her with worry. "Are they ready for us?"

"It's crickets in there."

Monty blows out a deep breath. "What do you think, Gordy?"

Gordy Williams is the middle school guidance counselor along with being the junior high girls' basketball coach. "They haven't had much time to process everything. It will be therapeutic for them to get on the court and compete. Just maybe not this quickly."

Gordy is stoic by nature. He is always casually well dressed and is utterly self-assured. Every varsity player had him as their junior high basketball coach. Similar to Mack, he commands respect by his demeanor along with his position as a guidance counselor. If you have to talk to him, it's serious business to middle school students, even if it really isn't. Monty is glad to have Gordy by his side. Not only because of his profession but for familiarity; he has been coaching in Hoover nearly as long as he has.

The three coaches share a "here goes" glance, and Monty leads them into the locker room. First, he gives the team an update on Mack, telling them what he knows for sure; he is stable at the moment. The girls aren't sure what that means. They have heard the different rumors floating around town and aren't fully convinced of anything anyone says in regards to Mack's condition. Monty decides against telling them at that moment that Mack has three fully blocked arteries and one that is 75 percent blocked. Heart surgery is likely. Since all the details are pending, Monty will wait and give the players the information once everything is confirmed. He doesn't think the girls need to be hit with another wave of emotions right before they are going to take the floor for the first game of the year.

Monty goes over the game plan with the team, the one Mack and him worked on so diligently. The Mustangs present problems, and they match up well with the Knights. They have a strong post player who won't back down from going up against Sasha, and they have solid guard play. While the Knights on paper are a better team, they know the Mustangs are gamers. They want to win just as badly as they do and will fight them with all their might for it.

The girls run onto the floor to a decent-sized home crowd for the first game of the season. The team's success last year sparked a lot of excitement around town. With word spreading about their fallen leader, it's likely some who were on the fence about needing to see the first game have shown up to give the team their support.

Before sending the starters out for the jump ball, Monty tells the team Mack will be eager to hear how the game goes so play hard and get a win for him. The girls nod apprehensively. It's go-time whether they are ready for it or not. They want to win for Mack. They know in the grand scheme of things it's just a game and it won't do anything to change the circumstances. The Knights break the huddle with a "together on three" shout to kick off the season.

The starters line up for the jump ball, looking hesitant at best. The crazy confidence they played with last year is nowhere to be seen. The ball is hoisted up in the center of the court and the season is officially underway. After two sloppy possessions by both teams, the Mustangs score the first points of the game. The Knights respond after trading turnovers with Mason Valley; Bentley feeds Sasha the ball inside and she scores a short bank shot from the low block.

Neither team looks crisp, but the Knights, the team crowned #1 to start the season, looks out of sync. It has been a long day for them, full of a vast array of emotions, and it shows in their body language. There are missed shots, turnovers, and lax defense. With the score stuck on 7-7, Monty takes a time-out with 4:57 on the clock and wonders how to get the players to wake up. Their reaction to Coach Mack being hospitalized was what he expected; he saw the tears and disbelief on their faces throughout the day. He can relate. Monty will tell his wife when he gets home later, "The last twenty-four hours has felt like an out-of-body experience."

Monty kneels down so he is eye level with the players. "Let's play the way we know how to. Let's settle down and play our way. There are a number of things out of our control. We need to put the off-court stuff at the back of our mind because the only thing we can control at this moment is how we play. And right now you guys don't look anywhere near the #1 team in the state. Don't forget who you guys are and how you got here. I know the circumstances are rough and your mind is on Coach, but the only." He pauses to look slowly around at every player. "The only thing you're able to do for Coach is to get a win."

The girls muster up some intensity when breaking the huddle, yelling "together" a little louder than usual, wanting to show their coach they desire the same thing; they don't want to feel this way or play the way they are playing.

As the starters walk back onto the court, Bentley yells for them to bring it in. With arms draped around each other, Bentley speaks: "This sucks but the game is going on without Coach. So the only thing in our control is to go kick ass." Her voice rises, "We kick ass and take names later."

They let go of each other with all of them feeling that edge that defined them a season ago. They are the mighty, aggressive, go-all-out Knights. They don't quite feel like it when the one who helped shape this team is hurting in a hospital room. They feel angry and hurt, and they don't understand why this happened to them, but for Mack they are going to try to summon the energy to get through it.

Bentley starts to push the rock on offense every time the ball is in her hands. The Knights establish the tempo they want, and the Mustangs try to disrupt their flow with a full-court press. Bentley and Zo shrug it off. Run right through it. They may not be feeling like themselves but they sure aren't going to let Mason Valley show them up. The intensity rises. The girls start to get lost in the game. No chance to think of anything else. They react and play. On defense, Krista and Sasha get aggressive; they record three blocks on one possession, and the third block leads to a fast break with a great finish by the new starter, Hayley.

Like it has been hiding, waiting to be activated there it is: the juice that makes this team who they are. The home crowd delights in the Knights' awakening. They look like the Knights they remember, the ones who play like a bunch of sugar-high kids, quick and free-flowing. When the horn sounded ending the first quarter, the score was 20-9, and the Knights went on a 13–2 run after the time-out.

Outwardly Monty shows no emotion, but inside he is ecstatic to see the girls break out of their funk. "I reckoned they just needed a minute," he says to Gordy before kneeling down with his clipboard in hand to talk to the players.

The second quarter has the Mustangs desperately attempting anything they can to get back into the game. While they are able to keep the Knights from running up the score, they can't get within single digits. Both teams are shooting the ball poorly. The Knights' offense still looks shaky, and Zo has been held to six first half points. Even so, the Knights take a 33–20 lead into halftime.

In the locker room the girls look more comfortable than they did during pregame. Monty does as well. He isn't used to being the main attraction. With all the girls looking at him, he feels some nerves. Monty always gets to play good cop while Mack often has to play bad cop. Monty understands the magnitude of his new role with all eyes on him now. This is a whole different ball game. He is the head coach at the moment. While it's going to take some time for him to adjust, he knows the team needs him to go with it, act it out, and they will follow. There is no other choice.

The Mustangs score the first two points of the second half. Down at the other end Zo catches a pass from Bentley and with no hesitation lets go a twenty-five-foot bomb that connects with the bottom of the net. As the quarter progresses, Zo starts to catch fire and look like herself. The whole team ups their aggressiveness, most noticeably on defense where they smother the Mustangs, overwhelming them with pressure on the perimeter and in the paint. The Mustangs look uncomfortable and agitated. The Knights keep extending their lead, and soon it isn't much of a competition at all. The Knights make their case that they are on a different level than the scrappy 1A team. The score is 55–28 at the end of three. Monty clears the bench for the fourth quarter giving the JV players some quality time on the court.

Zo, Bentley, and Sasha led the way tonight. Krista played well in her new starting role providing a spark on the boards. Her and Hayley will be looked upon to provide any boost they can in doing the little things to help the team. Hayley, starting in her first varsity game, played tentatively in the first half and was more at ease in the second half going three of six from the three-point line. Ellie got her first taste of real varsity action when she subbed in for Krista in the second quarter. She found out right away the varsity game is played much faster than it is at the JV level. More physical too. Each time Monty put her in the game she picked up a foul. This is an adjustment she will have to make and improve on as she gets varsity experience.

After the game, Monty tells Laney, the *Hoover Times* sports reporter, "I couldn't be happier with the effort these kids put forth. Our offense looked sluggish but our defense stepped up. Considering all the distractions I think we played awfully well. Mason Valley always presents a challenge. It was a fun game to start off the season." Monty pauses and adds, "It's the type of game Mack would have loved. In fact, I'm going to hustle out of here because I know he's waiting for me to call him and fill him in on every detail."

The locker room after the win has some life to it once again. There are smiles and happy exchanges, although in the back of their minds the players can't help but think about Mack, all of them wondering if they are going to have to get used to playing without him.

CHAPTER 5

The ball sails through the air a good three feet above Sasha's hands. The slap of the ball against the wall echoes through the gym. Bentley puts her hands up in the air. She pauses then brings them down to cover her face. Monty blows his whistle, indicating now is a good time to call it an evening, and the players walk off the court leaving the ball rolling in the opposite direction. Practice is a mess. The comedown from yesterday's rough news about Mack and the emotions of having to play a game is catching up with the team. So is the reality of the situation. Before practice started, Monty gave the players an update on their head coach. Mack is scheduled to undergo quadruple bypass heart surgery next Monday. He has a grueling five-day wait ahead of him with every operating room at the hospital booked until then. While Mack is in pain, his doctors say he isn't in any danger as long as there is no pain within ten minutes of each other.

The girls listened to Monty talk about the status of their head coach with sadness. They did show some relief when they were told Mack can fully recover; after hearing all the different rumors going around town about his condition, that is comforting news. Monty tries to keep expectations low when asked if Mack might return during the season. He doesn't want to get their hopes up and have them dashed if it never happens. There were some tears shed when they walked onto the basketball court after hearing the update. Practice wasn't productive, and the girls shuffled through it.

Practice the following day doesn't go much better. The kids aren't their normal selves; they are quiet and lack their typical boisterous attitude. The coaches show patience, knowing it will take time. As much as Monty wishes they could get a few more practices in, the season is here. There is no pause button. The following night the team will suit up for another home game; this time their opponent is the VMS Warriors. They are another team that lights up when playing the Knights. Monty doesn't know what he's going to get from this team going forward. With all the hoopla surrounding the Knights with the win state or bust talk, the #1 ranking, and Mack out, Monty feels like the pressure being put on this team is a lot. He had high hopes just like everyone else coming into this season; even so, listening to everyone talk about it he felt the brakes should be pumped a tad. Monty isn't a pessimist; he's just been around the game long enough to know it isn't easy to get to the state tournament, let alone get to the championship game, then win it, no matter how good you are. Heck, the best team in their conference, the Chesapeake Saints, haven't reached the state tournament in over seven years, and they are always ranked in the top ten in their class. So while everyone else goes straight for the state title scenario with this team, Monty tries to be realistic. An awful lot has to go right to win a championship, and more times than not the best team on paper doesn't end up winning. Monty's response is always the same when someone wants to talk expectations with him: "We'll just have to play and see what happens."

Monty ends practice on Thursday letting the girls play scrum ball. He watches every one of them bounce around with nothing on their mind except getting control of that ball and putting it in the hoop. They are aggressive and focused. Fully present. He even sees a few smiles. Monty tells Gordy it's nice seeing them play like this and not just going through the motions. Monty huddles them up before he sends them home and tells them to play like that tomorrow night. Like kids who are simply getting to play a game with their friends.

❧

Jemma waves Krista over when she sees her pop out of the locker room alone after practice has ended. Krista blushes when she gets near, knowing she may have crossed a line. Jemma can dish it and take it; however, she is still an authority figure. Krista puts her hand up asking to be allowed to speak first. "I'm sorry Jemma, I shouldn't have said that."

"Huh?"

"The boyfriend comment. I was just trying to get everyone to laugh."

In the locker room before practice, the girls discussed weekend plans. Jemma stays out of conversations unless they include her, but this time she thought it warranted her two cents when she heard where Krista was planning on going. When she advised the girls, "Nothing good happens after midnight," Krista responded that Jemma really needed to get herself a man. Of course that got an animated reaction, and everyone's attention turned to Jemma's love life or lack thereof. Jemma hasn't had a boyfriend since she broke up with Greg, Hoover's high school algebra teacher. Krista is sure Jemma wants to lay into her about the snide remark.

Jemma waves her hand in the air. "Oh I don't care about that." She softens her voice. "I know about your grades."

Krista slouches. This is even worse.

"Mrs. Pratt said she gave you a chance to do some extra assignments to get your grade up and you didn't. Greg told me the same thing."

Krista shrugs and sighs. She's uncomfortable in a way Jemma hasn't seen her. When Krista speaks her voice is gentle. "It's hopeless."

"No it's not, Krista. Look, I know it seems like a huge mountain to climb, but it's really not if you take it day by day and put in a little work and effort."

Krista raises her eyebrows. "Finals are in a few weeks."

"I know that. You can work hard and get A's in both classes with the extra credit available and acing the final. It's possible."

"Maybe if I change brains."

"Stop it Krista," Jemma says, shaking her head. "You can do it; you just have to believe. At the least you can get B's, and that's much better than a D or an F. Don't give up now. You're so close."

Krista bites down on her lip. "I'm going to end up going to junior college anyway, or better yet I'll probably only be able to get into Elmwood Community College. I'll be stuck working on the farm when I'm not in class."

"That's not true, Krista. Your grades are not that bad if you can salvage those two classes. Plus, there is nothing wrong with going to a smaller college like that."

Krista doesn't respond; she is too busy trying not to get emotional. She looks down and around to waste time.

"What's really going on? You know you can talk to me."

Jemma finds herself laughing out loud at so many things she hears come out of Krista's mouth. Not because what she says is always funny but because she reminds her so much of herself at that age. Unfiltered, talking more than she should, and putting herself out there.

Krista meets Jemma's eyes. "It's just a lot. I mean those two classes suck. Classes won't get any easier for me next semester. And basketball is a lot too. The other starters make it look easy while I'm on the struggle bus every damn day. And with Mack being gone…"

Krista starts to tear up.

"I thought you might feel like you were getting a break with him gone. Wow, I'll have to tell him even *you* miss him!"

Krista giggles and sniffles. "Please don't." She wipes her tears. "With him gone it's almost like I have no one to prove wrong. He pissed me off, but he made me want to prove him wrong. It was motivation, you know?"

"Well you can still do that. Make it so when he comes back he sees how good you got, that will really show him, right?"

Krista smiles slightly and wipes her eyes with the sleeve of her sweatshirt.

"And you *are* doing well in basketball. You know the team doesn't need you to be a superstar; they just need you to do your job and you're the only one who can do your job the way you do your job. The other starters can't do what you do. And look, there is plenty of time to get your grades up and apply to a state college if that is what you really want."

"Oh please," Krista says. "My parents told me they can't help with money. A university is way out of the question. My dad suggested the military."

Jemma can't help but giggle thinking about Krista in camouflage fatigues.

Krista keeps the frown on her face. "He's deadly serious."

Jemma shrugs. "It wouldn't be the worst thing in the world. You can get your college paid for after that."

Krista isn't amused.

"Well there are scholarships, Krista, and it doesn't have to be a university. There are a lot of different options. Community college. Junior college. But first things first, you have to get these two grades up. You are running out of time. Why don't you come join me in the mornings before school starts. You can work on your homework and extra credit assignments. I can help out if you need it. Or we can get you a tutor. Someone on the team would probably be happy to do that."

Krista grimaces. "I'm not having one of the nerds on the team be my tutor."

"Oh Krista," Jemma hisses.

"Okay fine. I'll come to your classroom before school starts, but don't be telling anyone, especially the team. And no nerds looking over my shoulder."

Jemma smiles. "Good. You can do anything you want, Krista, you just have to put your mind to it. I don't think you realize this."

"Yeah, yeah, yeah, Jemmers. I'm hungry. See you tomorrow." Krista turns and walks toward the exit.

"Bright and early at 7:00 a.m.," Jemma yells.

Krista stops and turns around. "Oh no way. I was talking about seeing you tomorrow for the game."

"Krista!" Jemma snaps.

"Lady, you just laid it on me! Let's start a clean slate on Monday morning."

Jemma shakes her head.

"I need time to prep my brain and body for this." Krista winks, swirls around, and continues walking toward the exit.

"Fine, but you better be there! And put in some serious hours on your own this weekend." Krista flips a thumb up in the air without turning back.

CHAPTER 6

Monty is speaking to the team about the target on their back before they take the court Friday night. He couldn't help but wince when he first learned they were bestowed with the #1 ranking. Maybe part of it was due to the fact he learned of their ranking the same morning he told the team Mack was in the hospital. The other part is the added pressure. This team went from unknown to the cream of the crop in a blink of an eye. A season ago they quietly surprised everyone. This year they are being told: you're best in class. The Knights are going from the underdogs to being hunted. It's not that Monty doesn't think they are deserving; he just wishes they were ranked a few spots down so they would feel slighted a bit. Feel like they still had more to prove to get the mantle passed on to them.

"With a #1 ranking comes great responsibility," Monty says.

Zo whispers to Sasha: "We're like Spider Man." Sasha gives her an eye roll, and a half smile before she goes back to paying attention to Monty.

"Everyone is going to be juiced to face you. Even the teams at the bottom of the conference. You are going to be their Super Bowl."

Coach Monty stresses there is absolutely no team they can overlook, no game they can take lightly, and no possession they can take off. Monty in no way is trying to get them riled up; he is just being matter-of-fact, but after the speech the girls are fired up feeling like he doesn't think they are capable of holding the top spot. The team gathers together in the hallway before they get ready to run out on the court in front of their home crowd.

Bentley sways back and forth. "They all want to take a swing at us." She stops talking to show her scowl. "They best not miss!" She punches her hand into her palm and takes off running. Bentley's teammates can't be sure if she is joking or really pissed off. They go with pissed off to be safe and rally right after her, sprinting on the court with serious game faces on. Unlike in the season opener, the Knights look more prepared to play when the jump ball is thrown up in the air. They can't just *get over* what is happening to their coach, but they can let the emotions they feel push them forward with some fight. They break their huddle before the tip-off with a "Mack on three" shout.

The VMS Warriors have a solid squad. They finished fourth in the conference last season with a lot of younger players on the roster. They are a short team. Their center is under six feet. They make up for it with their scrappiness and grit. Hoover always seems to bring out their best. That #1 ranking of Hoover's is more than enough to light a fire under the Warriors tonight, and in their huddle their coach is using the ranking to get under their skin. He is calling upon his team to be the ones to take that ranking away from the confident, bordering on cocky, Knights.

In the first quarter it looks as if the Warriors' coach gave a much better pregame speech to his troops than Monty did. VMS comes out looking like the top-ranked team and holds a twelve point lead at the end of the first. The Warriors are on fire, shooting a sizzling 80 percent from the field and are bringing it on the defensive end too; they held the Knights to ten first-quarter points on a dismal 20 percent shooting. In the huddle Monty tries to stay calm, even though the first quarter could not have gone any worse. He knows it's a long game and their opponent is bound to cool off while his players are bound to start making a higher percentage of their shots. Monty resists showing his disappointment and stresses to the team to up their defensive pressure.

The Knights come out for the second quarter in a full-court man-to-man press. The press was put in on Wednesday, so the team only had two days to prepare. The press wasn't met with any sparks of enthusiasm. It is another reminder that Mack isn't here and there would be some changes. The team seldom administered full-court presses in the past, and if they did, it was usually a zone press. Monty and Gordy Williams both have the same belief; defense wins championships. Being defense oriented they know they need something like this in their back pocket for such an occasion.

The press surprises the Warriors and takes them out of their offensive flow. To their credit, the Knights do their best to implement the zone just like Monty and Gordy stressed with so few reps to test it out. Monty predicted VMS wouldn't keep up their 80 percent field goal clip, and they didn't. The Knights start to warm up and connect with the basket better. Halfway through the second quarter Zo takes it upon herself to spark the team; she scores baskets on consecutive offensive possessions then forces a five-second out-of-bounds call to get the ball back. The Knights run an inbounds play, and Krista gets put in the perfect spot for an easy bucket. The six-point swing brings the Knights to within four points.

VMS calls a time-out while the Hoover fans in the stands bring the noise. In a small town a crisis attracts a crowd. Coach Mack's hospitalization is the biggest news in town. Hoover residents embraced the Knights last season, and they show up for them in a big way tonight. The gym is near capacity. The girls feel the glow of the basketball season upon them. It feels good. Strange knowing Mack is missing out. Their people are here though, and their cheers feel like permission to let it fly. They aren't alone. Play on; we got you.

The Warriors fight to keep the lead for the rest of the half while the Knights run their disruption-style defense. Sasha shows off her improved footwork when their point guard slips into the lane past Hayley. Sasha stays right with her when she performs a spin move and goes up for a layup, casually swatting the ball out of the air. It lands in Hoover's student section. The block lights up Hoover's side of the gym. Sasha's teammates go crazy leaping into her and getting wound up. Off the inbounds pass, Bentley steals the ball. She doesn't have the numbers for a fast break so she holds up and brings the ball out to the top of the key. When she drives into the lane with a full head of steam, a sea of VMS maroon engulfs her. Somehow in the midst of defenders converging on her, Bentley is able to fling the ball out to Zo whose defender left to help. Zo catches it a foot past the three-point line. Hoover's student section knows what's coming, and they rise to their feet. Zo's three-point bomb cuts the lead to one point and gives Bentley her seventh assist. Five seconds later the horn sounds, ending the half. The gym is rocking. The players run off the floor embracing the charged-up atmosphere.

The girls are animated at halftime from the momentum shift. Their renewed confidence is noticeable by the coaches when they walk in the locker room to address the team. It is night and day from the first game.

Still, Monty knows they are in a dogfight and doesn't want them to slip back into a funk. Mack always challenges them at the half when they are down, especially when they appear a little too fiery. Monty lights into them—well, Monty's way of that is mellow compared to Mack's. It still gets their attention. He tells them they can't let a team show them up on their home court. Monty reads off the poor numbers on his stat sheet. Most of it was accrued in the first quarter, but he omits that. Monty then challenges the team to up their defensive pressure and start attacking the hoop more. He isn't sure if this is the right approach and wonders if he is only taking it because of his fear of the team losing so soon on his watch.

The Knights stay alert when they walk back out on the floor like a pump of urgency was administered at halftime. They look ready to pounce. Once an underdog, always an underdog. The chip on their shoulder didn't slide off when they were tabbed the top team in their class. The players know what other teams in the conference are saying now: with their head coach out, they won't be as sharp. They also know what Monty told them before the game is true. Everyone is coming with the goal to knock them out of first place. To take something they earned from them. The challenge is welcomed by the Knights. They are going to fight for themselves and for Mack.

Bentley and Zo don't exchange any words; there's no need to. All they exchange is a familiar look when the third quarter gets underway. One they have frequently exchanged ever since a point in their early days of playing together when they discovered they both share the same will to win. When they found out they could count on each other to go fight. Like two junkyard dogs, they go into attack mode. Bentley steals a pass, and the Knights set up in their offense. The ball is worked around and when it finds Zo's hand she flashes to the middle of the lane and goes up against a post player. Her body contorts in the air to contend with her defender's height, and she flips the ball up on the backboard with one hand. The whistle rings out as the ball glides through the hoop. Zo's teammates celebrate her score with her before shoving her to the free-throw line. Zo makes her free throw, capping off an unconventional three-point play that gives her team the first lead of the game.

From then on it's all Hoover. The Warriors lose steam. Gone from the first half is all that adrenaline they had from being psyched up to play #1 Hoover. They struggle to get the ball past half court with the guards of

Hoover being relentless in their full-court press. When VMS does manage to get the ball across half court, they aren't hitting their outside shots. Krista and Sasha control the inside, not giving their smaller opponents any breathing room. Monty and Gordy share smiles on the bench, both thinking the same thing: this team has the ability to be really damn good.

When it's over, the Knights forced thirty-two turnovers on the night, easily won the rebound battle, and got by one of the sneaky good teams in their conference winning 71–57. When the coaches leave the locker room Bentley blasts music. A home win on a Friday night. There is nothing sweeter than the basketball season being underway. The girls bounce around feeling great about the win even though the absence of coach Mack isn't far from their minds.

CHAPTER 7

"It's called an open-heart surgery Zoey," Jemma says. "How did you think they would do it?" Zo shrugs and doesn't say anything. She flips to a new tab on her phone and searches for *quadruple bypass surgery*. She can't wrap her head around how the doctors are going to open up Mack's chest and keep him alive.

Jemma is at Zo's house hoping her niece will change her mind and go with her to visit Coach Mack before he has his surgery tomorrow. Jemma eyes Zo who is playing on her phone. "I think they have to stop his heart."

Zo glances up. "Seriously?"

"Yep. I think they connect it to some kind of a machine to keep him alive while they operate." Zo's head drops down, and her face turns a shade lighter. Jemma gets a sharp glare from Zo's mom, suggesting she dial it back a touch and stop trying to scare the kid. Jemma gives her sister a dismissive expression. Jemma has watched enough *Grey's Anatomy* to know anything can happen on the operating table. She *wants* Zo to be scared; if something happens to Mack she'll be even more upset knowing she had a chance to go visit him and passed.

Similar to her teammates, Zo doesn't talk much about Mack being hospitalized. Everyone close to Zo sees how it's affecting her. Basketball is her constant, her everything. It's basketball that makes her world normal no matter what else is going on around her. Zo's parents are worried about her. They are in the middle of ending their marriage, and while it appears she is handling that as well as a teenager can, Mack being hospitalized has been an overwhelming blow.

Zo looks earnestly at her aunt. The thought of Mack not making it through the surgery has her shook up. It hasn't crossed her mind once, and if she was being honest, she has been dwelling more on how Mack's absence affects her and her teammates than on what he is going through. Zo is crushed over Mack being gone from the team and can't stop thinking about how he is going to miss out on everything. Now Zo is thinking of the worst-case scenario and knows she has to go see him. The possibility that he might miss out on not just a basketball season but on his loved ones lives, especially his grandkids, brings things into perspective. Zo knows she won't be able to say what she feels when she sees Mack, so she takes a few minutes to write her coach a note and slips it into the card Jemma is giving him.

Once the two of them are on the road, Jemma wastes little time bringing up what Zo knows she won't be able to avoid.

"Did you guys have fun last night?"

Zo replies, "It was all right."

When Jemma stopped by Zo's house last night she wasn't there. When her mom said Krista picked her up, Jemma flipped out. She called Zo right away and with the mouth of a sailor wanted to know what Zo was thinking.

"I hope it was worth it."

Zo lays her head back on the headrest and closes her eyes. "What are you talking about? Why are you freaking out so much?"

"Zo, you went to see a band in Brookings on a Saturday night."

Zo opens her eyes and sits up. "Oh my gosh the horror. I did what a bunch of other kids did. I went to see a band."

"You can pull a fast one on your parents but not me. I looked it up; the band was playing at a *bar*."

"Yeah, an eighteen-and-over bar."

"You're not eighteen, Zo!" Jemma shouts.

Zo shakes her head. "My point is there were other high schoolers there. It's not a big deal." Jemma doesn't remember ever being this mad at Zo. Her two older brothers yes, but not Zo. Jemma rarely got to see her niece and nephews when they were younger, so when she did it was special. When they would show up to see their grandparents when Jemma was still in high school, Zo would want to sleep in her room. Jemma would make her laugh by making up funny stories about her brothers while rubbing her back to help her fall asleep.

Jemma drives in silence for one whole song before she lays into her again. "Do you seriously not see why I'm upset, Zoey?"

Zo has the seat reclined and is looking out the window. She doesn't respond.

"I just don't understand what you were thinking. During the basketball season. Really? That's not like you. I know you're upset about Mack and everything else, but acting out isn't going to make everything better. Do you really want to jeopardize everything you've worked for?"

Zo stays silent. She really hadn't thought she was doing anything wrong. On a whim she decided to go out Saturday night because it sounded like a good way to take her mind off things. Zo thought by going she was doing something normal and nothing was normal at the moment. A night with her friends seemed better than staying at home.

"You could have gotten busted for being underage," Jemma says. "You could have gotten busted for drinking. Krista could have gotten in a crash. A number of things could have happened. Do you really want basketball to be taken away from you?"

Zo thinks Jemma is being dramatic and lets her know by the look she shoots her.

Jemma shakes her head back and forth with a frown. "You think I'm blowing smoke, but I know because I was out doing that stuff when I was younger."

"Exactly," Zo says. "Why is it bad that I do it?"

"Because you have something to lose!" Jemma exhales and lowers her voice. "Don't you see that? Not just now but beyond high school. You get caught in Krista's car with beer even if you're sober you can get ticketed. You think college coaches will be impressed by that?"

"There was no alcohol in the car. Krista didn't drink at all last night. Nobody did."

"Okay, well a fake ID is illegal too."

"We didn't get fake IDs."

Jemma gives Zo a glare.

"Krista's friend let us in."

"Of course." Jemma sighs. "Well, regardless of the way you get in it's against the law. You never know, Zoey. Wrong place. Wrong time. What do you think Mack would say if he knew where you were?"

Zo already came to the conclusion she would never do it again. She won't tell Jemma this, or that before she even called last night she was already questioning her decision to go. Zo's stomach turned the whole night. She hoped with all her might something bad wouldn't happen. The venue was dark, loud, and packed wall to wall with people. Zo kept wondering who was a cop and who would recognize her. After two songs, she waited outside by the car with one of her friends.

"I can mention it to Mack when we see him. Get his opinion."

Zo sighs. "Can you chill? It's not going to happen again."

"Good." Jemma believes her. She can tell Zo feels bad. Jemma hands her the auxiliary cord as a peace offering and endures Zo's bass thumping mashups for the rest of the drive. By the time Jemma parks the car at the hospital they have moved on. Zo is locked in on getting through this visit. She started to feel queasy when they were on the outskirts of Sioux Falls. She doesn't want to see her coach in a hospital, looking sick and weak.

Jemma turns the car off. "It's going to be okay." She knows she doesn't sound certain and eventually says with more confidence, "After, you will be glad you saw him."

"Is he going to be, just lying there?" Zo asks.

"Ah yeah. He can't do much else."

"What will he be wearing?" Zo tilts her head to look at Jemma. "Regular clothes?"

"Yeah, Zo, he'll be lying there with his coaching shorts and shirt on." Jemma giggles. "No, he'll be in a hospital gown, you knucklehead."

Zo shrugs her shoulders like how is she supposed to know that. She makes a circle with her fist and blows into it. Jemma can understand her niece's feelings. She isn't thrilled to be visiting Mack in the hospital either. It's not something anybody hopes to do, and her giving Zo a full-court press to get her to come along had a lot to do with her not wanting to go see him by herself.

Jemma and Zo finally get out of the car and walk down the steps of the parking garage to make their way inside the hospital. Zo feels herself getting hot when they receive the room number from the nurse at the front desk and start walking down the hall. When they tap a soft knock then open the door to Mack's room there are familiar faces. Coach Monty and Coach Williams are both inside along with a few of their family members.

Coach Mack perks up when he sees Jemma and Zo. "Well, look who it is."

"Hey, Coach." Zo doesn't know what is proper etiquette. She gives Mack a shy wave. Having expected to see her coach all sick-looking and out of it she relaxes some when he still sounds and looks like Mack.

It's strange for Zo to see her coaches out in public. Zo thinks about it and can't remember another time she has seen any of them anywhere other than at school. She finds it odd. The same could be said of seeing them with their families. At school you don't take into consideration anybody has a life outside of those walls. There is an uneasy vibe in the room that keeps Zo's stomach queasy. She notices Mr. Williams's zipper is down. She wonders if everyone else notices this too. Then she wonders if he did it on purpose to take some of the attention off of Mack who has a group of people watching him lay in a hospital bed, all knowing his body will be cut open in the morning. She figures Mr. Williams, being one who works with people's feelings for a living, would know little tricks like this to lighten the mood. If it is on purpose, Zo thinks it's something she could never be bold enough to try since her fearlessness hasn't followed her off the court yet.

The tension is thick in the room. Gordy Williams's youngest daughter catches Zo's eye and fans a few dollar bills in front of her face. Zo gives her a thumbs-up. Her mom gives her permission to go with an assuring nudge. Zo and the girl quietly move toward the door with everyone watching. They are the only two kids in the room. One is sixteen and the other one is ten. Once they step into the hallway their demeanors change. They've escaped.

Zo looks down at the girl and asks with such enthusiasm, "What are you going to get with your money?" You would think they have been given permission to go on a shopping spree.

"Something good," the girl replies with a smile.

The two explore the hallways looking for a vending machine.

"Just look ahead and not in the rooms," the girl advises.

Zo smiles and assumes the girl was peeking in all the other rooms in a curious way when she first arrived here. Zo takes her advice.

At the vending machine the young girl takes a long time to make up her mind. Zo wants to delay getting back to the room as long as possible so she keeps the girl engaged and they go over the details of every selection. A few times. The girl gets down low to watch the candy drop after she makes her final choice. She grabs the candy with delight and informs Zo she will share with her. Something catches her eye, and she bends back down again. She reaches her hand all the way under the vending machine and pulls out a pink bouncy ball. Both girls look at each other, thrilled. Zo takes a look around then gives a nod, indicating she approves of seeing how much bounce they have to work with. The girl gives it a go. It's a decent bounce, not impressive. In a hospital they will take anything, so they start backing away from each other and start to play catch.

Zo knows Mr. Williams's daughter well from helping out at the Saturday morning basketball program when she was a freshman. Zo likes the kid. Likes that she is daring. Confident in ways Zo never was at that age. Wishes she could go back and tell her ten-year-old self it's okay to go for things you want. To speak up. Ask questions. Be brave. The kid is loving every moment of getting to play catch with her idol. The girl and her little friends follow Zo around after every home game. When the girl caught wind that maybe, just maybe, Zo would be at the hospital, she wasn't going to miss it. Her parents told her she could stay home with her sisters who thought it was quite weird she wanted to go waste a Sunday around sick people. She insisted on going, and here she is laughing in a hallway with the one and only Zoey Jones.

They play catch for a while. Zo knows they need to get back to the room. Knows Jemma is probably ready to get out of there by now, and she'll get an earful if she's gone much longer. Zo nods down the hallway and whispers, "Think we can get it all the way down the hall without it touching the walls?"

Surprised to know this is an option, the girl yells, "Yes!"

Zo always looks for a way to make things into a game. She wants to play above anything else. She holds out her hand for a fist bump and says, "Let's do it!"

A nurse sitting behind a desk halfway down the hall perks up hearing the girl's voices. Zo has her arm back ready to roll it when the nurse leans over the desk to give her a disapproving shake of her head.

"Ah busted." Zo shrugs her shoulders. "So close."

The two walk down the hall knowing the fun is over. When they pass the nurse she holds out suckers for both of them to grab and flashes a smile. "Believe me, I wish I could bowl that puppy down the hallway too."

The girls stop outside of Mack's door and prepare to go inside. The young one waves her prized vending machine snack at Zo. "Here, you can have this."

"Oh no." Zo shakes her head. "You keep it."

The girl takes out the change from her pocket and holds out her hand. "Then take this."

Zo smiles and starts to give her the same answer then pauses, realizing the girl just wants to connect with her. "Okay, thanks." Zo lets the coins fall into her hand with great pleasure. "Sweet!" She picks up the penny of the bunch and holds it up. "This will be my good luck charm for the rest of the season. Cool?" The girl's eyes light up. Zo will put the penny in her shoe for Tuesday night's game and every game after.

When the two of them walk in the room it goes quiet. Mack calls Zo over to talk. He knows Zo is apprehensive being here. So is he. There are few adults who can say they know how to get Zo to talk. Mack can. And there are few kids who can say they know how to joke with Mack. Zo can. Mack goes first, attempting to make light of the situation. He does his best. Zo admits she thought he would be wearing his coaching shorts. Mack tells her there is nothing that can keep him away from getting back to the team. Zo tells him she will see him soon on the basketball court. Before Zo walks out the door to leave, Mack says, "Keep shooting and winning."

After Jemma and Zo depart, others start trickling out. After not being able to have visitors during the week, Mack has enjoyed the company. It's been a tough week for him and his family. Mack is ready to get the surgery over and done with so he can get back home to recover. While he has been in a lot of pain, his family knows it's just as painful for him being away from the basketball team. Maybe even more so. When Monty and Gordy first showed up in his hospital room earlier today, all he wanted to do was to talk about the big matchup coming up on Friday with the #2 team in class 3A, the Chesapeake Saints. Were the girls ready? Monty tried to keep a poker face because he really didn't think they were anywhere near ready to play that caliber of a team so soon, with everything they were dealing with. What defense should they start in? Mack suggested a zone to see if the Saints would knock down any outside shots. The Knights play Tuesday at Skyline, one more game to get tuned up before Chesapeake. Mack has no concerns about that matchup and says they won't have a problem beating them. The three coaches discussed basketball like they would if they were gathered in the hallway back at Hoover High. Mack's wife had to remind him he couldn't get worked up, and the coaches changed the subject quickly but there wasn't anything else they wanted to talk about.

Monty prepares to tell Mack goodbye. He knows everything should go smoothly, and Mack should be just fine. He also knows you're never guaranteed tomorrow. Not long ago one of his high school buddies passed away unexpectedly. The suddenness hit him hard. Now he looks at Mack and makes sure he gives him a few heartfelt words before leaving.

When only his wife remains, Mack starts thinking about tomorrow morning again. Like everything in life, he likens it to the game of basketball. The uneasy feeling and the big buildup is sort of similar to what you experience on the eve of a big playoff game at the end of the season. One against an unknown team where you either survive and advance or lose and go home. Thoughts of all the possible scenarios play out in your head dominating your whole day and rendering everything else meaningless. At least that's what Mack was thinking earlier in the day. Now he is thinking this is nothing like the eve of a big game. It's much different. This is life and death.

CHAPTER 8

The players were told Mack would be out of surgery around 11:00 a.m. Monday morning. When noon came and they didn't hear anything they started to ponder the worst. A group of them went to Monty's classroom. He calmed them down by explaining this was likely due to delays in the surgeries before Mack's and it didn't necessarily mean anything went wrong. It wasn't until around 2:30 p.m. that word came in that Mack underwent a successful heart surgery. The team and the town let out sighs of relief.

With the good news, the Knights went out the next evening and easily won their game on the road at Skyline just like Mack predicted. Mack heard the news of the drubbing Tuesday night in the ICU ward where he was still recovering. Friday night's showdown with the Chesapeake Saints was postponed due to inclement weather that forced Hoover to take a snow day. Both Monty and Mack let out sighs of relief. It gives Monty and the team time to get their bearings, and it gives Mack a glimmer of hope that he might make it back to the bench for the contest depending on when the game gets rescheduled.

Mack got discharged over the weekend. His wife and doctor hound him to let basketball go and focus on recovery. Mack's sole focus *is* to recover, he assures them. This is his best chance to win a state championship, and he is going to do everything in his power to return as fast as he can. It's his dream to lead his team down to Des Moines and bring a title back home to Hoover. So yes, Mack tells them, he is only focused on recovering. Mack's goal is to be back coaching after Christmas. He is grateful to be home. Every little step is one step closer to getting back to his normal life. Of course Mack wanted to see Monty and Gordy right away to go over in detail everything he missed. They stopped by his house and watched game film together.

Mack was feeling really good for a few days until he wasn't. He woke up with pain in his chest again. It was accompanied by a horrendous cough and difficulty breathing. When his temperature rose past one hundred his wife drove him straight to the hospital. He was diagnosed with pleurisy, inflammation of the lungs. Mack was adamant, telling his doctor he didn't overdo it when he returned home. The doctor once again gave him direct orders to take it easy, warning him if he doesn't it will only further delay the time it takes to get back to coaching. Mack is not a happy camper knowing his goal of returning by the end of the month will no longer be met. He is allowed to go back home and ride out the illness there. His wife immediately enforces a strict no visitors and no phone calls rule. She also guards the remote and shuts down watching game film. It doesn't stop Mack; he writes up a scouting report on Chesapeake and plans to have his daughter mail it to Monty if the ban isn't lifted soon.

While Mack is in agony, the Hoover girls' basketball team plays on. Since dodging the best team in the league they remain undefeated. The shock of Mack being gone starts wearing off, and the new normal of having Monty as the head coach is setting in. There is no way to replicate Coach Mack. His prowess as an intimidating force on the sideline is unparalleled. Coach Monty runs practice similar to Mack, so nothing dramatically changes in that regard. He just isn't Mack. Monty is easygoing and soft spoken. Mack has a lot of sayings and analogies. Monty has dad jokes. The girls like Monty. If at times there is a "the cat's away the mice will play" vibe, the girls know when to be serious.

Monty has embraced his role as the head coach. He is proud of how the players have been able to focus amid the changes. He still has concerns about the weaknesses of their team. The most notable one is how the role players will develop. Monty sees how Zo and Bentley have gotten better. They are more polished from a year ago. Sasha has made the most improvement and is establishing herself as the conference's premier post player. Those three will carry the team, but they won't win a championship without other players stepping up. Both Krista and Hayley are getting their feet wet in their new starting roles. A few players are beginning to emerge as candidates to be able to give solid minutes off the bench; however, it's too early to tell how they will develop and look at the end of the season when everything will be on the line. Ellie's minutes are sporadic, but valuable. She is showing flashes of growth and toughness. Ashlyn Graves, a sophomore, is a JV player who looks promising. She is a good all-around athlete who favors the sport of golf. Mack isn't high on the kid. He isn't sure her heart is fully committed to basketball. Monty coached her on the JV team last year when she was a freshman, and he thinks once she gets some experience she'll be able to give them a spark. Ashlyn is what they call a tweener, a little small for a post player and a bit big to be a guard. She's a project like a lot of her JV teammates but one Monty thinks can blossom into something special.

At practices, the junior high coach Gordy Williams brings intensity when he shows up. The players agree Mr. Williams's junior high practices are tougher than Mack's. Not as strenuous, per say, just more meticulous. He loves defense and it's not a Mr. Williams practice session if they don't do the shell drill for an excruciating amount of time. He also believes teaching the basic fundamentals is key in development, so much so that he doesn't allow his seventh graders to play games against other teams. It's practice only. The kids might not like missing out on games but the results can't be denied. Going into eighth grade his players don't look down at the ball. The smelly passed-down goggles they wear in seventh grade that have the lower part blacked out ensures this. Their footwork is solid for that age, and if stats were kept they would have the least amount of turnovers from traveling or walking in the whole state.

Gordy is vastly different from M&M. For one, he still has three school-aged kids at home. He is an active participant in practice and often jumps into drills with his players. Another difference is their wardrobes. When Mack and Monty made a trip down to the eighth-grade gym to get a look at Sasha and Zo as eighth graders, they were wearing suits. The whole ensemble with coats and ties. Gordy was on the bench with jeans and a polo on. Sasha remembers being intimidated by the sight of the two high school coaches who looked to her like two detectives trying to put a scare into their suspects. She didn't think playing for them would be a pleasant experience.

Here at the varsity practices, Gordy says very little and defers to Monty knowing it's his show to run. He isn't afraid to challenge the girls though. Along with Miss Easton he takes the post players on one side of the court while Monty takes the guards on the other. One day, Gordy walked in with a surprise for the posts. He dug football blocking pads out of the storage closet. Gordy and Miss Easton use the giant square pads to clobber the posts while they try to make shots in the paint. The post players don't like this drill. Krista isn't afraid to make it known and tells her teammates in the locker room both coaches are putting some extra mustard into their forearm shivers. Games have started to get physical. Teams are having trouble stopping the Knights, and placing bodies on them is their new tactic. Gordy knows they will see even more of this as they get deeper into the season. The posts may not like Gordy's drill but Monty sure does. He thinks it's good for them. He sees the other teams attempting to muscle his players around. He sees them get away with it too. Especially against Sasha because she has an advantage. It's a fair one, but refs see a smaller body trying to compete with a bigger body and they take the little one's side. So Monty grins when Gordy Williams brings out the football pads. He's got his bad cop.

CHAPTER 9

Everyone who has ever played sports can tell you the bus rides are where some of their most memorable moments take place. Tonight the vibe on the bus is up a level. It's Tuesday, December 19, and tonight is the last game before Christmas break. A bonus for the Knights; they get to play on the road versus East Lyon—a pesky team that has a respectable 4–1 record in the conference. The Knights have breezed by their last few opponents and are yearning for a challenge.

Most of the players are already on the bus when freshman Mya Hendricks appears. The players had no idea she was going to be coming along. She got moved up to the JV team after two games, and now Monty is having her sit the bench for varsity games. With Bentley being the only true point guard on the team, he wants to cover the bases and make sure there is at least one backup on the bench. Mya is five feet nothing and has a mouth on her. With Hoover being a small town, they all know who Mya is. In fact, last year she was hovering around the starters after games along with her classmates, looking up to them in awe. Now, here she is boarding the bus about to join them. She feels like an imposter, knows she isn't that good yet, and that her dressing out for varsity games wasn't earned. Mya is determined to do something about that though because this has to be the coolest thing that has ever happened to her.

Mya takes a seat in the front of the bus where she belongs. The starters and upperclassmen sit in the back. Krista kneels up out of her seat and calls out: "Hey Mya, did your mom send like a booster seat or something for you?"

Laughter fills the bus.

Miss Easton, who is counting heads stops to give Krista a glare.

Krista shrugs. "Hey, safety first, right Miss E?"

Mya takes it like a good sport. It's something to be noticed by one of the starters. Mya doesn't dare share with the team now or ever how long her mom did make her sit in a booster seat because of her lack of height. It doesn't matter; the girls lovingly start calling her "Booster" from that moment on.

In the locker room at East Lyon, the Hoover players loosen up and easily go into their pregame pump up mode. Miss Easton covers her ears and has to go out in the hallway for some relief. Jemma joins her a few minutes later and tells her you get used to it. A student, one of the team's statisticians, walks in the locker room and walks right back out shaking her head. She asks Jemma and Miss Easton if *that* is how the locker room is before the game, what in the hell happens in there after?

The time they have to themselves before games is theirs, and they choose to play loud music. Sometimes they dance, sometimes they don't. It's always loud and some nights it's louder. The girls are especially excited tonight because Christmas is close and they know the Lions are out there waiting for them. Tonight they are going hard. It's a party atmosphere. Krista steals Bentley's phone. She's been telling everyone who will listen she has a song she wants to play during pregame. Krista finds it and cranks up the volume. Bentley and Zo groan; banjo's shouldn't be part of their pregame ritual. Everyone else lights up at the tune. Krista goes to the middle of the floor to sing. Her teammates clap along. Krista sings the words then yells them. Her teammates start to dance around her, even Bentley and Zo. The lyrics speak to each one of them, and by the end they are all belting out the chorus and scream when it gets to the part: "What do you want from me?" From here on out, this song has to be played before every game. It's mandatory. Jemma walks in to them going all out and with a wide grin tells them to get a hold of themselves because Monty is ready to come in. Bentley quickly turns on the song they always play last, and the girls settle into their seats.

Monty walks into smiles all around. He knows this night is different for them. This night is different for him too. After their first two games of the season they haven't had another game that has been even remotely close to competitive. It's been hard for him to tell how good this team really is. Tonight can shed some light on that, and he is eager to have a peek.

A rumble of crowd noise starts gathering steam when the starters get in their spots for the jump ball. East Lyon's gymnasium is old. It has an unusually low ceiling, which makes for a somewhat cozy or uncomfortable atmosphere depending on who you ask. Bentley commented before the game that she feels everyone in the crowd breathing on her when she plays here. On this night attendees drag in snow from their shoes, and the musty gym smell that's always present is stronger than normal.

The high school gym is the only place to be in this town on a below-freezing Tuesday night with Christmas just days away. It's the only place open besides the gas station on the edge of town, which will serve as the hangout spot for the local teenagers after the game. The gym is at capacity with kids home from college and relatives in town for the holidays. East Lyon's crowd stands for the tip-off. The Knights' student section is bigger than usual for an away game, and they stand up with them. East Lyon is revved up and ready to tango. The #1 team in their class is here to joust, and they want to knock them out of their top spot. Inspired by the bravado of the Lions and their crowd, the Knights' starters are lit up. They are craving competition, a real fight. East Lyon comes onto the floor appearing ready for the challenge.

The Lions look surprised by the speed of the Knights when Hoover wins the jump ball and takes off flying down the floor. The pace the Hoover Knights prefer is not easy for other teams to duplicate in practice. Because of this, the Knights tend to be the opponent who strikes first. Tonight is one of those times. Bentley and Zo are overflowing with energy at getting to play in a game like this. They love nothing more than to be confronted with a team and a crowd that wants to dismantle them. Both of them make transition buckets within the first two minutes. Sasha is crisp early making her first three shot attempts. Krista and Hayley, new to playing in a heated battle like this, take a number of possessions to settle their nerves down. After missing her first two shots, Hayley knocks down a three-pointer that boosts her confidence. Krista gets into a feisty exchange with her defender that heightens her senses. It's game on.

The Knights raced out to a 25–14 lead to end the first quarter. East Lyon doesn't shy away and adjusts to the Knight's tempo in the second quarter. They chip away at the eleven-point deficit. The Hoover coaches have become accustomed to seeing this trend; the Knights start out like gangbusters then cool off in the second quarter. Monty and Gordy aren't convinced it's always the other team being able to adjust to their pace of play. It seems to them the thrill of laying it on thick wears off and the team gets comfortable, or even somewhat bored. Whatever the root cause, the apparent coasting and playing down to the level of competition drives the coaches crazy. Tonight they continue the trend, and at halftime they are clinging to a narrow four-point lead.

The kids are calm in the locker room. Monty tries to sound urgent. Nobody on the team bats an eyelash. Almost as if they know they are good enough to win, no matter what, that East Lyon isn't a real threat, and letting them stay in the game is a game within itself. This doesn't sit well with Monty. He knows it stems from extreme confidence and that he will get their best when it's needed. He just doesn't like how they seem to pick and choose randomly when that will be. It makes every moment nerve-racking for him.

Both teams keep up the intensity, and the score remains close throughout the third quarter. The Knights aren't playing badly or with less effort; they just aren't hitting a high percentage of their shots and are playing a little loose on defense. The Lions are maintaining their fierce upset-driven attitude, showing that they could care less about Hoover's reputation. They have no top ranking to lose or any ranking at all for that matter, and they are playing like it.

A few minutes into the fourth quarter the gymnasium nearly shakes from the Lions fans responding to their team taking a two-point lead. A group of rowdy high school boys let the Knights hear about it and start the chant: "Overrated." *A bit soon*, is the first thought Coach Monty has after he feels his heart sink. The team he has been left in charge of is #1 in the state. If they lose to East Lyon, they may drop out of the top twenty-five. Being a head coach isn't for the weak. Monty feels his sweat-soaked shirt cling to his skin when he moves. This is new. He loosens his tie and immediately thinks of Mack. He smiles.

During the duration of the "overrated" chant, Bentley and Zo start playing chess with their defenders. It's their go-to move when they get challenged. The duo starts coming up with their own plays, ones they improvise, both reading the defense and getting each other open to make something happen. Both girls are athletic and have a knack for being able to change speeds and directions so fast that spectators' jaws drop in surprise, as well as in confusion. The two are not flawless, but the energy and competitive spirit they show frustrates opponents. Once they flip this switch, East Lyon, like the rest of the conference, struggles to contain them. Another constant when the going gets tough is to start forcing the ball inside to Sasha and let her go to work. In the first half Sasha saw a double-team after she scored ten points in the opening quarter. Her touches have been limited since. Sasha starts to get reacquainted with the hoop. The rest of the Knights start to raise their game with time on the scoreboard ticking closer to zero. Rebounds are secured, silly fouls cease, and they take the lead back.

East Lyon doesn't cower; they react to the Knights' surge by upping their level of play too. With their crowd helping them try to will a win, they keep within striking distance. They keep hanging around and when a three-point shot tickles the twine with a minute and fifty-three seconds left, it pulls them to within one point. A moment later they get the gift of the ball back with a Knight turnover. Time-out is called, and you can feel hope come alive in their gym.

For every spectator this game couldn't get any better. There are plenty of conference games played throughout the season that lack any drama or real competitiveness. This game has the feel of a game you get to see at the end of the year when it's win or go home. The Knights players don't look out of sorts when they make their way to the bench. There is no arguing over the missed assignment that allowed their opponent to make an uncontested three-pointer or the sloppy pass that gave them the ball back. There is no panic. Monty senses the confidence of his players and slows his voice down to a normal speed. This moment is what his team plays for. What they put in the work for. This is the fun part. At least for them it is.

Out of the time-out there is confidence in the eyes of the Lions players. They can feel the elation that will ensue if they can pull off a win. Hoover doesn't wait for East Lyon to set up; instead, they immediately bring intense pressure before the ref even hands the Lions player the ball. Bentley deflects the inbounds pass, and multiple bodies fly toward the loose ball. The Knights recover the golden egg and do what they do better than any other team in their conference: turn defense into instant offense. Hayley passes it ahead to Zo who takes it full speed to the hoop and goes airborne. She gets undercut finishing the layup and lands hard on the court while the ball lands in the hoop. The Hoover crowd reacts. Bentley, who is trailing the fast break, reacts too and dashes right in the face of the girl who took out her teammate. A ref lays on his whistle and steps between the two players. Bentley looks at him and puts her hands up. She then looks at Coach Monty still holding her hands up wondering, *What am I supposed to do?* Letting that go is not an option to Bentley. Not one that she can fathom.

Monty puts both of his hands up in the air and slowly fans them down in a gesture that says, "Take it easy, Bentley."

This is what Bentley's teammates love about her, and it makes her their leader. Bentley will be the first to make fun of you for coming into the locker room wearing mittens knitted by your grandma, but if someone on the other team tries anything, anything at all, Bentley has your back, never backing down even an inch.

Zo is slow to get up. She waves off Monty and gives him a thumbs-up. Zo's teammates surround her as she walks to the free-throw line. She holds her elbow tightly then extends it and shakes it out. With the home crowd trying to distract her with taunts, Zo drains the free throw with ease and extends the Hoover lead to four.

At the other end, Hoover continues to lay on the pressure. Thick. The Lions don't look confident anymore and are playing keep away from the Knights even though they are the ones who need to score. They are wasting a lot of time. A brave Lions player hoists up a desperation three-pointer that is nearly blocked by Bentley. Krista rebounds the miss and throws a long outlet to Hayley who goes full steam ahead to the basket. The Lions defender is late to contest the shot, resulting in another *and one* opportunity for the Knights. Frustrations are boiling over for the Lions. The game is out of reach with time close to expiring and both coaches wisely make substitutions. Krista puts a finger in the air stating their #1 ranking then waves to the East Lyon crowd as she's being subbed out for Ashlyn. When Krista sits on the bench Monty walks by and lets her know, "We don't need any of that."

The Knights are going into the winter break 6–0. The Lions players are deflated walking through the required "good game" handshake line after the horn goes off. They don't know what more they could have done. The Knights give them a nod of respect for challenging them. For making it difficult.

Monty keeps his speech short to the team afterward. They are wired up, ready to burst out of the gym and into their winter break. Monty tells them they played well enough to win but they have to start playing all thirty-two minutes of the basketball game the way they played the last few if they want to beat the great teams. Once Monty tells them "go have a great Christmas" and walks out, it's party time. The rush of adrenaline lingers. The girls are excited to be free and go off on their holiday break. Still, they take their sweet time to have some fun and jump around as their favorite songs play, taking a moment to relish the little taste of March they received on a frigid night in December.

CHAPTER 10

At 10:00 a.m. on Friday December 30, the team reconvenes. Monty decided against bringing the team back any earlier. He felt the girls could use some rest and some time away from everything after going through all they did to start the season. He knew he could use a break. His family traveled to northern Minnesota to visit relatives. It was a nice getaway even though his mind never drifted far from his basketball team.

An hour into practice, Monty starts to think he made a big mistake. Their focus isn't there. The players are in vacation mode. They look lethargic and show little enthusiasm for being there. The next day he gets the same results. Due to their state of play and because Mack has implemented this in the past as a way to see who prioritized the team over partying, Monty lets the girls know they will be practicing the following day. Sunday. New Year's Day. Bright and early at 7:00 a.m. The players exchange "you're kidding" looks when Monty makes the announcement at the end of practice. Monty is used to being the good cop and can't help but take the blame saying he should have brought them back a few days earlier to get back in the swing of things.

At 6:45 a.m. the morning after New Year's Eve, players start to show up. With sleepy faces they put their gear on. One by one they grab a basketball and start warming up. With a few minutes, until the clock strikes seven, Sasha starts to ask around about the only player who's missing, Krista. "Well, she's cutting it close," Ellie says.

"Um yeah," Sasha replies. "I'm not running up and downs for her getting to ring in the New Year properly."

"If Mack was here, she'd already be in trouble. You know his favorite quote: 'Ten minutes early not one second late.'"

Bentley walks by and says, "Her ass would be grass."

The girls keep glancing at the big hand of the clock in between shots, watching it tick closer to twelve. They are nervous for Krista and for themselves wondering what the punishment is going to be if she is late or misses practice altogether. A big boom by the outside entrance to the gym gets everyone's attention. Krista plows through the door huffing and puffing. Her basketball shoes shuffle snow slush in with her. Jemma rolls her eyes and takes off to get a towel from the locker room to clean it up. There are murmurs and hushed giggles. Krista wiggles out of her sweatshirt and walks on the court at the same time Coach Monty blows his whistle signaling the start of practice.

Bentley looks back at her in the layup line. "That was a grand entrance K-dog. Smooth."

Krista tries to hide a smile. "Suck it."

The coaches work the girls hard. Gordy and Miss Easton drag out the football pads. The post players look down and hide their eye rolls to each other. Thirty minutes into practice, Monty blows his whistle for a good ten seconds then throws his hands up. He's never lost his temper before. Without yelling he says, "I guess let's just run awhile. We aren't doing anything else right."

Monty senses the players losing their cool and blows his whistle for a water break. The players spill out into the commons area to get a drink and recover.

"What in the h-e-double hockey sticks?" Sasha yells.

Everyone slides down the brick wall to have a seat.

Mya's face is flushed, and sweat is trickling off her hair. "Is this normal?"

Ellie who is sitting beside her is too winded to talk so she taps Mya's arm and shakes her head no.

After a few minutes of silence, Bentley starts laughing and says, "Krista, you came running in looking like a scarecrow with its ass on fire."

When she catches her breath Krista replies, "You're damn right. How many seconds did I spare?"

Hayley giggles and says, "Like three."

Krista stands up to get another drink at the fountain. "You guys would have been proud of me though. I didn't drive or get in with anyone who was drinking. Promise." She takes one more sip from the fountain then walks back to take her seat against the wall. "I never went to the

Helton house either. Never made it. But I got home at like one, and a bunch of my relatives were still partying. So yeah, Krista's not feeling so hot. I got like two hours of sleep. My uncles and cousins kept me up. I put my practice clothes and hoodie on so I could keep hanging with them. Then later before my head hit my pillow I managed to get my socks and shoes on so I could just wake up and roll out the door."

Hayley stares at her with a mix of worry and wonder.

Maya raises her eyebrows and asks, "You slept in your shoes?"

Jemma walks out. "Get back in here, ladies."

Krista puts her fist up to flip her off then smiles and puts up her thumb instead. The girls groan and slowly rise up to go back in for more punishment.

Jemma giggles as they pass her by, "Happy New Year."

"This is Mack," Krista hisses. "You all know he's behind this."

Monty has the team run through their plays after the break. It's sloppy at best. When Ashlyn and Ellie forget how the play "wildcat" is run, Monty gives up. He sends them to the baseline to run again.

"They should snap out of it soon," Gordy says to Monty, in the most convincing tone he can muster. "They got used to staying up late and sleeping in until noon. They will adjust fast with school starting tomorrow."

"Well, we have a game in two days so I sure hope so," Monty says. "I should have brought them back sooner to get them back in the flow like Mack did last season. They seem uncharacteristically complacent, and I thought that before the break."

The players struggle to run their down and backs. Their pace reaches a slow jog. Monty blows his whistle and tells the team to stop for a breather. When she can bring herself upright Krista shrugs and in a barely audible voice says, "They obviously want someone to puke." She speed walks to the trash bin in the corner and puts her face in it. Sounds of deep suffering and agony fill the gym. Her teammates turn away and spread out immediately.

"Sheesh, Krista," Bentley yells. "Gross! Why did she do that here? She could have gone to the commons."

Hunched over the trash can with her back to everyone, Krista finally stands up. She wipes her mouth then turns to face everyone. "You want me to throw this?"

Across the court Monty doesn't move an inch. "Take it to the dumpster out back." Krista unwraps the black trash bag from the big plastic bin and hauls it away. Monty calls everyone over to him. Practice jerseys are drenched in sweat, and red faces gaze at their coach. "Look, I know it's early and I know it's New Years Day. I gave you guys a longer break because I thought you could use it. These last three days of practice have not been productive. Tomorrow we get back to normal. This week we play two teams that we can't take lightly."

The players eye each other. They know this means they aren't very good. Monty clears his throat to bring their attention back to him. "The following week we play Mason Valley at their place on Friday night and turn around to play the Saints on Saturday night. That is *somehow*, according to the powers that be, the only time they can fit in the makeup game over at Chesapeake."

The girls groan. Monty wasn't happy when he was given the information by the athletic director either. In fact, his groan was louder.

"That's two back-to-back nights of playing road games. Two excellent programs. Two of the best teams in the state in their respective classes." Monty looks around at the group of girls. "This is it, ladies. The heart of our year is coming up. I know to you all it can feel like a long season, but we basically have the month of January then shortly into February it becomes win or you're out."

Monty knows time for teenagers is interpreted differently. He remembers this from his own children and even his own childhood. Kids carry with them the notion that you have all the time in the world. They think their life will always be the way it is in the present. Monty wants them to realize it will be over in the blink of an eye. "Don't miss the moment" is what he used to preach to his daughters. Monty puts his hands up and everyone joins him. "Let's come to practice tomorrow and really get after it, ladies. Together on three."

The players walk over by the bleachers stacked against the wall. They grab their belongings and scatter as fast as they can. Most have their minds on going home and climbing back into bed. Jemma gives her niece a ride home. Zo sulks in the passenger seat staying quiet. Jemma, always talkative, engages anyway. "I guess Krista partied it up last night, huh?" Jemma maintained a serious demeanor all throughout the brutal practice session and flashes Zo her trademark smile. "That was disgusting."

Zo doesn't show any emotion and replies, "She didn't even throw up."

"Are you serious?"

"Yep. We thought she did too. Said she took one for the team."

"That little shit." Jemma goes quiet before adding, "I guess it worked. Shortest practice ever."

"Yep."

"So how was your brea—" Jemma catches herself. She knows how Zo's break was. She is one of the very few who knows what Zo is dealing with at home. Jemma switches gears. "I bet you're excited for games to start up again."

Zo shifts uncomfortably in her seat and says, "Yeah."

Glad to be in her driveway, Zo gives Jemma a hurried goodbye. Zo was the only one unhappy with all the days off Monty gave them. It was boring without basketball. Time froze without basketball. Winter break felt like a month to her. She just wanted to get on with the previously scheduled program. The bright spot of Zo's break was when she went with Sasha to visit Mack. It was a few days after Christmas and Mack's grandchildren eagerly showed off their Christmas presents. Sasha and Zo helped put together a giant Lego then played a board game with all the kids. Sasha brought Mack a glittery tin container full of homemade cookies she made with her mom. When Mack asked Zo where his Christmas present from her was she told him he would have to wait until March for it. Mack liked that answer.

Mack is progressing. He is starting to feel more and more like his old self and has his healing heart set on a return to the team soon. For him, time feels like it's running out. Mack wants back on the court and is targeting the end of January. He has resolved to keep this goal to himself.

CHAPTER 11

The Hoover Knights pick up right where they left off and win the first two games of the new year. The routine of practice and games is in full swing. The team still feels Mack's absence even if they don't say much about it. Krista and Bentley feel it more. This is their senior year, and Mack is missing it. Both are holding out hope he will return by the end of the season. It wouldn't be the same trying to accomplish their dream without him or ending their career with him never returning to the bench. Bentley is having her best season yet. She has the attributes of a steady, reliable point guard. She never tries to do too much. The coaches always know what they will get on a nightly basis from her: solid, consistent play. Even in games where she doesn't have big numbers, she always has a hand in every play. Bentley's teammates follow her lead. They take on her tough "you have to go through me" attitude. Mack gave Monty a letter to be read to the team when they got back from their holiday break. Monty, knowing Bentley isn't one to show any indication of suffering even in the slightest, gave her Mack's letter to keep. She placed it in a pocket in her backpack and reads it on game days.

Krista has been a strong contributor at the power forward position this year. She has earned her starting role. Her attitude and effort is noticeably higher than it was last season. Krista, who always seems to be at odds with Coach Mack, broke down the morning they were told he was in the hospital. She thought of all the times she was a pain in his backside—Mack's words—when she didn't really have to be. The two of them made big strides in their relationship since last season. At the state tournament, Krista didn't get many minutes, but they were important minutes and she rose to the occasion. She showed flashes of toughness and the coaching staff noticed her value. Mack softened his stance with

Krista since then, and the two of them even started to, on occasion at least, banter back and forth in a lighthearted way.

Krista will never say she misses Mack, but before a late practice in January she makes it clear he is on her mind.

"Hey Jems," Krista calls out.

Jemma is at the desk in the locker room office grading papers and can't even see Krista. Krista lets out a whistle. "Yoo-hoo!"

Jemma takes her time to appear in the doorway. "Yes, Miss Krista?"

"Isn't it weird that Mack has like no contact with us?"

Jemma looks at her with a blank reaction.

Krista shrugs. "Like don't you think it would be good for his recovery to see us or at least make some sort of contact?"

"You think it would be healthy for him to talk to *you*, Krista?" Bentley says, and giggles. "His doctor probably highly advised against that."

Sasha, Zo, and Hayley, the only other players in the locker room at the time, share a good laugh. Krista flips out her middle finger and waves it around at them before she looks at Jemma for a response.

"Honestly, Krista," Jemma says, "I think he doesn't want to be a distraction."

"Um, he pretty much had like a heart attack right before our first game of the season. I don't think him seeing us would top that."

Jemma shakes her head. The girls don't know if she's about to lose her patience or crack a smile. She stays serious. "He's following doctor's orders. He did stop by practice not long after his surgery, remember? He rebounded for you guys a little bit. You don't know this, but he had to stay in bed three days after that because he was so tired and sore. Plus, think about it, he doesn't want to be around until he can fully participate. It would burn him up not being able to do any coaching. Believe me he wishes he were here, and as soon as his doctor gives him the clearance, he'll be here 100 percent."

The girls are quiet. Jemma realizes how much they miss Mack and are keeping everything in. It's the first time Jemma has heard them talk about Mack in this way.

"He needs to focus on his recovery, and he wants you guys to focus on playing and not on him." Jemma pauses. "He sure hasn't forgotten about you guys one bit. He's keeping tabs on you for sure.

"So do you think he's coming back soon?" Bentley asks.

"Yeah, is it going to be soon?" Sasha asks. "I heard he was seen at our last home game, so like, if that's true I'm guessing he's getting close to returning."

Mack snuck into the gym to watch some of their first game after the break. His wife and one of their friends helped him make it up the side stairwell to watch from the upper deck. He hoped he would go unnoticed. It was a blow-out win, and he left right before halftime. He wore a hat thinking it would help hide his presence. It didn't.

"I have no idea," Jemma says. "I know if it was up to him he'd already be back. He has to be cleared by his doctor, and I don't know when that will be."

The girls drop it and change the subject. More of their teammates arrive, and they get ready to take the floor as soon as the boys practice is over. When they get on the court they bounce around with excited energy. This is the part of the day they look forward to the most. Getting to play. Smiles and chitchat fill the gym.

Monty calls Jemma over before practice starts. She stands next to him watching the team take warm-up shots. Monty keeps his eyes straight ahead. "They're messing with me, right?"

Jemma glances at him perplexed. She has no idea what he's talking about until she follows his gaze. Jemma watches Zo and Bentley for a moment. They are putting up shots and yapping their mouths in between. Shoot-around before practice is the last chance everyone has to talk to each other and goof around before the whistle blows and it's time to go to work.

"You're talking about Zo and Bentley?"

Monty looks at her out of the corner of his eye and nods.

Jemma works hard not to laugh. "What, did they tell you their DJ idea?"

Monty turns to her and says, "They aren't serious, are they?"

Jemma puts her hand over her mouth trying to contain laughter. "Oh yeah they are serious about that. They've been talking about it since before the season started. I'm sure they think with Mack away you might be easier to convince."

Monty can't help but smile. "Well, I wasn't sure they were being serious because the other day a bunch of them were talking about some kind of band or musician. I guess I pronounced the name wrong and now I have a new nickname."

Jemma laughs out loud with no restraint.

"Now those two jokers bring up getting a DJ for home games. Want the lights to be turned off for the starting lineups and have the DJ announce them with music and strobe lights flashing. They want time-outs to be a party for the crowd."

Jemma nods knowingly. She is well aware of the details. She has overheard all this discussed in the locker room.

Monty looks at her again and raises his eyebrows. "They want me to take their request to the school board to see if they will approve it. I thought for sure they were yanking my chain."

Jemma smiles. "Nope it's a real idea they dreamt up."

"That's exactly right; they'll have to keep dreaming." Monty laughs. He shakes his head and keeps watching his players toss up shots. "I feel a little bad about how I responded. They spoke about it with such passion. They've even come up with a fundraising idea to pay for it. They want to have a post-game concert in the parking lot and charge a cover."

Jemma shakes her head. "Oh that part is new."

"They even have the name of a kid out of Sioux Falls they want to use. His name is DJ Falls or Snow Fall, I don't know what the heck it is." Monty throws his hands up in the air. "I was sure they were messing with me."

Jemma turns around to burst out laughing. When she recovers, she turns back around. "Gotta love them don't you, Coach?"

"Oh, all of them. They have that special youthful hopefulness you kind of want to steal at least for a few minutes a day."

CHAPTER 12

Tonight's date with Mason Valley has vanquished any signs of complacency Monty recognized earlier. The Knights are going through warmups preparing for a wild encounter with the Mustangs and their small but rabid fan base. Hoover won their first three games of the new year all by more than twenty points and remain #1 in class 2A, while the Mason Valley Mustangs have jumped up to the #9 spot in class 1A.

The "cellar," the nickname given to the smallest and the oldest gym in the conference, is thumping with energy. Monty runs his hands through his hair on the sidelines. He looks at the Hoover crowd behind him that have filled up every seat available in their section. With such a small space for seating, the Hoover fans will get to feel like they are part of the huddle tonight. Monty can't help it and keeps thinking of tomorrow night's rendezvous with the Chesapeake Saints, a team that has been at the top of the conference for a decade. That game is all anyone wants to talk to him about, and that's been the case for the past two weeks. It bothers him that Chesapeake is playing a cupcake home game right now while his team has to play the second toughest opponent in the conference. The Saints' coach can sit his starters in the second half to get them rested for the twenty-four-hour turnaround if he chooses. Monty won't have that luxury.

The buzzer sounds. It's game time. The Knights are eager to play in this gym tonight. They walk out to line up for the tip-off with some bravado. They aren't the same young team that was outplayed in the season opener here a season ago. Even though they avenged that loss last year when the Mustangs visited their home court and beat them again at home to start this season, this is their first time back in this gym. Bentley and Zo haven't forgotten, and they know to get complete revenge they need to win on this court. For Sasha, this night is important too. She didn't get to play in last season's opener here because she badly sprained her ankle in practice the day before. Having to watch the loss, she knew what it meant to her teammates. Sasha is ready to put her own stamp on this rivalry game. Krista was the one who took Sasha's place in the starting lineup that game, and it wasn't a great experience for her. She, too, is anxious to get the bad taste of this gym out of her mouth.

The Mustangs make it known they have come to play. Tara Kleinhold, Mason Valley's center and best player, brings her arm in front of Sasha's to block her space in the center circle while the two wait for the ref to toss up the jump ball. Sasha is surprised but doesn't hesitate and returns the favor. The two do this dance over and over with the ref pausing to wait for peace before he releases the ball in the air to start the game. Kleinhold and the Mustangs don't like the Hoover Knights one bit. They got whipped up at Hoover to start the season, and they want to prove they are better than the score reflected. A mere 9.7 miles is all that separates Hoover from the much smaller town of Mason Valley. The Mustangs can't stand hearing all the noise about Hoover and their greatness. They want their own shine. If they can beat the #1 team in class 2A, they will earn it.

The ball is tipped and the two teams are off to the races. The Mustangs bring a pace to match the Knights. Having learned their lesson in the first contest, the Mustangs decided if you can't beat them, join them. The pace is blistering. The Knights don't mind it one bit. Chaos is encouraged. You want to go crazy? Let's party. Monty right away thinks Mason Valley's strategy is 'If we can't beat them, let us wear them out so Chesapeake can.'

The strategy doesn't pay off for the home team. The Knights are on high alert. The weekend challenge of facing the two toughest teams in the area brings out their best. They lead 15–8 after one quarter then go on a 12–4 run in the second quarter to extend their lead to 29–12. By the time halftime comes, the Knights are up nineteen.

Facing a big disadvantage, the Mustangs come out for the third quarter with some feistiness. They bring their best pressure defense and steal the ball from Bentley with an obvious reach in. After her opponent scores a fast break layup, Bentley lifts up her arm to inspect the red welt on her wrist. She doesn't look the refs way for an answer. She grits her teeth and brings the ball up the court with a determined look on her face. The ball gets swung around, and Hayley feeds Krista at the top of the key after a down screen gets her open. Her shot gets blocked from a guard who creeps up on her from behind. The Mustangs race to the other end and hit a short jump near the low block. A quick ten-to-three run to start the second half has Monty calling an early time-out and toweling off the sweat on his forehead. He tells the team to relax a bit. Ride this wave that is hitting them without overreacting. Monty glances at Bentley because she has on her face a "get even" look he disapproves of.

Zo finds Bentley on the walk out onto the court and whispers, "They got nothing on us, B."

Bentley nods and gets ready to get the inbounds pass. Bentley and Zo play with a fire inside them. One lets it shine outwardly, and one keeps it to herself. Both approaches give the other one confidence on the court. The ball is inbounded to Bentley. She stiffens her upper lip and charges into the lane. The Mustang center meets her to cut off her progress so she flips the ball over to Sasha who scores over their power forward with ease. On the other end, Sasha leaps up and blocks the shot of a guard who thought she had enough space to get the ball off. Sasha's fire is starting to be stoked, and teams are becoming very much aware they no longer have just the two talented Hoover guards to worry about. They now have a strong, skilled center to stop. Sasha is making Hoover nearly impossible to go up against. The sudden attention Sasha is receiving from opposing teams is nothing new for her. When you're always the tall one everywhere you go you get used to being the focal point. Everyone has something to say about you. It's the first thing you get noticed for. Strangers more times than not make the same obvious statement when they see her: You are tall. Sasha has learned to be ready for it. To accept people's wonder at the sight of her height. There is nowhere to hide and no way of avoiding it. Out on the basketball court Sasha has learned to embrace who she is, height and all. On the court she can shine. She can stand as tall as she is and be a difference maker. Tonight that is what she is being. Her and her teammates turn it up and don't allow the Mustangs to get within seven points. By the time the third quarter ends, they have a comfy fifteen-point lead. Two minutes into the fourth quarter they stretched the lead to twenty-three. Monty is pleased by how they weathered the run from the Mustangs. The Mason Valley coach looks up at the scoreboard wondering if it's correct. Just a moment ago they were in the game.

It's a great win for Hoover. They didn't shoot the ball well tonight. It was their defense leading to transition buckets that made the difference. They held the Mustangs to a season low thirty-eight points. Sasha came up big with a double-double; sixteen points to go along with thirteen rebounds. With the bigger game waiting for them tomorrow night, this game doesn't seem as significant. Monty liked what he saw tonight and is more relieved to get the win amidst the distraction of the buildup to Chesapeake. He could see the noticeable difference in the kids tonight. Their intensity level was high throughout the entire game. The coaches rode them hard in practice leading up to this contest knowing the importance of this weekend and the players answered the call. When the chips were on the line, they responded. In the locker room after the win Monty briefly praises them before he turns the attention to their next opponent. Tomorrow night will be the first time this season they will be underdogs.

Krista starts untying her laces then stops. "That's not fair. The Saints had to play Okoboji tonight. Big whoop."

Monty's hand is on the door. He turns back abruptly. "Krista, fair is a place with fried pickles and a tilt-a-whirl."

"And creepy carnies," Ellie adds, with a smile.

Bentley blurts out: "That's a *boyfriend* if you're Krista."

The girls laugh, and Krista's face turns red. "Shut up, Bentley. He was tamales!"

Monty has no idea what is happening. He only knows he doesn't want any part of it. Before the door closes behind him he changes the subject and says, "All right we have a big day tomorrow, so let's cheer on the boys' team, but right at halftime we're heading home."

Miss Easton and Jemma shoot Krista shocked expressions before following Monty out the door. Krista puts her hands up and says, "He was in high school okay!"

Bentley waits for the door to close and says, "I highly doubt it, and he wasn't hot."

Krista turns to Bentley and heaves her shooting shirt at her. "Thanks for bringing that up in front of the coaches, Bentley! And how do you even know how old he was or how hot he was? You never even met him."

"I *saw* him!"

Krista's eyebrows raise, "You did?"

"You brought him to the fair dance!"

Sasha giggles. "Oh Krista!"

Staying locked in on Bentley, Krista says, "And you didn't think he was cute?"

"Ah, no Krista I didn't."

Sasha starts giggling again. "What carnie isn't your type?"

Bentley puts her head down to laugh then looks up and says, "He was sketch-city."

Ellie's mouth drops open. "Oh my gosh I *remember* seeing you dance with a guy at the fair who I didn't recognize. He *was* cute. Wasn't he working there on his summer break from college or something like that?"

Krista points at Ellie and smiles, "Thank you!" She sticks her tongue out at Bentley.

"Don't do that!" Bentley stands up lightning fast and waves her finger in the air. "Ellie is just being nice. He wasn't in any school. Or something like that is juvie."

"Come on B," Zo says. "Maybe he was doing an internship or he's in med school and the fair is training."

Krista smirks at Zo. "Smart ass."

With no change in emotion Ashlyn chimes in: "It sounds more like a work release program."

"All you guys can suck it, okay." Krista tosses her shoes at her bag in frustration. She attempts to stay serious but it doesn't last; she starts to smile then doubles over in laughter.

"Oh sheesh," Bentley says. "You know this has to be good. Don't tell me, Krista, that you followed this guy from town to town all summer or something."

Krista doesn't respond.

Bentley's eyes go wide as saucers. "Oh my gosh did you?"

Zo twirls her jersey in the air and sings out, "Follow me and I'll hook you up with free corn dogs at every stop, girl."

Krista recovers enough to speak. "No, but he wanted me to come to the next stop in Vinton, and he was asking me to—." Krista can't get any more out; she covers her mouth and starts laughing again.

"Oh no," Ellie says. "Booster, cover your ears!"

Krista waves her off. "No he was asking me to buy him one of those—" She pauses to gather herself. "Gas station pre-paid phones so we could stay together."

Bentley loses it and starts laughing so hard tears roll down her cheeks. It's a ripple effect for the rest of the upperclassman. The JV players stay indifferent.

When it calms down Mya asks, "Well, did you get him one?"

Krista stares at Mya with pierced lips. "Booster, I swear you're like a little kid. All you do is ask a freaking zillion questions."

Mya smiles and asks, "Well, did you?"

Sasha laughs and mocks, "Yeah, Krista, are you guys together forever?"

"No, I didn't. Almost."

"Poor Booster," says Bentley. She changes her voice to a soothing one and adds, "Booster, don't be like Krista, okay? Be like Hayley."

Krista flips Bentley off then looks at Mya. "Hey, tiny."

"Yes, Krista?"

"These conversations don't leave the locker room. I hope you know that."

"Oh yeah, Krista, I can't wait to get home and tell my baby brother another Krista story." Mya likes the attention on her. She stands up to continue. "I tell my parents that story, *I* get grounded."

They move on and the girls make a conscious effort to try to reel in their amped-up energy. With no days off to recover, they are preparing internally for another game tomorrow night. One they are highly anticipating and one they will not be favored in. After getting snacks at the concession stand, they sit and watch the boys' game. Their bus pulls away from the Mason Valley gym at halftime like Monty promised. The players are going to their cars by 9:00 p.m. and advised to go home. Most do.

CHAPTER 13

In the quiet of the visitors' locker room, the Hoover Knights with their 10–0 record are getting ready to go to battle. Bodies and bags are scattered around. Loud music blasts through the speaker that Bentley placed in the middle of the room. The Knights are going through their usual pregame routine with something that hasn't accompanied the team as a whole this season: intense nerves. Across the building in the comfort of their home locker room the Chesapeake Saints, also undefeated, are taping ankles, tying bows, and tucking in uniforms.

This is the clash of the two unbeaten and best teams in the conference. While the Hoover Knights lost to the 3A Saints last season, they were the only team from the conference that went on to qualify for the state tournament. The Saints lost a heartbreaking game coming within three points of making it to state. So while the Knights were getting fawned over for making it to state and getting all the way to the championship game, the Saints had to sit at home with the sting of falling well short of their quest. They quietly went back to work and focused on getting better. Having only lost one senior starter from last year's team, optimism is abounding in Chesapeake. Like Hoover, they believe this is *their* year.

The styles of these two teams couldn't be more different. The Saints are disciplined, consistent, and have great depth. They patiently execute their offense with precision and play smart defense. The Saints are methodical. The Knights are chaotic. They use the court as their playground. They play off the cuff and in your face in a hurried fashion. Regardless of the conflicting styles, both have this in common; they win a lot and share the same dream of winning a state championship.

The noise in the Knights' locker room keeps rising. There is a serious, nerve-induced manner at which the girls bounce around the room. Jemma walks in and motions for them to kill the music. She announces the coaches will be coming in here in two minutes. Zo sways like a boxer, Bentley stalks the room like she is looking to fight, Krista keeps punching her fist into her hand, and Sasha is jumping up and down trying to get loose. Hayley, the only starter sitting down is locked in with her hands massaging her temples. The reserves are bouncing around feeling the nervous energy. This is their first time going against the Chesapeake Saints.

Chesapeake is ranked #2 in class 3A. The Knights are ranked #1 in class 2A. While no one would be surprised if Hoover came away with a win, most in the conference would agree that Chesapeake is the better overall team. When both teams pour onto the gym floor within seconds of each other, the Chesapeake gym lights up. Monty takes in the atmosphere and tells Gordy this feels a lot like Hoover's game to get to state last year. Gordy agrees, saying it has the feel of that special time of the year: tournament time. It's a welcome feeling. Moments like these are what you play and coach for.

The girls come to the bench antsy. Their nerves are at an all-time high. Monty has trouble addressing the girls because the crowd noise is deafening. The players feel the heat; the Chesapeake gym is bigger than theirs and they have a large intimidating home crowd. The Knights walk out to the center of the court feeling like villains. The ball is tossed into the air and so begins the clash of the titans. Both teams come out looking tight. Sasha gets fouled on an early possession. A shooting foul she steps to the line with a chance to score the first points of the game. The crowd noise is pulsating through the gym. Sasha misses both free throws, and the crowd noise goes up another decibel level. The Saints miss their first couple of shots too, and the score stays at zeros.

The Saints, feeling a little more comfortable being at home, loosen up first and make three consecutive baskets. With the score 6–0, the Knights feel the pressure. It's three minutes into the game and Hoover can't score. The Knights steal the ball down low and set up for another try. Zo unleashes one of her trademark bombs. The one that draws a loud reaction from the Hoover faithful to the effect of "No no no no. YES!" Zo's three-pointer quiets the Saints crowd for a moment and cuts the lead in half. During the next offensive possession for Hoover, Sasha redeems herself and makes a nice shot from the high post. The Knights start to settle in, and both teams start to trade baskets while the first quarter melts away. Before the horn sounds, Zo pulls up at the top of the key and hits another deep three to give the Knights a 16–15 lead.

Hoover came to win, and in the second quarter you can see they are feeling good. The nerves are gone. Bentley grabs a steal and finds Zo for a breakaway layup. On Hoover's following possession, Bentley drives right at the Saints' senior point guard, Brit Larson, and all she can do to defend her is foul her as she goes up for a shot. Bentley shakes her fist in the air then makes both free throws. The Knights are rolling. Krista already has four rebounds, and Hayley made her first shot attempt. Zo is on fire. She is carving the defense up, slicing into the lane and finishing at the hoop with ease. She is three of four from the three-point line. The Saints call a time-out to regroup and come out focused on stopping the Knights high scorer. Zo recognizes the new attention and finds Sasha in the post with beautiful looks for field goals on consecutive possessions. Since missing her free throws, Sasha is three for three from the field. The crowd is witnessing Hoover at its best; their inside and outside game makes them hard to stop.

The first critical moment of the matchup comes halfway through the second quarter. With the Knights playing seamless basketball, Larson wiggles into the lane trying to make something happen and gets all the way to the basket. The noise from the Saints crowd goes off the charts when Sasha is whistled for her third foul. Hoover fans rain down boos, feeling like it was a phantom foul. Sasha is a tough matchup for Chesapeake. Their tallest player is a good four inches shorter. Everyone in the gym knows the best chance for the Saints to be able to beat the Knights is to get Sasha in foul trouble. With three fouls to her name, they only need to draw two more to get her out of the game for good. Monty has a dilemma. If he takes Sasha out the inside game will be crushed. The Saints have two skilled, experienced posts who will be going up against two less experienced posts with Sasha relegated to the bench. If Monty leaves Sasha in and she picks up her fourth foul, he might need to keep her on the bench until the last quarter. Monty decides he has to show a little faith in the bench and sends Ellie in.

The Saints take full advantage of the open space in the middle. The Chesapeake coach knows how good Hoover's big three are. Even so, he knows Hoover can't win with any of them on the bench while his team can win with multiple starters out. With Sasha watching from the sidelines, he sends a girl to double-team Zo when she gets the ball and adds pressure to Bentley bringing the ball up. One star down, two to go.

Ellie plays as tough as she can, but she doesn't have the size nor the skill to be able to keep the floodgates from opening. The Saints play with new life knowing they are getting a gift with Hoover's imposing center on the bench. Krista is doing her best on defense, but her girl is quicker and more athletic. The Saints keep feeding their post players on offense and driving into the middle of the lane. On the Hoover bench Monty stews. This is the exact scenario they couldn't afford to have happen. With Sasha on the bench the game has drastically changed. The Knights were winning and in control before she went out. Monty steps over to one of the refs when there is a break in the action. The refs like Monty. He has developed a good repertoire with them over the years. This is one of the advantages of being an assistant coach. Good cop.

"Myron, why is my center watching this game next to me?"

The ref takes his whistle out, keeping it an inch away from his mouth, and says, "She went over her back, Coach."

Monty shakes his head and puts his hands up. "She was straight up and down."

This only gets an eyebrow raise from the ref.

"Don't punish her for being the tallest girl on the floor." Monty shakes his head in frustration. "Should I just tell her to get comfortable and eat some popcorn?"

The ref smiles and removes the whistle again. "She leaned into her. Got too much body, Coach."

Monty tilts his head and folds his arms. He doesn't agree. From his perspective, the Saints player went hard into Sasha's body. He isn't going to argue it anymore. "All right," he says in a quiet voice. He slumps down next to Sasha. "You just like sitting next to me, huh?"

"Oh yeah," Sasha says. "I might as well get some pom-poms."

"We will get you back out there, kid. I know it seems unfair, but don't lose your cool when you get back in."

Sasha shakes her head in frustration and drapes a towel over her head. Out on the floor Ellie picks up another foul, clubbing a Saints player on a layup.

"Doggone it," Monty yells.

Gordy whispers, "That's two fouls on her, Coach."

Monty looks down the length of the bench, stops himself from shaking his head, and yells, "Ashlyn, check in for Ellie!."

The Saints go on a 19–8 run to end the quarter taking a 43–31 lead into halftime. The girls are frustrated, knowing fouls are the main culprit. They *should* be winning this game. Monty makes it clear right away there can be no hanging heads. No excuses. Play hard and play the hand we're dealt. He walks over to the chalkboard, writes 23–12, and informs them this is how bad they are losing the rebound battle.

Monty points to the discrepancy and says, "Desire. This is what this stat is. Do you want it more? Get on the glass! If we want to win this game, we have to change these numbers in the second half. It's not just for the post players either. It's a team stat. Everyone should be crashing the boards."

The girls are engaged and chomping at the bit to get back out on the court. Monty says this before he sends them out: "We are up against a tough challenge. We can get back in this game. Chip away, little by little. There is no twelve-point shot. I don't want anyone trying to take one. Dig in and start chipping away."

Coming out of halftime, the Knights get the jolt of confidence they need. Zo gets free for a three-pointer to cut the lead to nine points, then Bentley steals the ball a couple plays later making a breakaway layup. They are locked in. Sasha blocks a shot on defense and throws a quick outlet pass to Zo who takes it the length of the floor and dishes it back to Sasha who finishes the break with an easy bucket. The Hoover trio is showing their potent combination of skills on the court again.

It's short-lived.

With three minutes left in the third quarter after the Knights cut the deficit to four points, the whistle blew. Sasha goes straight up to defend the Saints player barreling toward her. The girl dramatically bounces off her and onto the floor. Sasha doesn't hesitate; she starts walking to the bench knowing she will be blamed. Monty and the Hoover crowd can't believe the call. Monty knows pleading his case at this point isn't going to do a thing, so he begins urging Ellie to go play big. They will have to win with other players on the floor. He tells Gordy to get Ashlyn prepared to play. Sasha has just racked up her fourth foul, and Krista has three fouls of her own.

Sasha takes a seat on the bench. She learned last season from Mack that losing her temper wasn't an option. When teams started to resort to playing rough with the tall center in an attempt to try to level the playing field, Sasha reacted with anger not understanding that pissed off wasn't an acceptable response. She thought Mack of all people would understand her reaction; instead, he informed her she needed to take care of her rage or her bottom would be sitting next to him on the bench. Sasha worked hard after that to hold her tongue and to keep playing with no reaction when calls seemed unfair. Sasha didn't want to feel the wrath of Mack again, and more than anything else she wanted to make sure she could stay on the court. It wasn't easy to adjust, and tonight it's excruciating. Sasha sits next to Monty and asks, "What am I supposed to do? Just step aside and let her score?"

Monty shakes his head back and forth. "I don't know what to tell ya, kid, except be ready. You have one foul left, so when we get you back in again you'll have to make like a ballerina and tip toe out there."

Sasha gives him a deadpan look and says, "Oh yeah, you know I'm super graceful, Coach." Sasha being forced to the bench once again is a big blow. The rest of the starters can't help but feel deflated, and the Saints crowd can't help but celebrate. Hoover went all out in their quest to catch up, and now they have to try with all their might not to let the Saints pull away again. Chesapeake has the luxury of sending in a wave of fresh players. The new bodies focus on slowing down Bentley and Zo. The fresh post players for the Saints get wide-eyed knowing they have a chance to feast on the offensive end. Chesapeake surges ahead of the Knights, going back up double digits.

At the break between quarters, frustration is rising on the Hoover bench. Monty kneels down in front of his team. "Eight minutes left. One possession at a time. Sasha you're back in. Do the best you can to avoid the whistle. Believe me, their coach is telling them to attack you and get you out of the game for good. Guards, let's help her out and try not to let your girl into the lane." Monty nods at his team and adds, "We can only control how *we* play. Let's take our best shot."

The Saints switch strategies to start the fourth. They smell blood. A heavyweight opponent only goes down for good with a knockout punch. Chesapeake starts the quarter in a full-court zone press. Slow the game down, run time off the clock, and prevent the quick-scoring Knights from getting any momentum back.

Annoyed by the press and how the game has played out, Hoover shows little patience. They start to turn the ball over, and when they don't, the Saints prevent them from running their offense the way they want to. The zone limits their entry passes into Sasha who is being swarmed by three girls. Zo has cooled off with the extra pressure focused on her, and she starts to force bad shots. The Knights are clinging to life by playing scrappy defense. They go on a mini run to get within eight points. This is as close as they will get before the Saints take another comfortable double-digit lead. Hoover's big three do everything they can to try to get a spark going. Nothing will save this game. Time is running out. The Saints crowd, knowing a win is inevitable, starts to celebrate early. Monty pulls the starters out when the clock ticks under two minutes. Down thirteen, they appear to have a different way of looking at analytics than Coach Monty and are visually upset to be leaving the game with time left on the clock.

When you experience winning as much as the Knights have, one loss feels like the end of their world. Losing shows what they lack and to the players they hadn't been lacking anything. Reality is the Saints physicality bothered them, and the inexperience of the bench showed through. Chesapeake exploited their weaknesses. Monty isn't pleased with the result. He is proud of one thing; the kids didn't lose their cool when things went south. They played through it. He is hopeful this loss will make those flashes of complacency he saw disappear for good. To the players, though, all they know is the pain of defeat. There isn't anything worse.

CHAPTER 14

Monty liked the effort the girls gave on Saturday night even though he didn't like the result. He knows Chesapeake is a highly skilled basketball club. With the qualities they possess and Sasha getting into early foul trouble, the Saints did exactly what they should have done to Hoover. The margin of error is slim when you're trying to beat a team like Chesapeake. The players don't see it from that perspective. They believe they should have won the game. The players look at the loss as a blip in the road. Nothing more. They don't feel it's a true reflection of their team. Doesn't matter, they still feel gutted. Some take the loss better than others. There are a lot of *should haves* going through their minds. To their credit, none of them are discussed out loud. Mack and Monty never speak of excuses, and they wouldn't either.

On Tuesday, Hoover traveled to VMS for another road game. The contest provided no suspense due to the Warriors playing without their starting point guard who is done for the season after blowing out her ACL last week. The coaches aren't sure how the Saints' loss is going to affect their players going forward. It won't take long to find out. Friday is the rematch with Chesapeake in Hoover's home gym. Having to turn around and play the Saints six days after their first matchup is not ideal. The good news is they won't have to wait weeks for the hype to build up again. Avenging the loss this fast is welcomed by the Knights. The bad news is there isn't time to add any new wrinkles to their offense or defense. Monty watched the game tape of the Saints' loss several times. Besides Sasha's foul trouble, what stuck out to him was their defense. Chesapeake is skilled in patience, letting their offense unfold and executing with efficiency. The Knights' defense on the Saints was rushed and full of risks. Monty saw his team focus solely on getting the ball back

74

and getting a chance to score by any means necessary. This tunnel vision approach caused them to be out of position on the defensive end time and time again, giving Chesapeake too many easy shots in his opinion.

In the locker room before Friday night's rematch versus the Saints, Coach Monty stresses to his players the importance of playing solid defense for the full duration of the possession. Defense against every team in their conference not named Chesapeake is fun. Hoover can deflect passes, pick pockets, and easily force bad shots at will. When playing Chesapeake they have to keep focused for the entirety of the possession. Monty warns them if they don't commit on the defensive end tonight the outcome of this game will be similar to the first go around with the Saints. Monty raises his voice a bit to try to drill in this point. He can't be sure if the players are receiving any of the information he is spewing. The group is displaying a mix of hyperactivity and confidence along with a sense of uncertainty.

Out on the court, Hoover lines up next to Chesapeake for the tip-off. Having just played each other, the scene is so familiar the players avoid eye contact. None of the girls know anything about the other apart from their tendencies on the basketball court. It doesn't matter. They are enemies right now. Chesapeake thinks Hoover is a cocky bunch. Hoover thinks Chesapeake is a privileged bunch. The ball is tipped, and the two teams battle each other for the bragging rights of being the best team in the conference.

It's Chesapeake who strikes first and with authority. Having seen the success they had in pressing Hoover at the end of the previous game, they brought the full-court pressure right out of the gate. It catches Hoover off guard. The press causes early turnovers, and the Saints sprint out to a 10–2 lead. Hoover recovers after the initial blow and is able to shrink the gap. With four minutes left in the opening quarter, the Saints' lead is 13–10; even so, it's apparent Chesapeake is controlling the tempo. The Saints take the Knights' love of playing fast away. It dampens their spirits. Hoover is out of sync and out of rhythm.

Chesapeake's coach knows Hoover has three of the best players in the conference, but he believes he has the best team. He instructs his players to press the living daylights out of the Knights, knowing that he likes his chances if he can slow them down. The Saints goal is to take the open court away from the Knights and make them go through an obstacle course to get the ball up the court. Get them flustered and tired, then send in a fresh wave of bodies to keep the strategy effective.

Monty calls a time-out when things start to get out of hand. He looks at Gordy and they read each other's minds. They need a few practices to combat this tactic and a few more skilled ball handlers. Monty is kicking himself inside for not considering this approach as a valid option for the Saints' game plan. Chesapeake saw what the press did in their first encounter; it prevented the Knights from overtaking the lead when they made a comeback in a flurry. The Knights playing slow are not the Knights. Monty saw his players' faces when the contest began, and the Saints went right into a full-court press. Their reaction was similar to his dog's reaction when he realizes Monty is taking him to the vet. Fights it off with disdain and all his might. Monty's wife feels bad having to do this so it's always up to him to drag Bowser into the truck and force him to live out his worst nightmare. Trying to ease the players' minds, Monty tells them what he tells his pup: settle down. Don't fight it. Like Bowser, the girls can't quite get over it. Can't move on. They go back on the court and try to fight it even harder. Monty shakes his head on the bench. He usually tells his dog, "Relax, it will be over soon." In this case, the game is far from over.

The Saints pile it on. They lead the contest 28–15 at the end of the first quarter. Unlike the other teams in the conference, Chesapeake has the depth to sustain the full-court pressure. Two and three defenders continuously hound Bentley and Zo as they try to get up the court. The frustrations for the two normally high-flying guards start to show through. Hayley is being allowed to get the ball, and the press is agitating her. Zo and Bentley keep fighting back, expending so much energy trying to make something happen. Zo can't get into a rhythm with her shot, and the lane is clogged up. The Saints drop two girls down to double-team Sasha once the ball crosses the half-court line. When Sasha does receive the ball down low, she does everything in her power to dodge the darts of limbs poking into her. Sasha is used to getting beat up going against the football pads in practice, but she never thought this was going to become the norm from opponents. Sasha grazes a player—they blow the whistle, if they jab and slam into her—but nothing. She does her best not to allow her emotions to surface.

Nobody in the gym predicted the Saints would be leading the Knights 43–28 at halftime. Coach Monty is disappointed with himself because he didn't prepare the girls in practice for a press and with the team for the way they are reacting to the predicament they are in. He doesn't like their body language one bit. Monty goes to the chalkboard and writes 18–7, 12, then draws a heart.

"We're losing the rebound battle again, and we have twelve turnovers." Monty circles the number twelve. "I think ten of these are steals." Monty shakes his head. "We're not going to win games with these kinds of numbers. But this"—he circles the heart—"without this, we're nothing." He stops talking and takes a slow walk back to the middle of the room.

"I see some droopy faces. Some sulking bodies. I see some quit in you, and I know that's not who you are." He pauses to allow them time to think about that. "Anything is possible. We could catch up and beat these guys, or we could lose by a little or a whole heck of a lot. But I don't ever want to see you guys quit on each other."

Alert, solemn faces stare back at Monty.

"When you quit, that's when the season is over. No team wins a championship when that creeps in."

It's silent. The players make no movements.

"Now, you guys have a choice. Go back out there and throw in the towel. Quit. Or you can go back out there and give it your all against the odds." Monty holds up his arm. "What's it going to be?"

At once the girls rise up and huddle into a circle around their coach.

"We fight!" Bentley yells.

"Yeahs" echo her sentiment.

Sasha calls out: "We got this!"

Krista shouts, "Let's go balls to the wall!"

That cut the tension.

Monty half-smiles and says, "I like the enthusiasm but maybe a little less colorful, Krista."

Krista's face turns bright red. "I swear it's not bad! It's a military thing. Pilots used to say it. It's about the ball of the lever, I swear! It, like, means to go full throttle."

"Well, let's just say go full throttle then," Monty says. "Full throttle on three."

The girls yell it, then walk toward the locker room door with some bounce in their step. Sasha giggles and says, "Nice, Krista."

"I'm serious, you guys, it is not like that. My mom thought that too when my dad would yell it around us when we were little. Look it up!"

Out on the floor the team looks loose and determined. They were in a similar situation playing Chesapeake a week ago. They believed then a comeback was possible, and they believe it now, even if their psyche has been messed with. They come out for the second half with a chip on their shoulder and a score to settle. The Saints exposed them, and Monty challenged their hearts with the quitting talk. They play focused and bite back at the Saints right away. They make quick work of showing they are not going away. They go on a run that sees everyone get into the act. Sasha gets free and makes a nice post move in the paint for a score. Krista, who isn't known to look for her shot, scores near the block and two possessions later swishes a shot from just inside the free-throw line cutting the lead to 43–34. The Hoover crowd comes alive and gives their squad a standing ovation as the Saints coach calls a time-out to settle his team down.

Out of the time-out, Hayley steals the ball and goes the length of the court. Her shot is off the mark, but Bentley follows the miss and puts it right back up. The lead is now 43–36. Hoover is feeling a shot of adrenaline. Chesapeake answers with a three-point shot taking the lead right back to double digits. Bentley gets past the press, and Zo cuts to get free. Bentley throws her a lead pass. Zo jukes a Saints defender and takes it to the rim. Confronted by a post player who leaps in the air to contest her shot, Zo flips a no-look pass behind her head, leaving it to fall into Sasha's hands. Her bucket makes it 46–38. Another steal by Hayley leads to a long outlet pass to Zo who catches and lets a deep three-pointer fly. It swishes through the net cutting the deficit to five. The Hoover student section explodes out of their seats, and so does the Saints' coach who throws his hands together in a frantic T shape in front of the ref. Bentley and Zo leap in the air and bang shoulders on the way to the bench. Krista waves her hands in the air for the crowd to keep bringing the noise. Monty smiles at the scene. The whole game up to this point has been ugly from his point of view, and the way his team has played over the last few minutes is a thing of beauty. Later tonight and in the following days, he will choose that sequence to play over and over in his mind.

Hoover's run doesn't send Chesapeake into panic mode. Chesapeake plays the same way no matter if they are ahead by a big lead or behind. If a Saint player makes a mental mistake or misses a shot, they play on. The Saints send three fresh players out on the floor out of the time-out. The Saints work the ball around taking up time and getting Hoover to exert more energy. They take and make an uncontested shot in the lane then get set up in their press. The Knights want to hurry up and strike back. Zo forces a three. The ball is rebounded by the Saints, and they head to the other end to run their offense. Brit Larson hits a three-pointer extending the Saints lead to ten points. The Knights go back down, struggling but surviving the full-court press, and keep the ball moving. A short shot by Krista is blocked, and the Saints push the ball ahead. Larson pulls up for another three-pointer. When it swishes through the net, Monty calls a time-out in an attempt to stop the bleeding. He implores his players to keep their heads up and take the momentum back. The home side of the gymnasium is quiet behind them.

Hoover goes back on the floor determined to turn the tide. Nothing works. The supernatural flow they were in before doesn't return. On this night, Hoover has no more return punches to throw. The Chesapeake Saints press wears the Knights down, and they hold them scoreless for the remainder of the quarter. It's a Saints TKO at the end of three with a score of Saints 67, Knights 41. Monty empties the bench for the fourth quarter. With their evening done, the starters sit demoralized. The Saints coach takes his starters out of the game too, and they stop their full-court pressure defense.

Waiting and watching a full eight minutes of play from the bench is torture for the starters to endure. The second string for Chesapeake is good, and while it's a great experience for the Hoover substitutes, it isn't pretty. Ashlyn, who hasn't played many varsity minutes at all this year, turns the ball over two times in a row. With all the drama gone from the gym and with the contest already decided, it's quiet when her dad bellows out: "Come on, Ashlyn! Get it together!"

The next time down the court, Ashlyn misses a wide-open shot, and her dad gives her more grief. It's impossible for anyone to ignore. Later on she fouls the girl she is guarding, sending her to the free-throw line. With that, Ashlyn's dad stands up and yells, "Not good enough, Ash! Just not good enough."

The sound of his voice is gut wrenching. The players on the bench glance at each other. They thought there was no possible way this night could get any worse. If they had been good enough tonight, Ashlyn wouldn't have been the target of her dad's disdain in front of a packed house.

Ellie, the upperclassman of the bunch on the court, huddles her teammates together in the middle of the lane before the free throws are shot. "You're doing fine Ashlyn. Block it out." Mya pats Ashlyn on the back. They disassemble and line up. Ashlyn puts her hands on her knees and looks down wishing she was anywhere in the world but there. The players look uncomfortable, even the Saints players. All of them are trying to play a game, do their best, and not mess up. Ashlyn's teammates do what they can to keep the ball out of her hands to help her avoid any more embarrassment. The final horn is a welcome sound. The two teams shake hands. The Knights are distraught over the outcome. Chesapeake had a distinct game plan and executed it to perfection. There is respect between the two programs. Monty shakes his counterpart's hand and heads off the court with the only positive being they won't have to face the Saints again this year.

Bentley pushes the door of the locker room open so hard the handle is stamped with white paint. A bad loss slows everything down, and the usually noisy room is void of any sound. They share the wins with elation. Not the losses. Those aren't shared. They make you feel like you're on an island. No conversation. No eye contact. Most players sit with their head in their hands. A few lean back and stare into space. There is nothing for them to do but wrestle with their own thoughts and sit in misery.

The locker room stays silent until the soft sounds of Ashlyn sniffling surface. A few moments later it becomes louder. She is doing her best to hold it in and save herself more humiliation. It isn't working. Krista gets up and goes over to sit next to her. She pulls Ashlyn's hands away from her face and brings her into a hug. "Let it out, Ash. It's okay."

Ashlyn cries.

Sasha gets up to blow her nose in the bathroom.

Jemma walks in the room and speaks softly, "Coach is going to come in."

Sasha hands Ashlyn some tissue on her way back to her seat. Ashlyn sits up straight and works hard on gathering herself. She whispers, "Thanks, Krista."

"Anytime." Krista puts her arm back around her and gives her another squeeze.

The coaches walk in the room. Monty keeps his head down for a while before he looks up and addresses the team: "This is tough. Chesapeake is a darn good ball club. It just wasn't our night tonight. We have to start playing better for a full game. Too many turnovers, careless passes, and on defense we weren't locked in for more than a few short bursts. You keep playing like that, I'm sorry, but we're not going to be playing any games in March." He lets that hang in the air, knowing it will sting. "We just aren't." Monty shakes his head then keeps quiet for a beat before continuing. "If you play like you did in the first half at Chesapeake and like you did coming out of halftime tonight, for a whole game...I don't think there is a team in the state that can beat you. We have to work on putting everything together and finding that edge for thirty-two minutes." Monty takes a deep breath and puts his hands in his pocket. "I know this hurts. But there is plenty of season left. We have a choice to make. Feel sorry for ourselves and let this tear us apart or come together. I'll see you all on Monday."

Without a final huddle, the coaching staff exits the locker room.

One team is where the other one wants to be. Chesapeake has it figured out, and Hoover is still searching for something that's missing. Chesapeake plays united. There is no uncertainty. They know who they are. Hoover is still finding themselves, and if they want to reach their dream of a championship, they will have to go find the missing ingredient. Together.

CHAPTER 15

Jemma and Miss Easton are hanging out in the hallway when Laney appears. Having just wrapped up interviews for the *Hoover Times* with both head coaches, she lets out a whistle and says, "That was a rough one. The Saints were really impressive tonight."

"Yeah, they were on another level," Miss Easton replies. "We had no answers."

"They have so much depth," Laney says. "They can bring in new bodies in waves, and besides Zo, Bentley, and Sasha, everyone else was like a deer caught in headlights."

Miss Easton shrugs her shoulders and says, "All of them struggled tonight."

Jemma adds, "We were just off from the start."

"Heck of a game plan the Saints had," Laney says. "They totally controlled the tempo with the full-court press."

"Yeah," Miss Easton says. "That took us completely out of getting into any type of flow."

Laney smiles and says, "I like what their coach said to me though: 'If we play a third time and Coach Mack is on the bench, I'm not sure we would win.' I agree. I believe Hoover wins one of the two games if Mack would have been coaching."

Miss Easton and Jemma don't respond. Laney continues: "Two different coaching styles. I'm not saying either one is better. I just think Mack and his fall-in-line way keeps them sharper. There is an accountability factor Mack generates just by his notorious glare that I think the underclassmen are missing."

"Maybe," Jemma says. "But the girls sure like Monty a lot, and I know they are responding to him too."

Laney puts her right hand up like she's under oath. "Oh I have no doubt about that. I can see they like and respect Monty. I'm just saying when there is a change like that you can see some differences."

"From what I saw them do last year," Miss Easton says with a smirk, "I wouldn't count them out just yet." There is a hint of protection in her voice. Teaching and coaching at Hoover High is her life. Those are her kids. "I wouldn't be too quick to doubt them."

Laney smiles and replies, "Believe me I'm not. And the Saints coach agrees. He said they have a whole lot to play for with Mack out."

Speculation in Hoover is a hobby, and their high school girls basketball team is the main topic this time of year. Discussions like this one are going on all over town. With the two losses, the second one being a blowout, everyone has an instant reaction or overreaction on what the future holds for the Knights. Chesapeake looks bound for state to compete for a title, and Hoover, well, even though they are a class below, the two losses are making people question if they have what it takes. When you lose, everything is put under a microscope and everyone has an opinion. Is Mack's absence too much for the team to overcome? Some think so. Others think they can never win a state championship playing the style of basketball they play. Some will chalk up the defeats to off nights and believe the Knights will be fine. Only a few admit they have no idea how this season will end. Only time will tell.

CHAPTER 16

While the Hoover boys' basketball team is busy trying to challenge the Chesapeake boys in the gym, the girls' players are busy fleeing the scene. The mutual feeling is one of embarrassment. Bentley and Krista waste no time and leave separately, slipping out the side door of the school minutes after the coaches leave the locker room. The JV reserves scatter as quickly as they can. Hayley waits on Ashlyn; she wants to walk out with her so she doesn't have to emerge from the locker room alone. Zo turns her chair to the wall and zones out. Sasha and Ellie sit in their chairs next to each other stripping off socks and shoes at a slow pace. After an extended amount of time, Zo changes and makes her way out to the commons area to meet up with a young boy from Chesapeake named Jack. Zo promised Jack she would see him, and she isn't going to leave him hanging. They met last year when he approached their bus after they lost at Chesapeake and asked Zo for an autograph. Shortly after, Jack, a sixth grader, whose dad is the Chesapeake boys' varsity coach, sent a letter to Hoover High addressed to Zo. In it he thanked her for signing his shirt and told her he was working hard to be as good as she was. He left his email address and a bunch of questions for her. To his surprise, Zo reached out.

Zo finds Jack and one of his friends standing near the trophy case. The boys light up when they see Zo. Jack introduces his friend to her and says his other friend who wanted to meet her is hiding because he doesn't think Zo would want to meet him; being that his dad happens to be the Saints' girls' basketball coach. Zo tells Jack it's cool, and he calls out across the commons beckoning the boy to come join them. When he makes his way to the group Zo jokes with him and he relaxes. She asks the boys about their basketball season. They share details of their last game enthusiastically. They rib one another over mishaps and try to one up the other over who had the best plays.

Each boy is holding Hoover Knights' basketball gear in their hands. Once a season at Hoover they bring out boxes of retro athletic gear and put the items up for sale. The Chesapeake kids were thrilled to get their hands on a few old Hoover shooting shirts and red-and-white-striped breakaway pants. They get animated talking about how they are going to wear the ensemble next week to school on the same day. Zo is amazed the boys are proud to wear Hoover colors when her team just got whipped by their girls' team.

Jack tells Zo she had a good game and that her team will no doubt make it to the state tournament. Zo does her best to appear upbeat and unfazed by the loss. To Zo, this is the best part of a being a basketball player, and it's a nice pick me up after a disappointing defeat. Being a role model is something she doesn't take lightly. Zo vividly remembers being at Saturday morning basketball when she was little, and one high five from a high school player made her feel like she just touched the hand of a superhero. Now, as a high school basketball player herself, when any kid comes near her in awe, she happily engages, knowing she can pass on some power or at least be a positive influence in the moment.

Zo takes a picture with the boys and says goodbye. She goes back into the locker room to grab her bag and get out of there. Ellie and Sasha are the only ones left. Both are giggling because Ellie managed to get her shirt stuck in her zipper and is having a tough time getting it out.

"Ah finally," Ellie says. "Oh no." She throws both hands in the air and sits down. "Great, my shirt is ripped. That was brand-new too."

Zo sits contemplating her next move. She doesn't want to stay and doesn't want to go home either. She knows she will stay up late into the night and torture herself thinking about the loss. "Are you guys going to watch the boys' game?" Sasha asks.

"I guess," Ellie says. "It has to be nearly halftime by now. I'll probably go out and watch a little bit. What else is there to do?"

"I'm not going back in the gym," Zo says.

"I don't feel like going back in there either." Sasha zips her bag and sits down. "I don't feel like talking to anyone."

Ellie laughs and says, "You mean you don't want to hear everyone say the standard, 'You played well, we're still proud of you, yada, yada, yada?' Won't your boyfriend be mad if you skip it though?"

Sasha rolls her eyes and says, "He'll live."

Ellie starts brushing her hair. "Should we do something together?"

"I'm down," Zo answers.

"You know what we should totally do?" A big smile spreads across Ellie's face. "Let's stay at Evan's house. He's gone for the weekend. He won't care. And it's out in the boonies so you guys won't have to worry about running into anyone."

Evan is Ellie's older brother. He lives twenty-five miles northeast of Hoover across the Minnesota border. Zo lights up. Sasha is hesitant. It doesn't take much for her two friends to convince her this is happening. They let their parents know about their great idea with a text, and they take off from the school parking lot. They stop at the gas station on the way out of town because there is nothing close to her brother's house. Ellie picks up a pizza and soda along with a request from Zo to get Oreos and milk. She couldn't promise her friends that Evan had anything in his fridge besides beer and frozen meals. The girls drive away from Hoover, and the energy shifts. Getting away has a feeling of being teleported into a different realm. One where a loss isn't swallowing them whole. Out here on the dark country roads there is distance from what they know is happening in Hoover. Their defeat is hanging over the town and swirling through the air. In the car they talk about the last time they had a sleepover. They agree it was at the end of sixth grade at Ellie's house. There were at least a dozen girls there. They laugh, remembering how it was to be twelve years old.

Ellie turns left on another dirt road after what seems like a half an hour and lets them know it won't be much longer. Ellie has a brilliant light bulb-inspired idea and yells out, "Get ready!" She says it with such enthusiasm that Sasha briskly looks over at her from the passenger seat and sits up with a sense of alertness. Zo pops her head up from the back seat and asks, "What's up?"

Ellie calls out loudly, "3-2-1."

Everything goes black. Ellie turned the lights out, all of them, inside and out. Sasha shrieks. Zo stays quiet. After a few more seconds of darkness, Ellie flips the lights back on.

"Ellie what the heck?" Sasha screams.

"You guys have never played 'lights out' before?" Ellie asks, with a wide smile plastered on her face.

"Um no," Sasha says, staring at Ellie in disbelief. "The Hudsons drive with the lights on."

"We play this game on the country roads. They're so boring and quiet. Keeps you awake and alert—gets the blood pumping." Ellie giggles.

Zo, who can't think of another time when she was on a dirt road says, "That was insane."

Feeling alive and near death, she yells, "Do it again!"

Ellie flips the light switches off. Sasha yells until Ellie switches the lights back on. Zo and Ellie laugh at the rush.

"Ellie, not again," Sasha pleads. "Seriously, that is freaky and what if a car comes?" Ellie tells her it's part of the game, stating it hasn't happened before and the chances are slim. In fact, they haven't seen one car since turning off on the first gravel road. After another mile or so, Ellie turns into a long driveway. The girls spill out of the car as soon as it comes to a stop. The air is cold, and the night sky is clear. The moonlight and stars provide just enough light for Ellie to get the key in the door. She flips on the outside light. She is excited to show the girls something and leads them around the garage into the backyard. Using her flashlight from her phone she messes with a box by the house, and the backyard lights up. Zo gets excited at the sight of a line of haystacks with bull's-eye targets attached to them. Ellie explains that her brother and his friends are into bow hunting. Zo doesn't hide her desire to give archery a try, and Ellie is happy to show her how it works. Ellie goes into the shed and reappears before them with all the gear. Ellie demonstrates and hits part of the hay. She grabs another arrow from the quiver on her back and takes another shot, this time hitting space in between one of the rings in the middle. Zo and Sasha are impressed. Zo whispers, "Badass," then holds out her hands requesting the bow. It looks enormous in Zo's arms, and she struggles to keep it lifted. The arrow keeps falling off. Zo doesn't get discouraged; she keeps toggling it. When she manages to get the arrow to stay and gets a shot off, the arrow sails off far away from the hay bail. Zo tries and tries again. Doesn't want to stop. Won't until she hits one of the bails. Ellie tells her it took her a long time to get the hang of it too and it's still hard for her. Zo finally hits a part of the hay. It's nowhere near the paper target. It doesn't matter; Zo is hyped up. She puts the bow down and throws her hands in the air. After Zo celebrates, she rubs the area where the bow string slapped her arm. Ellie informs her it will leave a mark.

Ellie asks Sasha if she wants a turn before she packs up the equipment. She shrugs and gives it a try. It's easier for her to hold up the bow and keep it in the correct position. Her first shot hits the corner of the hay.

"Of course Sasha hit hay on her first attempt," Ellie comments.

Zo whispers, "Superwoman."

Ellie nods, "Go again."

Sasha takes another arrow from Ellie and concentrates. The arrow hits the paper inside the last ring.

Zo pumps her fist in the air and yells, "Damn, Sash!"

Sasha flashes a brief smile. "That's a lot harder than it looks."

After Ellie puts everything away and turns the backyard lights off, the three girls go inside and sit at the kitchen table. They start eating their pizza that has cooled off. Ellie takes a bucket of her mom's famous green slush out of the freezer. She scrapes out a cup for each of her friends, and they light up remembering this treat from their sleepover in middle school. They talk about that night some more and laugh at all the funny memories like when everyone freaked out when they saw Ellie's house had a pop machine in the basement. It blew their minds. There was candy, baked goods, and of course, the slush. Zo ate handfuls and handfuls of root beer barrels that night, saying, "you're not the boss of me" to everyone who told her to slow down. Talking about that night gets them in a cheerful mood until Ellie brings up Ashlyn's dad yelling at her. They feel horrible for her and wonder if that is how her dad talks to her in front of hundreds of people, then how does he talk to her at home? Now it makes sense why Ashlyn's favorite sport is golf.

With the pizza devoured, Zo starts to dip her Oreos in a large Minnesota Vikings mug with the gusto of a little kid. While Zo is attempting to drown her sorrows with cookies and milk, Sasha is texting with her boyfriend, Bryce.

"They win?" Ellie asks.

Sasha rolls her eyes. The Chesapeake boys team, like their girls team, is at the top of the conference. The Hoover boys have a record hovering around the .500 mark.

"He said it wasn't a blowout, and he had eleven points."

"So, kind of a win." Ellie laughs.

The three girls start to talk about random stuff: the test they had in social studies, the breakup of a couple that went out for one week, and Ellie's ripped shirt. It's nearing midnight when they go into the living room and each take a section of the big **U**-shaped couch. Ellie gets out blankets and pillows she finds in the hall closet. They get comfy sprawling out on the spacious couch. The trio choose an old horror movie even though none of them are fans. It's the only type of movie that won't allow their minds to wander back to the horrifying loss they suffered earlier. They haven't said a word about the game. When you win, everyone wants to own it. When you lose, you are left alone to feel it and deal with it internally. To Sasha, Zo, and Ellie it's comforting to share in the defeat together. Along with Freddy Kruger. They try to watch and think of nothing else. It works until they hear sounds.

Sasha sits up. "What the heck was that?"

Ellie pauses the movie. "I heard it too."

Sasha flips the lamp on. "Um, it sounded like it was coming from *inside* the house."

"Shh," Ellie whispers and stands up. "I think it was by the back door."

There is another noise. Ellie shakes her head and whispers, "It's definitely inside. I think someone is in the basement."

All three of them are alert in an instant. They are in the middle of nowhere. The closest neighbor is nearly a mile away. Who is here with them? Could it be an enemy of Ellie's brother? Zo is used to Hoover where no possibilities of danger exist. They hear the noise again. It sounds like something or someone moving around below them in the basement. Ellie holds her finger to her lips and dashes off. Zo rushes over to sit next to Sasha. They whisper to each other about who could be in the house and if they should call 911.

Ellie appears, and Sasha's eyes go wide. "What the hell, El?"

Ellie is holding a gun. Zo looks at Ellie, freaked out and intrigued. "Is that a real gun?"

"Shh! Yes," Ellie whispers. "And trust me, I know how to use it."

"Maybe we should just call the cops," Sasha says, raising her hand. "Am I the only one thinking this?"

"It will be at least thirty minutes, if not longer, before anyone will make it out here," Ellie responds. "If somebody comes through that door,

I won't miss." Ellie stays calm and points her gun at the interior door that is shut. Behind that door are two steps that lead down to a small entryway where you can go left to the kitchen, right to go down to the basement, or straight to go out the door into the backyard.

The lamp and TV go black. The girls jump and gasp. The power is out. Sasha and Zo reach for their cell phones so they have some light. Ellie keeps her eyes and the gun focused on the door.

"What the freak is happening?" Zo asks in a quiet, shaky voice.

Ellie whispers, "Someone shut off the breaker downstairs."

Sasha and Zo instinctively take cover behind the couch. Zo reaches over to grab a blanket and puts it over her head. They hear a faint creaking noise, and the girls stay quiet, bracing themselves.

"Okay, Ellie, this is serious," Sasha says in a raised whisper. "Someone is definitely in here. Maybe we should run out the front door and jump in the car to hightail it out of here!"

"We don't know what or who is waiting for us out there," Ellie replies. "I have a full round. I feel safer staying here."

Zo peeks out the blanket and gives Sasha an alarmed look. "Farm kids are gangster." Zo's tone of voice makes it sound more like a question than a statement.

"No." Sasha shakes her head. "Ellie is just crazy. I hope the next time we see her it's not during visiting hours in a prison."

"Guys, quiet," Ellie hisses.

The girls go silent. After what seems like an eternity, Ellie speaks: "I think they are gone."

"Okay," Sasha says. "But what else did they do besides turn off the power?"

"Yeah," Zo says. "And what if it's been quiet because they are hiding in the basement waiting for us to make a move?"

Sasha's phone chimes, and she lets out an audible exhale, then says, "No bleeping way! I am going to kick his ass!"

"What?" Ellie says.

"It was Bryce and Ben. It's them. They were in here, not homicidal maniacs trying to kill us."

Ellie lowers the gun and relaxes.

Zo throws off her blanket and stands up. "I need a root beer barrel."

Sasha reads off more texts from Bryce that are coming in rapidly. "So they thought it would be funny to scare us."

Ellie laughs. "Yeah really funny until I put a cap in their ass."

Sasha can't laugh; she is too livid. "I told him we were having a girls' night. I can't believe they came out here and messed with us like that."

"What was he thinking?" Ellie says. "He knows we hunt! Oh my gosh, tonight could have turned out really bad, Sash. I'm glad I didn't shoot your boyfriend." Ellie collapses on the couch.

"Ah yeah me too," Sasha says. "I'm really glad I decided to text him. I thought I should make contact so at least someone knows what happened to us if we were never heard from again."

"What did you text him?" Zo asks. She's back from the kitchen with the tub of slush and the scraper in her hand.

"I texted: 'Someone is in Evan's house and cut the power! Ellie got a loaded gun out!'"

Ellie smiles. "So including the gun in the text was what made him realize 'oops I better tell them.' So, you kind of saved his life." Ellie laughs again. "Don't let him ever forget that."

"Oh believe me when I get a hold of him he's not going to forget any of this."

The girls hear a loud vehicle out front. From the texts Bryce sent Sasha, they know the two boys parked far away and walked to Evan's house so their loud truck wouldn't give them away. Bryce texted they were going to come say sorry in person. Ellie goes downstairs to flip the breaker back on to give them power, then she goes with Sasha outside to confront the boys. Zo is over it. She stays inside and flips through the choices on Evan's TV trying to find a comedy to watch. Bryce and his friend stay by their truck, which is stopped halfway down the driveway. They wisely keep their distance. Sasha chews them out and sends them away. They leave swiftly with their tails between their legs.

When the girls get back in the house, Ellie bursts into laughter. "You ripped him a new one!"

Zo laughs too. "That was epic. I could hear it in here."

"Yeah well, he thinks it's funny to pull off a prank not realizing you've got a loaded gun ready to shoot down a legit robber or killer."

"I've never seen you mad like that before," Ellie says.

Bryce hadn't either, and tomorrow morning there will be a lengthy apology letter from him taped to Sasha's windshield. The girls go through the events that transpired one more time because they are still amped up on adrenaline. It takes them a while to settle down and let sleep overtake them.

When they wake up, rays of sunshine are lighting up the living room. Finding a box of pancake mix only requiring water they have breakfast before tidying up the place. It takes some time to find all of Zo's arrows. Once they do they drive back to Hoover. When they see the town's water tower come into view, those familiar emotions from last night's loss return. They pull into the high school parking lot half expecting to see debris littered around. Some kind of remnants from last night's rout. That's not the case. Nothing has changed. The parking lot is empty except for Sasha's car. The Knights are still the Knights. One off game during their season isn't the end of the world. They don't need to beat the Chesapeake Saints to win state. As bad as the entire team feels, their goal is still alive.

Basketball, like life, goes on.

CHAPTER 17

Monday morning the Knights lose their #1 ranking. Racking up two defeats within seven days they drop all the way to #6 in the newest poll. Later in the week, Mack asks Jemma to pay him a visit. She knows he wants to check on the morale of the team.

Jemma gives Mack a light hug when she walks through his door and asks, "How are you, Mack?"

"Getting closer and closer, young lady," Mack says. "I'll be back driving you crazy in no time."

Jemma giggles and says, "Can't wait." She notes to herself that Mack looks healthier. Not frail or tired like he did the last time she saw him.

They step into the living room and take a seat. Mack turns serious right away. Jemma is not surprised. She knew he would waste little time getting to the gist of this visit, and he is not known for small talk.

"How are the girls handling everything?"

"You know," Jemma says, then pauses to sigh before she proceeds. "On Monday at practice it was bad. They were pretty down. Then Tuesday they played really well and took everything out on Central. Walloped them. Yesterday and today at practice it's like the losses to the Saints never happened and they're unstoppable."

Mack cocks his head and contemplates this information.

Jemma continues, "After practice today, a few of them stayed and played jig. Monty needed to leave to pick up his wife, and I told Gordy to take off to go eat dinner with his family. I let the girls stay and play awhile, but they wouldn't stop. I finally got them out of there by shutting off the lights."

Mack beams, and says, "They're responding to adversity with optimism. That's the heart of the underdog in those kids. The fight. It burns them up as much as me, and you're going to see them respond in a big way."

Jemma isn't expecting this interpretation. She stays quiet and smiles.

Mack leans back in his chair. "They are going to be just fine. They got knocked down a peg. Life is a lot about how you handle losing. How do you respond? Do you fold or keep going for what you want? Our girls won't give up. I think if anything it lit a match under them."

Jemma smiles and replies, "I like how you can spin a butt kicking into a positive."

"Well, I've seen it over and over through the years. Teams that have an undefeated record that don't get challenged during the regular season…they get to the postseason and they get into a close game—" Mack stops to shake his head like this angers him immensely. "And you can see they have never been there before. They steamroll teams all year, never getting challenged, and then it gets close or they get behind in a win or go home situation, and they have no experience with that scenario. They tighten up." Mack whistles then says, "Our girls just gained some experience. They have formed some new armor, and now they have a bone to pick."

Jemma smiles and lets Mack keep talking. He's fired up. Frustrated with the losses, he feels he should have been there. His team didn't perform well, and the Saints look to be at the top of their game. They look "March ready" according to Mack. Only a few people saw him sneak into the upper level and watch the game on Friday night. Mack felt helpless watching his team sputter and take a tough loss on the chin. He snuck out at the start of the fourth quarter. He didn't go unnoticed, and word of his presence at the game trickled around town making the players feel even worse about their performance.

Mack discusses both losses to Chesapeake with Jemma in detail. Next he asks Jemma, the unofficial den mother, about each player. He wants to know how she thinks Ellie is handling her reserve role. Is Ashlyn fitting in when she gets into varsity games? He heard from Miss Easton that she is the leading scorer on the JV team. Does the freshman kid deserve a seat on the bench? He hears she got the nickname Booster because she's so darn quick. He leaves the starters for last. Was Bentley on a warpath at Monday's practice? He hoped so. Is Zo maintaining her quiet swagger after being held to a season low? Is Hayley gaining confidence? How is Sasha's development? The Chesapeake coach called him raving that Sasha is the most improved player in the region, maybe the state. Is Krista staying in line? Is Monty showing signs of stress, or is he keeping his happy-go-lucky attitude?

Mack knows this season is more challenging and unique for everyone involved because of the circumstances. Enduring the grind that comes along with being a coach takes a village. Mack is grateful for the family around him and for the town who puts their arms around the team. This is a perk of living in a small town. You know everyone, and you're like a big family whether you want to be a part of it or not. This team gives a sense of pride to the town of Hoover. A Knights loss becomes the town's loss. Hoover is on the map because of girls' basketball—no longer another small town you've never heard of. The Hoover Knights are not even the best team in their own conference, even so they have a way of drawing people in. Whether you like the style the team plays or not, they are never boring to watch and people from around the conference mark their calendars to make sure they don't miss the Hoover girls when they roll through town. It's been hard on Mack missing out on being a part of this magical feeling. He is eager to rejoin the show.

Jemma knew coming over here that she would eventually have to cut Mack off or he would keep her there all night talking basketball. Being away from the team has been torture on Mack, and she can see he is overflowing with an urgency to get back. She rises from the couch and states: "Well, I know everyone is excited to get you back but don't rush it, Coach."

Mack stands up and casually waves his hand at her. "I'm as good as new. Don't you worry about me." Mack's smile disappears. "Honestly though." He clears his throat. "I have an appointment with my doctor coming up soon. I really think I'll be cleared. I'm feeling good, and everything is on schedule. So, God willing."

"Well that's good to hear." Jemma wraps her scarf around her neck to prepare for the elements she will face once she steps outside.

Mack opens the door for her. "I need to get back to the team."

Jemma turns around when she reaches her car door. "Well, listen to your doctor, Mack, and take all the time you need."

Jemma smiles. Mack doesn't. He stares at Jemma with alert eyes and says, "I don't need any more time. March is coming."

Krista sashays across the locker room with a smile. "Oooh, Bentley!" She points her finger and shakes it at Bentley as she gets closer to her. "You are so lucky I was with Shawn yesterday." Shawn is a local police officer, so Bentley flashes her a worried look. Krista swings her bag off her shoulder, sending it crashing into the chair.

"He would have busted you big time." Krista's smile stays plastered on her face. All eyes are on her.

Bentley pulls her practice clothes out of her bag trying her hardest not to act nervous. "What are you talking about?"

"You were going like twenty-five miles over the speed limit on Highway 9."

Bentley blushes and gives her a puzzled look.

"He was for real going to flip on the cherries, and I asked him to bust the next one."

"Where at?"

Their teammates are hanging on every word.

"Right when you come over the hill by the mound. Off to the side on that dirt road."

Bentley laughs, then her voice hitches as she replies, "I thought that was a 65 mph zone."

Her teammates let out "yeah right" laughs.

"Wait, that's still going on? You and the copper?"

Now everyone looks at Krista.

Krista raises her eyebrows and retorts with a smile, "We are friends, okay?"

Bentley flashes her an okay gesture and calls out: "Yeah, sure, just friends."

"We are!" Krista yells. She gives Bentley a glare, then her face softens into a smile. "I *would* marry him tonight if he asked."

The girls give Krista grief about his profession and his age.

"Calm down, y'all," Krista yells, cutting off their outpouring of comments. "And relax. Shawn is only twenty-five. He's a sweetheart and interesting too." She sings out: "He's an ex-marine." She leaves this hanging there for a moment, proud of the fact. Feeling like maybe she should validate this adds, "He's traveled the world."

It's silent for a moment until Sasha clears her throat and says, "And you haven't even traveled Iowa."

Bentley spits out the water in her mouth and cackles. Laughter reverberates around the room. Krista keeps her lips tightened. She can't prevent a smile wiggling out and bobs her head up and down, acknowledging Sasha had a good hit.

After it quiets down, Krista turns her attention back to Bentley and says, "Well anyway you're welcome, Bentley. I knew it was your truck right away by the color and I told him 'You can't pull her over. That's my point guard, like we need her eligible.'"

"All right," Bentley says. "I guess I'll get you guys a rice cooker or some crap like that for your wedding."

Krista grins and says, "Make it something fancy like a fondue set."

Jemma walks in surveying the room with a scowl. A couple of the players have made their way out to the court for practice, but there are way too many lingering for her liking. She wants to yell but her voice comes out calm when she says, "What's the holdup, ladies? Coach Monty isn't very happy you haven't made it out yet."

Bentley points up at the clock and says, "We have like seven minutes until practice starts."

"Well usually you guys are out there warming up at least fifteen minutes before."

Bentley shrugs and replies, "We're helping Krista plan her wedding."

Jemma rolls her eyes while the players giggle.

"For real, the copper. She's got a thing for a man in a uniform."

Jemma doesn't break; she stays serious: "Just get out on the court please. I swear, you guys are going to give me a head full of gray hair."

"Oh, Jemma." Krista walks by her and gives her hair a light tussle. "You love us. We keep you forever young, babe."

While the coaches are having a hard time getting the girls on the court these days, they are having an equally hard time getting them off the court once practice ends. The coaches know it's their way of reacting to the losses. Each and every one of them was a part of the butt kicking the Saints handed them. While the big three still led the team in statistical categories, their play didn't make any difference. It was a collective group effort that dealt Hoover their horrendous loss. The players are getting over the loss the only way they know how, by digging in and doubling down. It's their way of making a statement to their coaches and each other: we aren't quitting. They are trying to make up for the losses or at least not waste them. They are taking that chip on their shoulder and letting it dig all the way in as deep as it can go.

Monty is encouraged by their demeanor. He knows when losses start to appear it's easy to see finger pointing and players start to go separate ways. Monty took from the losses an urgency to hold the cracks together and build this team back up. He is pleasantly surprised to see the players doing that themselves. He sees a different team than the one he saw over break. This one is finally showing a trait that kickstarted them last year at this time: hunger.

CHAPTER 18

When Hayley walked into the locker room tonight she knew something was amiss. She couldn't put her finger on it at first. Being the young one starting on varsity she has less experience playing with and being around her older teammates. She is also the opposite of them in the locker room: quiet and reserved. At times she feels like an outsider. Someone who is still being considered worthy enough to be accepted into the group. Hayley finds herself observing her older teammates with fascination. She notices things. Like how Sasha rolls her eyes a certain way to show her feelings. Or how Krista bites her lip when she is stuck in a jam whether it's in a conversation or out on the court. She watches Zo and Bentley communicate with each other using only facial expressions, like they share a telepathic connection. Hayley notices the way everyone maneuvers around one another and the way in which their different personalities collide.

After a few minutes, it becomes clear to Hayley what is off tonight. Something is wrong with Bentley. For starters, Bentley walked into the locker room quietly with her head down. On game days, Bentley has an electric energy that goes along with her stride regardless of her mood. A confident eagerness you could call it. As if she has a plan she knows won't fail and she can't wait for the moment to prove it. On this night, Bentley walked in the room like she was trying to slip in unnoticed. She didn't go into her normal routine of taking her sweet time to put on her socks, shoes, and accessories while music played. Most game nights there is a chill vibe in the beginning while they get ready for the main event. A calm before the storm. Tonight is different. Bentley sits for a while before she gingerly stands up. She takes a step, grimaces, and sits back down. Her face says it all. Hayley looks around. Nobody else is paying attention to Bentley. They are in their own zone getting ready.

Hayley waits for Zo to finish getting her uniform on then taps her shoulder and whispers, "Hey, Zo." Zo looks up surprised, then raises her eyebrows for her to proceed. Hayley covers her mouth slightly and leans close to tell her: "I think something is wrong with Bentley."

Zo gives a glance in Bentley's direction. She watches her for a while then nods at Hayley. Bentley has her chair facing the wall with her back to everyone. She has her hands on her knees and has not yet changed from her regular shoes into her basketball shoes.

Zo steps over to Sasha and whispers, "Yo, ask Bentley if she's okay."

Sasha looks perplexed then gives Bentley a hard stare. She shakes her head, then shrugs her shoulders and says, "Um, that's all you, kid."

Zo takes a few steps, gently inching closer and closer to Bentley until she is right next to her. She gives Sasha a pleading look of help that is returned with a hand gesture urging her to just do it. Zo peeks around to see Bentley's face.

"Hey, B." Zo waves a hand below Bentley's eyeline. Zo takes a step back before asking, "You all good?"

Bentley looks up. She grits her teeth and looks back down. "I'll be okay."

Zo, Sasha, and Hayley share alarmed glances.

Ellie is near and calls out, "What happened?"

Bentley twists around to face her teammates who have inched in closer to her. "Ah it's stupid. My freaking water bottle fell on my foot. I set it on the top of my truck and when I opened the back door to get my bag it fell off. Landed right on the toe next to the big one."

"Ouch," Ellie says.

Sasha puts her hand over her mouth, "How bad is it?"

"Freaking hurts pretty bad."

"Can you play?" Zo asks.

"Oh I'm playing," Bentley responds. She stands up and puts some weight on her foot. She clenches her teeth, and a hissing sound comes out.

"Um yeah, you might want to rethink that," Sasha says. "Have you looked at it?" Bentley shakes her head no. She's too scared to assess the damage. The thought of missing a game is the worst thing she can imagine. Sasha and Ellie urge her to check it out. Krista walks in and gets filled in on the situation. Bentley is wearing a thin canvas sneaker.

Luckily she wasn't wearing flip-flops or slides, which she is known to wear even in the harsh winter weather. Everyone coaxes her into taking a look. Bentley removes her shoe at a slow pace and everyone hovers around her. She closes her eyes and takes off her sock.

"Damn, Bentley!" Krista yells.

"It's already swollen," Sasha says. "Like a lot."

Bentley opens her eyes and takes a look. Her eyes go big and she points her finger in the air at all of them: "Nobody say anything to the coaches!"

Sasha gets low to check out the black-and-blue toe up close. "It looks like your toe is about to explode. You should really like raise it up and get some ice on it."

Bentley lowers herself to the floor and lies down. She props her foot up on the chair. She covers her eyes with her arm and lets out a scream. Ellie searches for some aspirin in her bag while everyone stares down at Bentley.

"You can try to tape it up," Mya suggests. She receives some eye rolls from her teammates. "No really, I hurt my finger last year and Coach Williams taped it to the finger next to it. He let me play. It was annoying but it helped."

Krista finishes tying her shoes and steps in between the wall of players surrounding Bentley. "Well, let's get some tape already!"

"Wait," Ellie yells. She puts her hand up. "Can you feel your toe, Bentley? Like can you move it at all?"

Bentley wiggles her toes the best she can.

Ellie reaches down and touches Bentley's hurt toe. "Can you feel this?"

"Yes, drama queen, I feel it. It feels crushed. So yeah I feel it."

"I'm just checking because we would have to take you to the hospital if you couldn't feel it."

"Okay let's get ice and tape stat!" Krista shouts and looks over at Mya. "You're up, Booster."

"Why me?"

Krista gives her a glare.

"Okay," Mya says. "Where do I get it?"

"Wherever, run to the General Store if you have to, just go!"

Mya puts her arms up at the request.

Zo snaps her fingers. "Boys' locker room! They have a room with first-aid stuff."

"They sure do!" Bentley confirms with enthusiasm. "Right when you get in there it's the door on the left."

"You seriously want me to go into the boys' locker room?"

Krista glares at Mya again. "Ah yeah, Booster, just do it."

"No way. I'll get in trouble and I don't want to see anybody's junk."

"Grow up," Krista says. Her glare softens and she winks at her. "You'll live."

"The boys' basketball team won't be in there yet," Ellie assures her. "It's way too early for any of them to be here."

Mya isn't budging. Sasha comes near and hovers over her. She says in the most serious tone she can muster up: "You know if Bentley can't play you're starting at point guard, right?"

Mya straightens up and sighs, "Okay fine I'll go."

Krista instructs Ashlyn to be Mya's lookout. The two of them dart out of the locker room. Bentley covers her eyes with her arm again. Not playing isn't an option for her. She will just have to manage the pain.

Ellie leans over close to Sasha and whispers, "Maybe we should tell someone. Like Miss E or Jemma."

"No," Bentley barks. "They won't let me play if they see it."

"My gosh how did you hear that and also can you even play?"

"I have ninja hearing and yes I can play."

Mya and Ashlyn come running into the locker room laughing. Mya has an ice pack and a roll of tape.

"Nice." Krista nods and gives them two thumbs-up.

"You owe me, bitch." Mya glares at Krista and hands the supplies to Sasha. "The whole wrestling team was in there!"

Laughter rings out.

"Yeah, real funny."

Krista smiles. "Did you see some nice junk, Booster?"

"No! Just Marcus in a towel." Mya shudders. "We locked eyes then I ran into the supply room. The rest of them were still in the showers thank God."

Sasha puts the ice bag on Bentley's toes.

"How does it feel?"

"It's throbbing."

The girls start making their way onto the court to warm up. The coaches typically don't watch much of the early shoot-around session, and if they do it isn't with much intent. The players agree that Bentley should take that time to keep ice on her foot and not worry about the coaches noticing her absence.

Today of all days each coach wanders in the gym. The girls are nervous; none want to be the one who gets asked where Bentley is. They shoot up shots with a heightened sense of anxiety. The players are relieved to be clear of any conversations with the coaches when they burst back into the locker room. Bentley is sitting down ready for tape to be applied so she can test out her foot. Ellie does the honor and tapes Bentley's two toes together. Bentley puts her socks and shoes on as delicately as she can. She gets to her feet and slowly takes a step, then another. Her teammates watch, witnessing the verdict. Bentley is in obvious discomfort and is working hard on walking normally. Jemma appears and everyone freezes. The music is low, which is not normal. Jemma is used to them acting weird but not this weird and not during their ritualistic jam session.

"We're good," Krista says. "Just trying out a new pregame vibe. Bringing it down a notch."

"Okay." Jemma smiles. She cocks her head to the side and decides not to say anything else. She goes into the office to grab her clipboard.

Bentley walks back and cranks up the music to the normal high level. She tries gently jogging and lifting off her foot. It isn't great but she can tolerate it. She puts a thumb up in the air. Somehow it's a go for her. A few teammates make eyes at each other questioning how she came to that conclusion. They know Bentley though, so they don't say a word.

After the coaches come in to speak to the team, they make their way onto the court where Bentley knows she will find out how bad her foot really is. In the layup line she cringes. This isn't going to be easy. She isn't close to full strength, but there is no way she is missing a game, any game.

After a few minutes of watching the pregame warm-ups, Coach Monty calls Bentley over. "How long have I been coaching you, Kramer?"

Bentley shrugs. "Awhile."

"You think I wouldn't notice there is something wrong with your leg?"

Bentley shrugs and looks off in the distance.

"What's up, kid?"

Bentley shakes her head. "It's dumb."

"Try me."

"My stainless-steel water bottle fell off the roof of my truck right on my toe."

"Which digit?"

"The one next to the big one." Before Monty can react, Bentley blurts out, "I can go, Coach!"

Monty knows Bentley at 50 percent is better than no Bentley at all. He tilts his head. "Have Jemma take a look at it first." Monty walks over to Jemma to tell her what's going on. Jemma and Bentley take off for the locker room. Once there, Bentley gingerly takes off her shoe and sock.

"Whoa," Jemma says. "So *this* is why you knuckleheads were acting odd pregame." Jemma shakes her head. "Who's the wise one who taped you up and didn't use any foam wrapping underneath? It's going to hurt like hell to peel that tape off."

"Please just leave it," Bentley begs. "I promise it hurts but I can do it."

Jemma touches the top of her toe. "Can you move it? Feel it?"

"Yes," Bentley says. "Don't worry, Dr. Ellie and friends already went over that." Jemma gives Bentley a worried look.

"Trust me, Jemmers."

Jemma knows it isn't her call. They walk back out on the court. Jemma tells Monty about the tape and how swollen the toe looks.

"How do you keep a kid like that out?" Monty asks Jemma and the universe. "That kid is as stubborn and tough as they get." He exhales and looks at the scoreboard. Less than a minute remaining until the game begins. "Look, I'll let her start but if she can't go, she can't go, and she will just have to accept that."

Skyline is pesky. With Bentley not at full strength, they will get wide-eyed and confident over the opportunity to pull off an upset. The Hoover players realize this and pretend to be nervous in the huddle before they walk out for the tip-off. The reality is they are thrilled. They thrive when the stakes are raised. It sharpens their focus. Since losing to Chesapeake they have been rolling over their opponents with not one suspenseful moment. The thought of a real challenge is exhilarating.

From the get go it's clear to everyone in the building that Bentley is favoring her leg. Skyline does what any team would do when they see their opposing team's point guard playing hurt; they try to exploit her and run her ragged. Bentley is pissed off by the circumstances and is locked in. Her teammates do their part taking pressure off her by making things happen when the ball is in their hands. The first quarter is a dog fight with the Knights trying to establish their queens of the court dominance while Skyline is aiming all they have at chipping away at their armor. The whole spectacle is a sight—the helter-skelter knock-down drag-out pace and Bentley hobbling around the court. The Knights are thriving off Skyline coming at them with full force, and Skyline is playing up to the Knights' level.

With two minutes left in the first quarter, Monty sends Ashlyn in to relieve Bentley and instructs Zo to be in charge of bringing the ball up the court. Bentley is fuming on her way to the bench. Monty sits down beside her and puts his arm around her shoulder. "Relax, kid. I'll get you back out there. Take a break and a breath."

Bentley doesn't want either. A sinking feeling shoots to her stomach while she sits and watches the first string play without her. She feels like throwing up when the second quarter starts and Monty keeps her on the bench. Zo takes the reins and gets them set up in their offense. More times than not she keeps the ball in her hands at the top of the key and motions for Sasha to set her a screen. The two of them make a fun game out of the pick and roll. With Bentley sidelined, the Knights maintain their high intensity and are playing well. Ashlyn is getting valuable minutes with Bentley relegated to the bench. Skyline uses her defender to pay attention to Zo. Twice Ashlyn gets the ball on the wing with nothing but daylight in front of her and she freezes. Not an outsider shooter, her teammates urge her to take the ball to the hoop. On the next possession she goes for it and fumbles the ball then recovers enough to flip it over to Krista to avoid a turnover. When there is a break in the action, Zo talks to Ashlyn. "You're way taller than the girl guarding you. Go post her up. I'll get you the ball. She can't guard you down there."

The next time Hoover has an offensive possession Zo follows through with a pass to Ashlyn down low. Like she predicted Ashlyn makes a strong move to the basket and scores. Monty and Gordy share a knowing look. Ashlyn can be a Swiss Army knife; not only can she give them some solid minutes on the wing, but they have another body that can fill in for Krista and Sasha.

The made bucket gives Ashlyn a jolt of confidence. Since the humiliating episode with her dad during the Saints game she has made positive strides in getting more accustomed to being on the court for varsity games. It helps that her mom barred her dad from attending any of her games until he could promise he wouldn't make a peep. He is already back in the stands and so far is abiding by the rule. Ashlyn doesn't know if it will last. It doesn't matter as much because Ashlyn has something she didn't have before, a team behind her. When she sat crying in the locker room Ashlyn thought her teammates felt the same way her dad did; she wasn't good enough to play with them. She assumed her teammates would look at her as weak. They didn't. The varsity players—except Hayley, who was her friend and classmate—were intimidating to her. Krista, who was the scariest in Ashlyn's eyes, was the one who comforted her by showing a genuine act of kindness. The varsity players reacted as if they understood what she experienced or at the least cared about what she was going through. Ashlyn felt accepted by them. They were there for her at her lowest point and were on her side. It felt good to not feel alone. Ashlyn knows it's likely she will let her father down again, but she is motivated to do everything in her power to never let her teammates down.

With the Knights not skipping a beat with Bentley on the bench, Skyline goes into a full-court press to see if that can rattle them. Since Chesapeake installed the full-court press and was successful, every team Hoover faces implements a press at some point. Most teams start the game out this way but soon realize they can't administer a full-court press at that intensity for the entirety of the game. On the first trip down the court, Zo slices through the press with ease and finds Sasha at the end with a sharp no-look pass that draws a loud gasp from the crowd. When Sasha gets her hands up to handle the heat of the pass, there are more gasps. Sasha keeps the ball raised high and puts it up on the glass and in. Sasha runs back down the court while loud cheers echo through the gym. She doesn't hide a smile when she points over to Zo giving her props for initiating the jaw-dropping play.

Skyline starts three short, scrappy guards who are like gnats nipping at Hoover's ankles. The press starts to wear the Knights down. They force Zo to give the ball up early and make someone else handle it. A Hayley-to-Krista pass sails out of bounds, and on their next possession Skyline picks off the inbounds pass and scores two points uncontested. Monty calls for Bentley to check back in. She leaps off the bench and attempts to hide any hobble on her way to the scorer's table. She is getting used to playing with her foot throbbing, and the intensity of the pain has started to fade. Skyline keeps their full-court press in place, and Bentley joins Zo in trying to bob and weave through it. The press is effective against Hoover because they are dangerous in the open court where they are free to push the ball and stay in control of their motion. A press makes them stop, assess, and think. It makes them play slow. Breaking a full-court press is now a part of every Hoover practice. Monty and Gordy are having a hard time getting the team to understand the importance of switching gears. They tend to resist and try to keep up their frenetic tempo, which results in turnovers. While the Knights haven't fully embraced this change, they are showing improvement. The press still helps Skyline keep Hoover in their sights. The Knights take a slim 36–27 lead into halftime.

In the locker room Monty lets the girls know he isn't happy with the way they are letting Skyline stay in the game. The Knights have been playing very well lately, and Monty doesn't want them to get a bit lax waiting for the most valuable time of the season to arrive. Monty decides now is as good a time as ever to tell the players the rumors are true; Mack is officially coming back. With Monty sharing this information and reminding the players the postseason is only a few weeks away, the Knights come out for the third quarter fired up. They pull away little by little and before Skyline realizes how it even happened Hoover has a comfortable twenty-plus point lead. Monty subbed out Bentley halfway through the third quarter to ice her foot for the rest of the game. Mya walks on the court thrilled and nervous to take Bentley's spot. Hayley helps her fix her uniform; her shorts are twisted up. Her teammates on the bench chant "Booster" when she makes the first three-pointer of her varsity career. The student section follows their lead and starts to chant "Booster" every time she touches the ball. When she scores on a breakaway layup with under a minute left in the game, it brings the house down. She won't score another point in a varsity game again this season. It doesn't matter; she's a Hoover Knight now. One that will be remembered forever not by the name her parents gave her, but by the one her teammates did.

CHAPTER 19

Mack is back. It's whispered quietly in the hallways and loudly in the locker room. The girls are anxious to see him. It's been awhile. There is a lot of buzz. It's a big deal around here. On the court Mack is speaking with Monty when the girls walk out to warm up for practice. Smiles light up their faces. Mack's too. It's genuine. You can tell because he holds it there like he wants this moment to last a while. A nod of gratitude for getting through this with him. The players don't know what this game means to him. How it brought him back. What he went through. Or what they mean to him. The smile is all they will get. It's enough.

Mack let's Monty be the vocal one. He has to be on his best behavior and he is, only raising his voice to show excitement when Krista does a drop step without traveling. Everyone laughs, even Krista. It's good to have him back in the building. Healthy. No longer any "will he or won't he return" discussions. During a three-on-three drill, Booster stops in the middle of the lane and puts up a floater. It's something she sees her older, more skilled teammates do. It's a shot she's never attempted and is trying in hopes of impressing the head coach. The one who wasn't here when she was brought up to sit on the varsity bench. Booster's floater goes up in the air and comes right back down without touching any part of the basket. Mack says, "Nice floater" in his trademark monotone voice. Everyone laughs, even Booster. Mack wasn't trying to be funny, and an embarrassed smile washes over his face. It's genuine. You can tell by the flush of his cheeks.

Mack lets Monty take the lead. Doctor's orders. There will be no changes. Monty will lead the pack, and Gordy Williams will keep his role; he'll help out at varsity practices when his schedule permits and have a seat next to Monty and Mack on the bench during games. It's odd at

108

first for the girls to have Mack back at practice. Besides, when Mack tells a group close to him to do one thing while Monty is heard calling out a different set of instructions, everything goes smoothly. Mack didn't make it back as fast as he wanted. It's February and there are only three regular season games remaining on the schedule. He is thankful to be back at all and in time to participate in his favorite season, the postseason.

On Friday night Mack returns to the bench for his first game back. He smiles ear to ear before the contest starts and shares handshakes with everyone from the refs to the opposing coaches. Mack stays calm throughout the contest. The only time he stands and yells at the refs is when he thinks Sasha is getting beat up in the post. "Stop sucking your whistle; it isn't candy!" That line gets a big smile from Monty and Gordy who are glad to have him back. Besides that lowkey outburst, the game lacks any chance to show much emotion. The Knights made the game easy, opening up the contest with a 26–8 first quarter. They won by more than thirty points.

The following Tuesday the team makes quick work of an average conference opponent. Mack is surprised by how well the team is playing. He states they look like they are primed for playoffs. The girls play carefree. Monty kept the ship on path, and he is being praised by everyone for stepping up the way he did. Monty stays level headed as always and deflects the attention. He gives credit to the players for handling the adversity and for the assistance Gordy, Miss Easton, and Jemma provided. With the return of Mack and the postseason so close there is an increase of anticipation. The time is near when the Knights will have to show if they have the goods to win a state title. To be the last team in their class standing. Soon everything will reveal itself. Does this team have the *it* factor or not? *Potential* was the word used most for the core of this group when they were younger—when Bentley was a sophomore and Sasha and Zo were only freshmen. They had growing pains to get through. Potential affords you space and freedom to develop. Their ascension from unknowns to taking the state tournament by storm a year ago was swift. They went from being unranked for most of last season to being tabbed #1 at the start of this season. They went from being the chasers, the team with nothing to lose, to being the chased, with everything to lose. From potential to the cream of the crop in a blink of an eye. Potential is comfortable. The sky's the limit. When you have *arrived*, freedom and space evaporates. In its place comes expectations, pressure, and results. You're now supposed to perform well today, tomorrow, and always.

The players have not shied away from everything that has come their way: the expectations, the losses, the absence of their head coach. With Mack back, everything they have gone through has led them right where they need to be. The Knights are heading into the postseason playing their best basketball of the season. The swagger they are playing with reminds their fans of how it felt to watch the Hoover team play last season when they were gearing up to pull off an impressive postseason run. Gordy Williams sees a difference though and shares it with the rest of the coaches: "Last season they were playing with pure passion. This year they are playing with a purpose."

CHAPTER 20

Tonight marks the last game of the regular season and the last of the coveted Friday night home games at Hoover High. It's been tabbed "senior night." On top of all this, a win will give Coach Mack his four-hundredth career victory. Jemma and Miss Eason had a plaque made for the occasion. They ordered it a week before the season started, anticipating Mack would reach the milestone the third game in. Jemma has kept it in the bottom drawer of her desk, hoping all year she would be able to dust it off and hand it over to the girls to present to Mack. With Mack back, it feels like basketball season has been heightened. Everything seems more important. More magnified. When Mack was away it always felt like a little something was missing.

There is a celebratory vibe in the gym before the game starts. Bentley could care less about the asterisks that accompany tonight's contest. She wants no part of senior night. Bentley doesn't think about this being the last regular season game she ever plays on this court. Can't. Won't. She is a Hoover Knight at the moment and that's all that matters to her. When she gets announced before the game with her parents by her side and receives flowers from Miss Easton, she glances around embarrassed at the spectacle being made. She hands the flowers back once she gets to the bench.

"What am I supposed to do with these?" Miss Easton asks her with a playful snarl when they land in her hands.

"I don't care," Bentley replies. "Give them to the cheerleaders." Bentley turns her back to Miss Easton and reties her waistband.

"Your mom would appreciate them."

Bentley turns back abruptly. "She doesn't want flowers either."

Jemma giggles listening to the exchange. She motions for Bentley's kid sister Sadie to come down to the bench. Miss Easton hands the flowers off to her to give to their mom.

Jemma smiles. "That is so Bentley. I'm going to miss that kid next year."

"Yeah me too," Miss Easton says.

It's moments before the players go onto the court for the tip-off. There is strategy talk between players, coaches, and last-minute uniform adjustments. Everyone in an anxious frenzy of sorts anticipating the start of the game.

Miss Easton flips her thumb toward Krista and comments, "And look at that one." Krista is pointing up to the rafters making eye contact with someone she knows, then performs a little spin and slides her lucky wristband on that she started wearing during the game after the loss to the Saints. She messes with it, getting it just right, then flips her ponytail before sitting down next to Sasha to hear the last-minute words from the coaches.

"What are we going to do with her?" Miss Easton says.

Jemma laughs and replies, "Try to get her to graduation without incident."

Miss Easton chuckles. "Oh we will."

"I know." Jemma smiles. "I'm going to miss that one a whole lot too."

The players sit listening to Monty give out the opening plays he wants them to execute. Sometimes the plays he calls get run; other times something better comes up and they improvise. Freelance is their favorite way to play. Tonight Zo and Bentley are feeling even more daring than usual because they are wearing brand-new basketball shoes. They are bold and futuristic. The two can't get over how cool they are expressing their excitement to everyone in the locker room earlier. They hopped around and said a lot of words like "fresh" and "sick." One of them even commented on how fast they were going to make them look. With the music pumping and them bouncing around, they were sure their new shoes gave them super powers.

It's not just the shoes; it's the whole team that seems to be full of superpowers. The Knights run circles around their final regular season opponent. The team shows their home crowd they are more than prepared to take on any team standing in the way of them and the state tournament. The final tune-up is a clinic. Mack's words. Bentley starts the game by stripping the opposing point guard's pocket two consecutive possessions, resulting in her driving the length of the court for layups taking flight in her new kicks. Her bruised toe is completely healed, and she ends the evening with twelve points, ten steals, and seven assists. Sasha nearly notches a triple double too: seventeen points, twelve rebounds, and eight blocked shots. Zo goes 5–8 from three-point range and has a team high twenty-eight points. Hayley is 2–3 from three-point range and perfect from the free-throw line. Krista had a solid overall game even though her highlight came when she tripped seemingly over her own feet and still managed to recover to save the ball from going out of bounds. She took a bow and the student section gave her a standing ovation.

Monty and Mack are confident the team is ready to start the postseason. The Knights have taken their game to a new level since losing to Chesapeake. The losses were an instrumental part of the team getting to where they are now. Monty has to admit while they were tough to swallow, the defeats were necessary. If they had beat Chesapeake, he hated to imagine how sky high in the clouds the players would be. They probably would have petitioned for that DJ and went to the school board on their own. Losing made them get real with where they were at. They were not as good as they thought. The losses allowed them to shake off any thoughts of them having to be perfect. They never stopped believing and kept their sole goal: a championship. The Chesapeake Saints changed their whole defense to stop the three Hoover stars, and the Knights weren't able to adjust. The three stars needed to see they weren't going to be advancing far unless the rest of their teammates could rise up with them. They had to learn to trust each other more and dig in. Now the Knights are playing with unflappable confidence. A lot of it stems from the improvement of the new role players. Hayley made important strides with her comfort level as a starter and is making wiser decisions. Ellie is finding her flow by using her body better and reducing her foul count. Ashlyn shed some of her hesitancy and is giving them quality minutes when she gets in. The rest of the players on the team are helping in other ways. Miss Easton's JV squad has improved since the beginning of the season and provide the varsity starters with higher competition in practice. The Hoover Knights look more like a unified team. Far from the one that took the court without their coach to start the season.

Tonight they win the last game of the regular season by thirty-seven points. After the game is over, they have to pull M&M back out on the court because neither of them knew Mack just notched his 400th win. The players present him with the plaque at the center of the court. Mack is genuinely surprised by the gift and graciously holds it in his hands. In the locker room after the win, nobody acknowledges senior night. There is, however, an ambush that takes place when Bentley and Krista walk in five minutes after the rest of them thanks to Miss Easton having Laney hold them back for an interview. Their teammates drill them with Super Soaker water guns when they appear. The girls use every inch of their small space to have an all-out water gun fight. The war ends with everyone soaked and gassed.

Krista and Bentley each have a gun in their hand. Krista holds hers high in the air and screams, "Victory!" Then drops it on the ground. She grabs a towel and wipes her face. "You guys suck." She laughs. "That was pretty good though. I didn't want any mushy crap."

"No kidding," Bentley says. "That was perfect."

The Knights fight, laugh, and play without any mention of this being the end. It's a new season. The best season. Their favorite time is officially here. Everything in their world comes down to what lies ahead.

CHAPTER 21

The exterior door to the gym swings open. Bentley and Krista walk out with the frigid air hitting their warm skin and damp hair. The jolt from the extreme temperature change refreshes them. The girls hold their winter coats in their hands like badges of toughness. Practice wrapped up moments earlier. Like usual at this time of night it's dark, cold, and quiet.

Bentley pauses on the sidewalk and searches the pockets of her backpack for a piece of bubble gum. "Weird not having a game to play on a Tuesday."

The team tips off the postseason tomorrow night in their home gym.

"Oh my gosh," Krista says. "It's Tuesday!"

Bentley raises her eyebrows. "What is wrong with you?"

"Taco Tuesday. I can finally go."

Bentley smirks. She finds a piece of gum, and the girls continue to walk to the parking lot. "No, for real I'm stoked. It's my uncle's bar. They have the best tacos, and I always get to eat for free." Krista drops her mouth open then snaps her fingers pointing at Bentley. "Girl, you are totally coming with."

Bentley gives her a dismissive glance.

"For real you are coming. They will love having us; plus they make some dank tacos."

Bentley shrugs. "That does sound good right now. I'm down."

They jump in Krista's wagon and fire it up. Bentley rolls down the window to yell at Sasha and Ellie who are walking to their cars. It doesn't take much persuading; the pair throw their bags in the back and hop in excited to be going on a road trip that will end with food. Krista pulls out of the parking lot. Sasha spots Zo near the corn field walking home, so Krista loops around to catch up with her. Zo is thrilled to join them and gets thrown in the middle of the backseat between Sasha and Ellie.

Krista's car "The Slick Ick" is truly something to behold. Below Zo's feet is a hole that's covered up by a shingle sheet. With a little work you can pry part of it up to reveal the live view of the road below. The feature gets a strong reaction from first-time guests. Tonight is no different when Zo flips it up to show Sasha and Ellie. They can't stop giggling.

"Where exactly are we going?" Ellie asks.

"It's not far. Like fifteen minutes tops. It's right outside Mason Valley."

The girls stare at Krista. She looks around the car. "What?"

Bentley glares at her. "Dude seriously, *Mason Valley?*"

"So Bentley isn't really allowed within city limits," Zo says, and laughs. "Mack's orders."

"No kidding!" Bentley perks up then bursts out laughing. "We had an office visit about this. It's been requested by Lord Mack that I make nice with the Mustangs, even though I didn't even do anything. I'm not sure I can do that if they're eating tacos at the table next to us."

"It is not *in* Mason Valley; it's out in the country. It's just the closest town. So chill. And this is a Hoover-friendly bar. I doubt any Mustang players will be there."

"Bar?" Sasha says. "I thought it was a restaurant."

"It's a bar slash restaurant. I swear it's cool though; you can be under twenty-one to eat there."

Krista takes a detour when Zo suggests they get some air before leaving Hoover. Sasha and Ellie have only heard the stories of The Slick Ick going airborne. They don't know what to expect and brace themselves in anticipation. The girls scream when Krista nails the gas to get some speed. The station wagon lifts off the ground and immediately crashes down. Zo and Bentley laugh uncontrollably. Ellie and Sasha are in shock. It sounds like something below broke.

Krista leans up in her seat and looks in the rearview mirror. "You girls good back there?"

Sasha smirks. "Well, my head almost went through the roof, but other than that I'm amazing."

"Holy cow, Krista," Ellie says. "How is this thing still running?"

"I have no idea."

The girls are happy to be on a road trip together and for the post-season starting. They are getting antsy for tomorrow night's game. This is the moment they have been waiting for since their season ended a year ago. The chance to play for something special: a title. It's hard to explain the thrilling feeling this time of the year generates. None of the teenagers attempt to articulate it with any dialogue. They just know they feel it in their bones.

Krista is driving awhile on a lonely dark road when she slows and turns into a gravel parking lot in the middle of nowhere.

"This is it?" Sasha asks.

"Yeah."

"I have driven by this place a bunch," Bentley says. "I never knew what it was."

"I have seen this too," Ellie adds. "I thought it was abandoned."

Krista turns the car off. "Okay, guys, for real, don't judge a book by its cover. The place looks a little shady but it's decent inside. My uncle and his friends are biker dudes. They look real hardcore, but they are super sweet so don't be scared." Her teammates stay quiet. Krista looks over at Bentley. "What?"

"No comment. I'm just here for the grub."

The girls walk across the patches of weeds, dirt, and gravel to approach the low-lit standalone building. They stall at the door waiting for Krista to be the one to go in first. Krista calls them chicken shits before she plunges ahead. She swings the door open and steps inside. The air is warm and smells of greasy food mixed with spilled beer. There is a long bar to the right, and to the left are six tables scattered around. One pool table sits by the back wall. Every patron from the handful of men sitting at the bar to the three tables full of people turn at once to look at the girls. They stare at them. It's not in a *what are they doing here* way but in a *I can't believe they are here* way as if they are celebrities. A guy at the bar shakes his head and smiles at Krista for a beat before he jumps off his stool and pulls her into a big bear hug. When he finally lets go, Krista turns to her teammates. "Guys, this is my uncle Tiny."

The girls giggle because he's the size of a Mack Truck. Krista starts to say the names of everyone, but Tiny stops her and says, "I know who they are. It's nice to have you ladies here. Krista, I'm shocked you showed up!"

"Well, it's the first Tuesday I haven't had a basketball game, so hey, I'm here to eat tacos and to see you."

"So cool of you. Sherry is going to be so surprised. Come on let's get you guys a table, and I'll let her know to get a stream of tacos flowing your way."

The group sits down in the back next to the pool table. The patrons return to drinking and eating while shooting the group an occasional glance here and there. When Krista's uncle comes back to the table he brings along a friend with him. The man is younger than Tiny with a thick black beard. He is wearing a black leather biker jacket and cowboy boots.

"Everyone," Tiny announces, "this here is my buddy Grizzly. He's a big fan." The girls give the guy a puzzled look like they can't believe this intimidating gentleman is a fan of theirs let alone has even watched a single girls basketball game in his life.

Krista stands up and gives the guy a hug. "My Grizzly bear, how the hell are ya?"

"It's so good to see you in person." Grizzly lifts Krista off the ground and sets her back down in a smooth motion. "I never see you except on the news when they show all you all's highlights." Grizzly pulls up a chair in between Sasha and Bentley.

Sasha eyeballs him and says friendly but sarcastically, "So big fan of girls basketball huh?"

Grizzly smiles. "Not really. Just a big fan of your team." He points to Tiny. "This guy made me come with him last season and watch the game where you all made it to state." He shakes his head thoughtfully. "That did it, man. Hooked. That shit was wild."

The girls laugh.

"True story," Tiny says. "He stormed the court along with everyone else. I think he gave a few of your high school buddies concussions running out there."

"Hey something came over me, man. You girls are badass. I was at the edge of my seat. That ball rolled off the rim and I lost it. I felt like I was a part of it." Grizzly winks at Krista. "And then you know I've known this little hell raiser since she was like ten."

"You guys are famous around these parts," Tiny says. "Sherry, the one making you tacos in the back, is flipping her shit over you guys being here."

The girls don't know what to say so they stay quiet and smile.

Grizzly smooths out his beard and turns serious. He lowers his voice and says, "Hey, do you all need protection for state? We can do that. I can run that detail no problem. We can surround your bus on the way down. Make it a mini Sturgis rally. Stand guard in the hallways and outside the locker room. We'd do a stellar job."

Bentley laughs out loud. She puts her hand over her mouth, embarrassed she couldn't hold in her reaction. She recovers and manages to get out: "I'm sure you would."

"That would be baller," Krista says.

"Our coaches would love that," Sasha says, sarcastically.

Ellie comments: "Well, we have to make it there first."

It gets quiet. The girls know making it to state is the only option; they made it that way and want it that way. Not only that, they boldly let it be known that *winning* state is their only aim. Now that the time to follow through on their bold proclamation is right in front of their face, it's becoming real. Nothing is guaranteed. Saying it is only saying it. It's easy to be a shot caller. Will they back it up? Will they or won't they is the question everyone in northwest Iowa is asking now that March is near.

Grizzly stands up and puts his hands on the back of his chair. "Oh you'll make it." His wallet chain jingles against the metal. "Got the opposite of a curse on you all; got fairy dust paving the way."

The girls look at him like they still can't believe any of the words that are coming out of his mouth.

Grizzly looks Sasha's way and nods. "I've seen this one block a shot ten rows into the stands, people ducking for cover and shit." Grizzly gets low and looks both ways doing his best impression, then points over to Zo who hasn't said a word since they walked in. "That one's a *real* girl Air Jordan; haven't seen anything like it in my life and you—" He taps Bentley on the shoulder. "I was ready to empty my pockets when I saw you walk in. Just take it all. She'll pick your pocket like a magician. Leave you wondering what the hell just happened."

The girls are enjoying Grizzly's thick drawl and enthusiasm. All of them are grinning from ear to ear as they listen to this man they never met before beam with pride over their basketball feats. "And you too," he nods at Krista. "I know your blood. Not just Tiny here but your cousin Bones and your daddy Big John. Don't mess with Krista! She don't scare. And you, don't think I don't know who *you* are." He is pointing at Ellie. "I'd be scared to play you one on one; you'd shank me, no regrets."

The girls burst into laughter.

"That other girl's not with you all but the short one, she starts. The Bell girl. She's a tough little whippersnapper too. I know her granddaddy. You all have a squad. So yeah I have my money on you guys getting to state. I'd bet the farm on it."

Tiny is smiling. A proud uncle. The tacos arrive. Grizzly and Tiny leave them alone to eat in peace. The girls eat the tacos and the other items that show up happily. They keep eating until they have to beg Tiny to end the stream of food coming their way. One of the patrons finally works up the courage to come talk to the players. He lives close to Skyline and tells the girls he watched them beat up on his home team both times this season. Says it's a pleasure watching them play basketball, and before he can say any more, another gentleman from his table starts talking them up. Then another. They have questions and share their opinions. Mostly though they ask about the path they have to take to advance to the state tournament. Tiny brings a menu over and asks the girls to sign it for Sherry who is too embarrassed to come out and meet them. By the time they leave they have talked to every person in the place. Before exiting, they pop into the kitchen to thank Sherry, telling her how good the tacos were. She blushes and can only manage a quiet "thank you." Later that night, she'll tell Tiny over and over again that she can't believe the Hoover girls' basketball players actually came to eat here the night before their first game of the postseason. She'll frame the menu they signed, and it will hang by the pool table until she takes it with her the day she retires.

The girls jump in the wagon after telling Tiny bye. Krista stands there for a few moments talking to her uncle.

"Thanks, Uncle T, this was fun."

"Anytime. You guys just made Sherry's year and probably everyone else's in there." Tiny lights a cigarette. He blows a big puff of smoke out. "Hey, I hear your ma saying you might not go to college. That true?"

"Really? You too?" Krista lets out an exaggerated groan. "I honestly have no idea what I'm going to do."

"Well that's okay. You have time. But for your uncle's sake, consider college."

Krista's face scrunches up.

"Now listen, it's just that I know what a degree can do for your paycheck. And I'd like to see you get away from here too, you know?"

Krista doesn't respond, opting instead to look down at the ground.

"Hey, I'm not trying to make you feel bad. I just know you can do something good, Krista. Go away to find out what it is, and if you want you can always come back."

Krista rolls her eyes. "Yeah I don't know what that something could be but we'll see."

"Come on. I can think of some things. Maybe something in the medical field. Like an EMT or something. You like to help everyone out and you have no fear."

Krista raises her eyebrows. This is news to her.

"Just think about it. When CJ rearranged his face in that four-wheeler accident, who helped him when everyone was freaking out? It was you. You took care of him and drove him to the hospital. Remember the fire at Grandma's way back when?"

Krista nods.

"You were the one who put it out! In a room full of adults you took charge."

Krista raises her eyebrows contemplating what she's hearing.

"Don't sell yourself short, Krista Rae. That's a skill and a needed one."

"Thanks for the advice, Uncle T. Hey, I have to get these girls home. Game tomorrow night and all."

"Yeah you guys have a state title to chase. Hey, after you win it all, come back here again. We'll celebrate."

"Don't jinx it, dude."

Tiny laughs. "Never. But for real though, good luck making it there. The biggest thing I had going on in high school was—I mean nothing compared to this. I made some pretty solid pieces in shop class. That's about it."

"You wrestled."

"Yeah sure but that didn't amount to anything. You guys actually have an effect on people around here." He takes another pull of his cigarette and exhales. "I guess what I really want to say is that if it ends tomorrow, still be proud of what you've accomplished."

Tiny opens the car door for Krista. She gives him a big hug before she gets in. Waiting for the car to get warm teeth chatter. It's pitch-dark when the wagon turns out of the parking lot.

"Your uncle's bar is pretty dope," Zo says. "Thanks for taking us."

"I told you guys Taco Tuesdays is where it's at."

Bentley puts her hands up to the air vents. "When did your uncle open this place?"

"Oh Tiny doesn't own it."

"Just runs it?"

"No."

Bentley smirks. "You said we were going to '*my uncle's bar.*'"

"Yeah, it's his favorite bar. He practically lives there."

Bentley shakes her head. "You made it sound—never mind."

"It *was* super fun, Krista," Ellie says. "And they *were* really sweet."

"I can't believe everyone in there knew who we were," Sasha says.

"Is it weird to you guys that so many people outside Hoover know us?" Ellie lets out a laugh. "Who knew we had a fan in a biker named Grizzly?"

Bentley looks back at Ellie with a big smile. "That blows my mind."

"And it's like that everywhere," Sasha says. "If my grandpa and his buddies saw us walk into their morning coffee powwow they would be like giddy fanboys."

"Oh I believe it," Ellie says. "Even my cousin's best friends who go to *Mason Valley* went nuts when they found out my cousins were related to someone on the *Hoover girls' basketball team.*"

Bentley looks back at her teammates with a sudden seriousness. "And they're all waiting to see what we do." She turns to look straight ahead again and watches the faintest of snow flurries hit the dash and disappear.

"No pressure at all," Sasha says.

It's quiet for a while until Bentley leans her seat back and it collapses into Ellie's lap. Both girls shriek from the surprise. Bentley struggles to get the car seat to stay upright again. Once she does, she razzes Krista for the wonder that is her car.

"Seriously, why is this car so psycho?"

"Why are you trying to put the seat back anyway?" Krista glares at her. "Don't touch anything in here!"

"I wanted to rest a bit."

"Rest? It's like eight o'clock."

"Well, I just downed eleven tacos. It's hitting me."

Krista sighs. "You guys don't get to sleep while I drive. Sing with me." She cranks the radio up. They cruise along, jamming out. With no warning whatsoever, the hood of the car flies open. Krista punches the brakes and pulls off to the side of the road.

"Holy shit!" Bentley shouts.

Krista gets out of the car, leaving the rest of them sitting there in silence. Bentley looks back at the other three, and after a few seconds they burst out laughing.

"Did it get mad that I called it psycho?" Bentley wonders.

"Did anyone else almost pee their pants?" Ellie manages to ask while she continues to laugh.

"Guys, we could have died!" Sasha says.

"This car is freakin' bonkers!" Zo's eyes are wide. "It's a living legend."

Bentley laughs. "Yeah a living *urban* legend."

Krista opens the car door and yells, "Hey, come help a girl out. Why are you guys just sitting there?"

"Oh we're just thinking about the things that flashed before our eyes when we thought we were goners," Bentley replies curtly.

"Oh chill out, you are fine!"

They get out of the wagon and join Krista by the hood. They flash their phones so she can see better. Krista fumbles the latch trying with her all her might to secure the hood back into a closed position. She can't get the loop to latch and takes a break to shake out her hands. She paces next to the car and lets out a big coyote call into the sky. Her teammates breath into their hands and discuss who would be the best person to call if they can't get the hood back down.

"I'll get it; just give me a minute," Krista says.

"I take it this has happened before," Sasha says.

"A couple times. It only does it on the highway though."

"Oh good," Sasha giggles. "That makes me feel better."

Krista returns to the front of the car for another attempt. Her teammates huddle around her. With a group effort they get the latch to hook. They break their unintentional huddle with a cheer for The Slick Ick living another day, then pile back into the car. The cold air they were exposed to and the adrenaline from the scare is enough to keep them lit up the rest of the way home.

The girls part ways in the parking lot with each of them internally looking forward to the following night when they will lace up their high tops and start their desired march to state. Even so, nothing at the moment seems real significant to them, because nothing unfolds at once. To them they are simply living life, and each new moment is all there is. They don't realize how significant of a time in their lives this actually is or how the teammates you grow up with will always hold a special place in your heart.

CHAPTER 22

Zo walks through the double doors that connect the high school to the middle school. The familiar smell brings up numerous memories. Not many good, not bad either. Zo walks much taller as a high schooler than she did back when she was a student here. It seems like many years ago when in fact it's only been three. Zo opens the door to Jemma's classroom and strides in with a cocky look on her face. Lips puffed up. It's game day, and there is only one person in the whole town that she acts this way around. Zo's eyes go wide and her demeanor changes. Gordy Williams and Miss Easton look at her with amusement. Zo doesn't say a word. Her quietness amazes Miss Easton. When she first saw Zo play basketball she couldn't believe what she saw. The freshman girl who sat silent in her classroom and was timid in the halls came alive with a basketball in her hands. Miss Easton wondered how someone so shy could take over center stage on the basketball court with all eyes drawn to what she was going to do next.

"Hey you," Jemma says. She has a silly grin on her face because she loves seeing her niece embarrassed. "Feeling yourself a little bit?" Jemma giggles.

Zo's face goes red. "Hey."

Gordy and Miss Easton smile at Zo then go back to what they were discussing. After a few minutes, Miss Easton has to get going and leaves the classroom. Jemma and Gordy start a new conversation, one that leads to Jemma trying to explain her relationship with her father. Zo sits on top of a desk looking disinterested. Gordy is fond of Zo. It was a pleasure coaching her in junior high. When Zo came along, Gordy found a player who exemplified his spirit on the basketball court: play to win, do it the right way, and have it be for the love of the game. He had a front-row seat to watch her before she turned into one of the leading scorers in the state. Back then there was no hoopla over their eighth-grade team when they played in small middle-school gyms in front of sparse crowds. Gordy knew right away Zo was on another level than other kids her age when he first saw her play during a Saturday morning basketball session when she was in elementary school. Young girls normally don't perform double pump shots or have that much hang time. Being such a quiet kid there was zero drama with Zo, just a strong desire for playing basketball. She never wanted to leave after practice was over. Eighth-grade practices were short and so was the season. Zo wanted to get in as much basketball in as she could. So did Gordy and he would stay late to let her keep playing. A high school senior who quit the boys' basketball team helped out at practices. Gordy and him would go one on one with Zo who craved the challenge. Gordy was never one to raise his voice or be a cheerleader, and his favorite saying was "There is always going to be someone better than you." Having her first coach be Gordy, who understood her desire for the game while instilling the importance of not resting on your laurels, was influential to Zo.

That eighth-grade class of Zo's was the best class Gordy ever coached. There were enough kids out for an A, B, and C team. Most kids at that age are all potential. Two of those girls were Sasha and Ellie. To Gordy, it wasn't about winning as much as it was about teaching. He enjoyed seeing the girls improve and seeing them play basketball the right way. They were pretty good too. They were so good that new rules were pulled out of thin air and enforced when they would show up at away games. Gordy's favorite was one coach telling him before the start of the game that pressing wasn't allowed in their gym. Of course, looking at Sasha, more than a few made the declaration they don't begin games with the ceremonial jump ball. Gordy took it in stride knowing it didn't matter much what other teams wanted to do. He was more concerned with what his team was doing well and where they needed to get better. Winning wasn't the top priority, and he made sure everyone got quality minutes even if it meant the score wouldn't favor them. They still won plenty, and the highlight of the season for Gordy was a victory over a team he had lost to over and over through the years. Walking off the opponent's court that day with a convincing win was about as satisfying of a moment he has experienced as a coach.

In Jemma's classroom, the conversation turns to Hoover's first playoff game tonight. Jemma and Gordy know what this postseason means to Zo.

Now that the time has arrived, both of them hope her and her teammates' dream of a championship comes true. The whole town shares this sentiment, especially the youth in the community. Gordy, who gets to see all the problems young kids have to deal with, is happy these girls have become positive role models and are setting a positive example. This is what he likes the most about the girls stirring up a basketball craze in this town.

"Tonight is step one," Gordy says in a matter-of-fact tone.

"Oh my gosh," Jemma says, fanning her face with her hand. "It's starting."

Zo only offers a nod. She doesn't appear nervous or hyped up. She's calm while Jemma has been biting her nails off, and it's only 4:00 p.m.

"Let me ask you something," Gordy says, looking at Zo. "Why do you love basketball so much?"

Zo doesn't know if this is a trick question or not. Gordy has a way of appearing serious when he is attempting to be lighthearted. "Because—" Zo hesitates to see if he'll clarify his intent. He doesn't. "It's fun."

Gordy tilts his head waiting for more. He knows Zo is uncomfortable sharing. He isn't going to let her off the hook though and waves his hand out, a nudge to expand her answer.

Zo looks at Jemma, Gordy, and then down at the ground. She clears her throat and lifts her head up. "When I'm out there it's quiet. Silent. And I don't know, I guess it's the only place I feel like myself. Like I get to really be me." Zo is speaking slowly and pausing a lot as if she is making sure it's safe before she keeps going. "There isn't much else that interests me. I don't like school or being social. I kind of feel like there's nothing else really for me. But when I step on the basketball court, that's mine. And win or lose. Do well or don't do well. Out there, everything makes sense. It's easy. And it's fun to me. It's like a secret language only I know. And it's like, I don't know, it's like I can just make magic. And it doesn't always work, but the cool thing is I get to keep trying. And out there with my teammates, it's like we're alike. We all want the same thing. Just to play and win. There's just nowhere else I would rather be than just playing basketball."

Gordy smiles warmly. He knows exactly what she means. Out on the basketball court Zo can be bold, aggressive, and wild. All the things they tell little girls not to be. On the court there is no thinking, no talking; it's you and the game in the present moment. To Zo, the court is a quiet place where she can be loud and express herself.

Jemma stares at Zo with a smirk on her face, surprised her niece actually shared this with them. It makes her happy that she gets to be a part of something Zo loves so much. Zo gives Jemma an embarrassed glance then begins to nag her about leaving to go pick up her pregame sandwich. Zo turned sixteen over the summer and got her driver's license. She still chooses to get rides from Jemma and her teammates during the season. Jemma will ask her why when they walk out to the parking lot. Zo will tell her it's fun. When Jemma presses her to elaborate à la Gordy, Zo tells her it's more fun doing that sort of stuff with others. While everyone thinks the basketball season is long, she thinks it's short. Every game this season is precious to Zo, and she is going to make the most of all the big moments and the little ones in between.

🐦

One thing you can't say about these basketball players on the floor—both the Hoover Knights and the VMS Warriors—is that this basketball game doesn't matter to them. Both teams play their hearts out. Both teams give what they can. Both sets of coaches sitting on opposing benches are all in. Both crowds intensely watch the game play out, rooting for their side. One team is turning in their uniforms tomorrow, and the other one is just getting started. The Knights pull away early and never look back. The Warriors have no answer for Hoover's big three who come out playing like it's the last game they will ever play together. Because it could be and they never want this to end. The win awards the Knights another opportunity to play on their home court and takes them a step closer to their goal of making it back to the state tournament.

Most people in attendance predicted the outcome would be an easy Hoover win. They still came out to watch the show. This Hoover team is special. Everyone is saying so. A year ago this team's potential was still unknown. The run they went on in the postseason was a pleasant surprise to the community. This year the weight of high expectations have been planted firmly on their shoulders from the first day of practice. Their town wants them to return to state and bring back bigger hardware than they did a year ago. Instead of feeling the pressure, the Knights take it as

128

assurance. A push of confidence by the ones who witnessed their elevation. Proof they aren't alone in their beliefs they can win a championship. That it *is* within reach. To them the high expectations are confirmation of the confidence and swagger they feel has been earned.

VMS exchanges high fives like good sports after Hoover ends their season for the second straight year. VMS's all-conference guard Ruby Wilson, who is always tasked with guarding Zo and does better than anyone else in the league, gives her a glare in the handshake line.

"I hate you," she says, sarcastically, then breaks into a smile. "If you guys are going to beat us like this, please do us a favor and go win the whole dang thing this time."

Zo smiles. "Bet!"

The two of them became friends when Ruby attended a Hoover basketball camp in the fifth grade. Too young for cell phones, the two swapped emails and have been staying in contact that way ever since. They have never met up outside of playing against each other in various sports through the years; even so, they have a mutual respect for one another as athletes. After VMS lost to Hoover earlier in the year, Ruby's email to Zo ended with: "Thanks for making me better." Zo replied, "Likewise." The two have always been rivals while realizing—the only way eleven years old can—that winning isn't the only thing that matters.

There is no breakdancing in the locker room after their opening round win. Nor had there been one of Jemma's famous pep talks beforehand. Her pep talk tonight was walking in and telling them they don't get one for this game. Take care of business. VMS is a conference opponent they beat twice during the regular season. One who is playing with a backup point guard. The Knights didn't take the Warriors lightly. No, the Knights took them by storm. Now they are focused on the next round. They talk to each other about Saturday's opponent in the locker room after the game. They are wound up with anticipation for what lies ahead. They warn Monty in the hallway they will be "dipping into his classroom" tomorrow so they can watch game film. Monty doesn't want them to know how thrilled that makes him so he contains his smile. Wondering why he doesn't want them to know their excitement for this time of year is reciprocated, he calls out to them in a playful voice and says, "Come ready to study film and not to fall asleep!"

Krista turns and walks backward. "Oh Monty, we can multitask."

"I'll bring pillows," Ellie says cheerfully. "Oh, someone bring snacks."

Sasha raises her hand.

Monty keeps smiling long after the girls walk out the door. His wife will say one day that being the head coach for this season nearly turned his full head of hair gray. She'll also say it opened his heart up wider than she ever could have ever imagined.

CHAPTER 23

It's the last night playing in their home gym. This is a guarantee. From here on out, the Knights will be playing many miles away from Hoover. Jemma passes the players on her way into the locker room. They are heading to the court to get some shots up before they return for the much anticipated pregame pump-up ceremony. Jemma wants to take some of their confidence for herself and save her anxiety for the next game. It's not working. She is jittery.

Miss Easton is sitting behind the desk in the locker room office when Jemma walks in. She lights up. "How do you know it's tournament time without knowing it's tournament time?"

Jemma raises her eyebrows. "Um, the hammer in my bag?"

Miss Easton smiles. "Okay that, and I think Bentley levitated her way in here tonight."

Jemma laughs. "Yeah their excitement is off the charts. Zo was like a freakin' kangaroo bouncing around getting her pregame sub. Even Mack came into my room like five times today, all antsy. He even told me a joke."

"Impressive. So you ready to pump up the troops?" Miss Easton's eyebrows raise.

"As ready as it gets."

The two coaches prepare the locker room for their pregame activity. This started last year when Jemma, looking for a way to get the girls pumped up for their postseason games, took it upon herself to give the team a pep talk. They won and it was demanded that Jemma come up with something for the next round. M&M were oblivious to the pregame events Jemma orchestrated. Mack walked into the locker room before one game and couldn't believe his eyes. Jemma didn't get everything from

131

their little powwow cleaned up in time. Mack wasn't sure what to make of the mess he saw and assumed the players were horsing around. He had never been so furious with a team in his life. The Knights were moments away from an important game that would determine if their season would continue. Instead of erupting on the players, Mack put his fury into coaching them to a win. If he would have walked in five minutes earlier, he would have seen eggs flying through the air and heard the whole team savagely chanting: "Be the wall." They won the game, and to his credit Mack never said a word about the mess.

Jemma and Miss Easton are attempting to *keep* it a covert operation again this season because the players love it so much and because there are some things M&M don't need to know. It will work. Mack and Monty won't find out until decades later these pregame sessions existed and were one of the highlights of being a Hoover Knight.

The girls come back into the locker room psyched to find out what Jemma and Miss Easton have planned for them tonight. On the ground is a two by four piece of wood with the name Fairfield Tigers written on it. The team gathers around ready to have some fun. They can't keep quiet, so Jemma yells at them to shut up. Miss Easton can't help but giggle watching her coaching pal take charge. The girls are giddy with joy hovering around Jemma like she is going to unveil the greatest secret ever.

"It's going to take a team effort to keep your dream alive. To keep playing for a chance to make it to state," Jemma says. She grabs the zipper of her bag, and before unzipping it she takes a moment to build the suspense. "Every one of you is important and will be needed to end Fairfield's season." She pulls out a bag of nails then a hammer. The girls approve by the noisy reaction that ripples around. "One by one you get to put a nail in Fairfield's dreams."

The girls start taking turns hammering a nail into the piece of wood. There is cheering and shouting. When it gets to Ellie's turn she takes a big swing that connects with the nail. She winds up for another one to finish the job, except her swing doesn't land on the nail. It connects with the floor.

"Ellie!" Jemma yells.

"Sorry! I guess I got too excited."

Jemma and Miss Easton share nervous glances. The players inspect the destruction.

"It's not that bad," Sasha says.

Miss Easton bends down and picks up the chipped pieces of the floor. "Anyone have any super glue?"

"Monty's shop room," Ellie replies.

"We can't ask *him*," Krista retorts. "He and Mack will have shit fits if they find out we're hammering away in here."

Miss Easton gives her a disappointed look, and Krista says, "Sorry they will not be happy. Not one bit. They will blow a gasket. They will fly off the handle. Is that better, Miss E?"

"Yes, thank you, Krista dear."

"Home ec room," Ashlyn says. "Miss Ode has super glue."

"She lives an hour away," Ellie says. "Her classroom is locked."

"No, she's here because she promised us she would stay for the game."

Jemma bolts to the home ec classroom while Miss Easton checks on M&M's ETA. Bentley turns the music back on to maintain the pumped-up vibe they created. Halfway through the song Jemma hustles back into the room and applies the super glue. It works well enough. You have to look close to see any difference.

The coaches walk in to prep the players for their second-round game. The girls look ready, having just swung out some frustration. They want on the court to take down the Tigers for real and to keep marching ahead. On Thursday, the players were introduced to the Fairfield Tigers in Monty's classroom. They watched game film of the unfamiliar team. Both Monty and Mack liked to hype up their opponents. Watching game film, the players weren't impressed. They are determined to show their coaches when the game starts how they feel about their scouting report.

Playing in front of their home crowd for the final time, the Knights jump out to a 16–7 lead by attacking the hoop. The guards drive and keep it or dish it inside to Sasha who has eight of their points. This prompts their opponent to change their defense into a 2–3 zone. Scoring easy baskets gets cut off, and at the end of the first quarter the score is 22–17.

Fairfield takes the lead in the second quarter. They have turned this into a slow-paced half-court game by using the whole shot-clock and playing their zone defense. Zo and Hayley struggle from the three-point line, making this defensive tactic effective. The Knights are having a hard time getting an entry pass into Sasha with three Fairfield players collapsing in the lane to surround her. The Knights come to the bench during a time-out looking annoyed, not flustered. Mack, however, is quite flustered and implores them to "stop playing with your food." Monty preaches patience, saying they are trying to do too much all at once. Relax and work the ball around. The team came out a little too worked up wanting to get to the state tournament in the first quarter. Monty reminds them: "We are a much better team than Fairfield. Take it one possession at a time."

Fairfield dictates the pace. They play slow. The tactic keeps the game low-scoring and close for the first half. In the second half, Hoover is able to break free of the sluggish pace by creating a few fast breaks with their defense. Sasha's size, strength, and ability are too much, and she wears down her defenders going on a mini run of her own. Sasha even breaks out a hook shot and gets an animated reaction from the crowd when it swishes through the hoop. It's a move her dad threw into her drills over the summer, one Sasha wasn't psyched to try. Her dad told her nobody would be able to stop it. He played basketball in college, and he tells her the throw-back shot is underrated. Sasha's hesitancy over the old-school move prompted him to make her a deal: "You make a hook shot in a game, and I'll give you $100." That deal was too good to pass up. Later that night when Sasha gets home from getting pizza with her teammates, a crisp hundred dollar bill will be waiting for her on the kitchen table.

Hoover jumps ahead twelve points in the third quarter, and they never look back. A win is a win even if the girls call it the most boring game of the year. Afterward in the locker room they feel a little bit disappointed that a playoff game didn't generate any thrill-inducing moments. M&M could care less. They are glad to be done with Fairfield and advancing on. Two down, two to go.

CHAPTER 24

When Hayley was in elementary school, her mom knew her tell instantly. She would make a clicking sound with her mouth. Hayley's mom would hear this and drop what she was doing to ask her daughter what was bothering her. Hayley would eventually let everything spill out. One time the clicking sound was brought about because Hayley saw a boy at recess get hit with a hard-thrown ball to the face. Another time it was because a teacher had called Hayley up to the whiteboard to answer a question she didn't know. Hayley has always been a kid who feels everything. Deep. Then she keeps it sitting inside until she can't take it any longer and it starts to come out any way it can. The clicking sound is no longer the first noticeable sign that something inside her is making her feel anxious, scared, or uncertain. Now she cracks her knuckles.

Hayley sits in the locker room tonight preparing for the biggest game of the season. Music and nerves are in the air. Her teammates are getting loose around her. Bentley and Zo are messing with Booster, bobbing and weaving around her. The three of them have smiles on their faces. Krista is doing some karate kicks in the air getting laughs. Sasha is stretching her arms and legs out. Everyone is getting the weight of the game they are about to play off their mind while Hayley is sitting with everything racing through hers. The Knights brought the show on the road tonight, and it will be this way for the rest of the season. Hayley knows tonight and every game after will be the biggest game of her life. Pressure then more pressure. Zo, Sasha, and Bentley are the stars. Hayley and Krista are the two players people have questions about. Hayley can't stop cracking her knuckles nor can she break free from the voices inside her head:

"She's good but she's too small and young to make a big difference on varsity."

"Those three girls are all-state caliber players, but what about the other two starters? Can they win a championship with them?"

"Maybe, because you could put just about anyone next to those three the way they are playing right now."

Hayley has heard tidbits of these comments and assumes the rest because when you hear one doubt your mind likes to run wild. She tries to calm herself by listening to her breath. The music makes it hard. The breathing is what her mom suggested when she was young and agitated by something: breathe slowly in through your nose, hold it, then let out a big breath like a lion. Tonight she skips the lion part. The music is cut, and her teammates depart to go warm up. Hayley takes a few moments to herself to breathe in peace before joining them.

The vibe in the gym is electric even though the majority of the fans have yet to arrive. The players warm up, feeling anxious and hyper. Being in a gym they have never been to before adds to the drama. The fact that their community is traveling here to fill this gym up to see them play a game isn't something the players can even process. Not now. Not when they are living in the moment. One day maybe they'll think about the people who cared so much and about what their team meant to their town. How this game they play generated hope and good feelings for people. Right now though, only adrenaline is shooting through their bodies.

Last shots are put up in a flurry before the players run off the court with fans now coming in by the droves. The girls' mouths drop open when they walk in the locker room. Jemma and Miss Easton's creation hangs before them. A large unicorn piñata with bright sprinkles and a rainbow-colored horn twirls in the air above them. Jemma knows the girls would expect something new, and she doesn't want to disappoint them. She and Miss Easton have been conspiring for weeks over ideas; usually the brainstorming is conducted on the bus rides home from away games.

Jemma holds a bat in her hands and says, "We couldn't find a bulldog so this will have to do." Written on both sides of the unicorn are the words: "Brighton Bulldogs," the team Hoover is facing.

"It's time, ladies," Jemma yells. "The time is now. Brighton has come here, to this gym, to take your spot at state."

Jemma speaks in a harsh tone like she has the power to will these girls to succeed. A nervous wreck all day, Miss Easton thought Jemma was going to throw up before the girls came into the locker room.

"It's up to you to stop them. To show up, win, and keep going."

Bentley reaches for the bat and takes it out of Jemma's hands. "I get first swing." She eyes the unicorn, plotting which part she is going to strike first.

"Hold up, Bent!" Jemma steps between Bentley and the unicorn. Even though Jemma specifically bought this piñata after reading various comments from parents who pointed out even they had trouble cracking it open, Jemma sees the fire in Bentley's eyes. "Everyone needs a chance to hit it before it breaks. One attempt per person."

Miss Easton gives Bentley a strict point of the finger then swings it around to the rest of the group and says, "One swing, everyone."

Bentley cocks the bat back, making sure to put everything into her single attempt. Bentley hits the unicorn across the face with force. It leaves a good size dent near the left eye. While the girls applaud, Krista steps forward. Each player takes a turn giving the piñata a hearty hit. A few of them make a comment while others stay quiet. All of them share the same body language when they finish striking the unicorn. They express self-assurance. It is as if the hard swing released everything inside—the doubts, the chatter, the pressure, the insecurities—and left only one thing remaining, power. They are on a revenge tour to get back to state and win the championship. To go finish what they failed to do last season. They are on a mission, and it isn't about the opponents they face. They are not out to prove everyone wrong. They are playing to prove themselves right; they can be champions.

The starters are realizing they didn't plan this right. The piñata is about to burst open, and it won't be one of them doing the honor. Booster steps up, and there are a few groans. They cheer her on anyway. She has a big smile on her face to go along with the big bat in her hands. Her whack doesn't do the trick. The unicorn dangles in the air mocking them with its resilience. Booster asks for another shot, saying the bat slipped. There's no chance of that. Bentley takes the bat from her before she can even finish her plea.

Ashlyn raises her voice, "Hayley hasn't gotten a turn yet."

The girls look surprised. They didn't know Haley got skipped over and call for her to step up. Ashlyn pats her back and pushes her forward. Bentley hands her the bat. "You got it in you. Take it down."

Everyone starts to chant Hayley's name. She holds the bat in her hand for a moment. Feels the weight of it. Hayley looks around at her teammates. Nerves, adrenaline, and thoughts are swirling through her body.

"Quiet," Jemma yells. "Miss Hayley. The floor is yours. Do you have anything you want to say?" Jemma knows what she is doing. Hayley won't speak unless prompted. Being naturally reserved and the young one around the seasoned upperclassman, she is used to listening. The moment is hers.

Hayley's face is flushed. She struggles to find the right words. Her teammates are surrounding her waiting. She takes a breath in and releases it. "Okay. I guess I'll say nobody outside this circle knows what we can do. What we're made of. We got here together, and we will do whatever we end up doing together. So, this, this is for us."

Hayley swings the bat, piercing the unicorn and shedding it open. Packs of gum rain down, and the girls erupt in pandemonium. Feeling the power course through them, the Knights run out on the court as a pack ready to pounce as soon as M&M gives them last-minute instructions.

The winner of this matchup moves on to play Friday night for a trip to the state tournament. Brighton's crowd is large, and a rowdy group of their students came out prepared for the occasion with props and costumes. It's a big deal their girls are playing in this round and playing Hoover. Everyone wants to get a look to see what the fuss is about with this team, and of course they want to be the ones to end their season. The Brighton players were nervous all day, anticipating their shot at Hoover. They watched them on TV last season, and now they are taking the court next to them. The Hoover crowd doesn't show up all that early. They don't bring the same numbers or amount of noise as the Brighton crowd does. They've been here before. They believe they will get more chances to see their team play. They aren't intimidated by the force the opposing crowd shows when the ball is tipped and they go wild. They have no doubt their team's play will speak for the whole town of Hoover.

On the court the Knights look comfortable in this atmosphere. This gym that sits an hour drive away from them instantly is a special place because right out of the gate they stake their claim to it. The Brighton Bulldogs heard the talk, the hype, the folk lore if you will, about this team that plays like no other girls' team you'll see. They prepared the best they could. In person it's not what they thought it would be. Coach Smith, Brighton's head coach, who is a gregarious fellow, sees the helpless look in the eyes of his players in the huddle when he calls his first time-out. He eases their pain by saying, "You are not playing bad. They have some talented players over there, but even talented players can make mistakes. Don't quit. Stay close. Keep fighting."

The Hoover Knights' big three put on a show. Sasha is owning the lane, Zo is going between her legs and around her back getting to the hoop, and Bentley is patrolling the perimeter with her knack for being everywhere all at once. Krista and Hayley are playing solidly. Krista's focus has improved. It shows in the stats; over the last four games she is averaging nearly ten rebounds a game. Hayley has emerged as a gritty defender and tonight is being tasked with locking up Brighton's leading scorer.

Finding themselves down by thirteen points, Brighton stops defending the Knights one on one and switches to a two-three zone. They want to cut off their drives into the lane and push Sasha as far away from hoop as they can. Hoover starts settling for threes, and they are not connecting. Brighton's defensive switch helps them cut the lead to seven.

Monty calls a time-out to discuss the zone. "We stopped attacking," he yells, because the buzz in the crowd hasn't subsided one bit. "Ball movement. This will bust up the zone. Keep moving, penetrating, and dishing."

Mack jumps in. "Stop lollygagging on offense. You can't stop being aggressive just because you see a zone. We can't let a team like this hang around. Krista, get the lead out of your shorts, and Hayley, shoot with some confidence."

The starters listen intently. Sweat trickling down their faces. They rise up and put their hands together joining their teammates to break the huddle.

Gordy Williams pulls Hayley aside before she goes back out on the court. "Hey, take some of this magic gum."

Hayley's eyebrows raise.

"I never lost a game when I chewed this." Gordy smirks. "Back in my D1 days when I was the starting center."

Hayley breaks into a big smile. Gordy Williams, like Booster, is still waiting for inches to show up. She reaches for the gum.

"Warning, it *will* make you play big."

Hayley smiles again, "Thanks, Coach."

The perimeter players stop shying away from avoiding the zone. They pass and cut nonstop trying to catch a defender sleeping. Bentley slithers into the middle of the lane. Zo creeps down by the baseline, and Bentley puts a bounce pass right in her hands that sends the zone shifting. Zo shot-fakes and passes it under the basket to Krista who holds her girl off her to score. On the next offense possession, Hoover does the same thing. They keep the ball moving. This time, Hayley drives baseline and hits Krista at the free-throw line. She pass-fakes to the wing then throws it up high for Sasha to go get. Sasha has to tip the ball to herself to save it from going out of bounds then goes straight up with it for two more points. Hoover breaks out of their lull and takes a commanding 37–22 lead into halftime.

Finding themselves with their backs against the wall, Brighton comes out fighting in the third quarter. They go on an 8–2 run to get the deficit down to single digits. Brighton switches their defense up and goes into a 2-1-2 zone attempting to do a better job of keeping the Knights from doing damage around the basket. They are daring Hoover to beat them from the outside. Zo only had one three-pointer in the first half. She's never shy with shots and starts letting it fly from deep. She misses consecutive attempts, and the Brighton faithful feel like they have a real chance to crack Hoover's code. The gym gets loud with hopeful energy. Hoover's offense again goes stagnant. On one possession, Bentley forces her way into the lane and gets bumped, causing her to lose the ball, which leads to a fast break. Mack thinks Brighton is getting away with fouling Hoover's slashing guards. He stands up and has a word with the official. His face gets red, and he loosens his tie. He puts his hand up when Monty walks toward him and says, "I'm good. I'm calm. I just can't let that go. They are holding and banging our players around."

Monty calls a time-out to regroup. Mack is working hard not to lose his cool. He lets Monty talk to the players for a bit then kneels down, eye level with the girls and says, "Let's put this game away." The starters on the bench are frustrated. Zo stands up. She wants back on the floor to settle the score. It's not about what Brighton's players are doing; she wants to shut up their cocky crowd. The one that is behind their team like their lives depend on it. They have more confidence than the five players on the floor, and Zo wants to quiet them. Her teammates feel the same way. While walking back on the court Bentley gathers her teammates together and brings her hand to her mouth to shield her voice from carrying past them, "Let's go looking for dinner."

It's on. The Knights go into attack mode. Everyone in the gym can feel the shift. Bentley wills her way into the paint and dishes it to Sasha who has to fight off two girls to secure the ball. Mack, Monty, and the entire Hoover crowd want a foul. Sasha doesn't hesitate; she keeps playing, bringing one of the girls up with her on a shot. The ball goes in, and Sasha shrugs her shoulders on the way down the court feeling lighter. Mack is irate; there was no foul called on the play. Monty puts his hand on his shoulder. "Easy, Coach. Thanks to me we're at zero technical fouls on the season, which is a record."

Mack gives him a sideways glance. Monty isn't sure if Mack's proud of this fact or thinks now is a perfect time to change it. No matter, there won't be any more reason to get up in arms over anything. Bentley steals the ball and lofts it ahead to Zo who avoids her defender by going up for a reverse layup. On defense, the Knight's switch to a two-three zone. Brighton's offense stalls. They are wearing out. Sasha records five blocks in the third quarter alone. Krista is snagging every weak side rebound. Hayley makes two consecutive open shots, forcing Brighton to pay more attention to her. Bentley has six steals on the night. Zo is on fire. She drains a long-distance three ball. The next time down her defender picks her up from deep, so Zo drives at her then hits her with a step-back three-pointer that swishes through the net. Ellie and the bench mob break out their new celebration: the bow and arrow. A few possessions later, Bentley pokes the ball out of her opponent's hands and hits a streaking Zo who pulls up and swishes another three-point bomb to beat the third-quarter buzzer. That's game. Hoover leads 60–41 after three quarters. The starters play the first two minutes of the fourth quarter before they exit for good. Another check mark for Hoover. One more game to go.

The coaches are pleased with the in game adjustments they made. Before they leave the locker room, they tell the players Friday is going to come fast. They already know their opponent—Maple Falls. The girls have no reaction because they don't know much about them. Mack responds by telling them Maple Falls is the only undefeated team left in class 2A, and they have the state's leading scorer on their team. "We have to show up or they are going to wipe the floor with us."

The players want to roll their eyes because that contradicts what they are thinking about any team they face right now: "They got nothing on us." When the coaches leave, the girls crank the music. The players keep it low key, knowing winning this game tonight means nothing if they don't win the next. Mack's words work; they start thinking of the challenge ahead and share the same attitude: let's not *get* ready, let's *stay* ready.

Laney catches Mack in the hallway. He winks and says, "Nothing like a close game to get the juices flowing. *Now* I really feel like I'm back."

"Hmm, you call that close, Coach?" Laney laughs then rattles off numbers that state otherwise.

"Well hey, compared to our other games it felt like it. There were a few instances where they crept in the picture and it was enough to feel that spark. This is the best time of the year. If you can't feel the juices flowing, you don't have a pulse."

"You're right about that," Laney says with a smile. "One more win, and the real fun starts."

The two discuss Friday night's matchup. Mack is excited for what he says should be a "barn burner." Unlike moments ago in the locker room, he is brimming with confidence in his team. He can't hide how proud he is of his Knights. Yes, Friday will be a heated battle but one he feels his team will win. Mack knows those girls. He saw their eyes when he told them Maple Falls had a perfect record with the leading scorer in the state on their roster. They want on the court to shoot their shot against them right now.

After their chat, Laney finds Coach Smith to congratulate Brighton on a nice year and get his thoughts on Hoover. He heaps praise on the Knights: "They gained some fans tonight. My players were in the locker room after the game talking about some of those plays they made. They're sad the season is over and in awe at the same time. I told them to be proud of how they played. Hoover is the real deal. They lived up to the hype. I mean, the Jones kid made some threes from the parking lot along with crazy circus shots. Then you got Sasha Hudson, who dominated the inside and even hit us with a baby hook shot. I couldn't believe it! I had to ask my assistant if I saw that right. Their point guard runs the show and harassed our guards to no avail tonight. Then those other two…I didn't think they would hurt us but they did. I wish them the best of luck."

The crowd in the gym is lingering. Hoover's fans are basking in the win, and Brighton's are staying to give their girls a pat on the back for a solid season. Miss Easton comes into the locker room to tell the players there are parents and little kids waiting for them to come out. The girls hustle up to enjoy the scene before they jump on the bus for the long ride back to Hoover.

One team lives to play another game. The other team is going home. In a few weeks, Brighton's girls' basketball team will gather for their annual banquet. At the end they will watch a video that splices together their best highlights from the season. Since playing Hoover was their pinnacle moment, Sasha's hook shot and all of Zo's deep threes make the final cut.

CHAPTER 25

Red and black is everywhere. The freshman basketball team decorated the bus. They did this for the last game as well. Today they put more into it. Streamers, balloons, and the Knights' rally cry are scribbled on the windows. The varsity players jump on the bus with youthful exuberance. Because of the magnitude of the matchup and the fact that this game will take place far from home, they bring more with them. Their bags are stuffed to the brim. The bus goes silent after they get out on the country road because they brought their dreams along too, and those require peace and quiet.

It's the first time all season they don't feel alone in route to an away game. This isn't about just them anymore. A town is following. Some are leading the way. All ascending on another town most have never stepped foot in. There is a sense of wonder and an element of surprise this creates that adds to the anticipation that is in the air. Walking off the bus has a different feel. Tournament time does this. The players walk into the foreign school and take in the surroundings, laying eyes on the site that will be the location of new memories after tonight. Happy ones, they hope.

After a light shoot around, the players return to the locker room. Miss Easton beckons them. They follow her voice past the showers and bathrooms wondering what is in store for them. Miss Easton stands solemnly at the exit door because this game will send one team off to where every high school basketball player wishes to be and will send the other team home where their dream will stay a dream. She asks in the tone of a drill sergeant, "Are you ready?"

The players stay quiet and offer convincing nods. Miss Easton sees in their eyes they want this. They are ready. She opens the door, and they pass by her into the dark of the night. They turn to see flames. Jemma is standing next to a dumpster with a fire pit down at her feet. One you would see in a backyard. Makeshift for sure. Doesn't matter, the girls are beyond satisfied this is what they get. Jemma and Miss Easton went big. The players are psyched. The girls form a circle around the fire pit. Ellie asks what everyone else is thinking, "How did you guys get this here?"

"Don't worry about it," Jemma says. "Your job is to be focused on the game." What they don't need to know is that Jemma played in this gym when she was in high school. That is how she knew there was a back door to the locker room and knew this idea would work. Miss Easton needed some convincing. This *was* better than trying to do it inside with a lighter and the chance of setting off fire alarms. The two are proud to be pulling this off.

Jemma hands out paper and pencils and tells the team in a shaky voice, "This is the last hurdle to get to state. You want to win a championship, right? If you are going to make that happen, you have to leave some things behind. Let go and move ahead. I want you to write down something you know you can't take with you. Because if you want to be champions, there is something that has to be burned and left behind."

Jemma lets them think about this and adds, "It can be something you're beating yourself up over—a bad play, a bad game, a bad habit—or it can be something else entirely. Just think of what you need to let go. What can't make the trip to state with you if you're going to be your best."

Jemma gives them a minute before telling them they have to hustle up. Some of the girls are struggling to decide what to write while a few were done in an instant. Jemma looks up at Miss Easton who is holding the door open so they don't get locked out. She holds up seven fingers indicating how much time they have left. Jemma nods and asks the girls who wants to go first.

Bentley speaks up and tells everyone she'll do the honors. She crumples up the paper and says, "I'm not sharing what I wrote." Nobody prompts her to change her mind. They know this is too personal for any of them to share. "It's one word. That's all I'm saying." She lifts her hand over the flame and releases the paper into the fire. "Bye bye."

Each player goes and keeps what they wrote on their piece of paper to themselves. Last one up is Krista. She doesn't have a piece of paper in her hand. Krista glances around the ring of fire. She puts her hand on her forearm and peels off her wristband.

"What are you doing?" Bentley asks.

"That's your lucky wristband," Ellie adds, in case she needed reminding.

Krista shrugs. "Yeah, I keep telling everyone it is. But it's just a wristband. It's not luck. It's you guys. It's us. We are the ones beating teams. I don't need this. It's starting to smell funky anyway." Her teammates are not sure what to think. Krista has been vocal about her wristband being lucky ever since she started, wearing it after they lost to that team. The one they won't say by name. "Look, we're not going to win a state championship because of this." Krista holds up the wristband. "Or because Sasha has to eat her pregame meal at her grandparents' house before every game. Or because Zo taps her heels together three times with special coins in her shoes or because Bentley has to eat a peanut butter and jelly or banana or whatever the hell kind of sandwich it is at a certain time before tip-off. Hayley, you have Ashlyn braid your hair the same way before every single game, and Ellie, you have to brush your teeth every time we start our pregame jam session. The JVers, I have no idea what you weirdos do except for the two of you who stopped shaving your legs when the postseason started. That's gross by the way, but whatever. That stuff and all the other stuff and this wristband doesn't have us playing for state. Nobody can touch us when we play together. It's us, y'all. So F this wristband!" Krista dangles it up in the air over the flame. "You guys showing up is all I need." Krista's teammates start to chant "do it." Krista tosses her wristband in the fire. The girls put their arms around each other and sway back and forth watching it burn. They do their usual sounds when in this formation: loud *ahs* that get louder and louder until they end with a big nature boy woo-hoo. They go back inside to get ready for Mack and Monty to address them. The two head coaches look sharper than usual when they walk in. New suits and intense expressions make them look like they are preparing to perform a particularly tricky audit. They tell the team they have worked hard for this opportunity and if they execute the game plan they will be playing at the state tournament next week. With a hint of a campfire smell covering them, the Knights bolt out of the locker room and bask in the thrill of charging onto the court in front of a packed-to-capacity audience. The Knights pace around during warmups with a chip on their shoulder and a hop in their step.

They love being the underdog. Maple Falls is ranked number three in the state while Hoover is fifth. M&M did everything in their power to try to galvanize the team by talking up their opponent every chance they got. The Hoover players are sick of all the noise leading up to this game about the elite team they are facing—the one that boasts a perfect record, averages seventy points a game, and has the top scorer in the state on their roster. Every player took Mack and Monty's words as a throwing of the gauntlet. Hoover's starting five walk on the court bursting with energy waiting for the ball to be in the air so they can respond.

With a trip to the state tournament on the line, the intensity in the gym is off the charts. Sasha makes her presence felt, scoring the first four points of the game. Maple Falls takes a few possessions to score, and once they do they go on a seven to zero run. Hoover doesn't worry about it. They are bringing a confidence and aggressiveness that Maple Falls can't match. On offense, the Knights start connecting with the basket as a result of broken down plays. They thrive on improvising. So much so that Hoover's style gets called backyard ball by many, and tonight they show off this trait by going on a 12–2 run to end the quarter. With them leading 16–9, Monty and Mack share a pleased look with each other before they address the team. This is going better than they could have scripted.

The second quarter sees Hoover take command of the game, sucking out the tension in the air. Powering their surge is their harassing defense. Sasha takes her block count up to four, and as a result, Maple Falls stops entering the lane. The team records seven steals in the quarter. Bentley leads the way in that category like usual. She and Zo are relentless in their pursuit of shutting down their opponent's leading scorer. They work together to make her night miserable. She only scores two points in the half, and Hoover goes into halftime with a nice 34–16 cushion. In the locker room the players stay intense. There is no chance for a letdown, not with the winner of this game advancing to state. The team that came in as underdogs are keeping that mentality. Sasha yells at some of the JV players who are joking around and laughing. This is serious business. The starters know they can't treat Maple Falls lightly with two whole quarters left.

Maple Falls comes out of the third quarter playing for their season. They scrape and claw their way into making the game competitive. Hoover shows trust in each other when the lead dwindles down to eight.

With two minutes and change left in the quarter, the Knights take back power. Zo drains a deep three-pointer. On defense, Sasha gets her fingertips on a shot attempt; Krista dashes to grab the ball and without thinking flings it with one hand to the opposite side of the court. The crowd gasps at the decision. Krista knew what she was doing, and like a magic trick Bentley appears when it lands. She gets the ball off the bounce and puts it up on the glass for two points. Everyone in the crowd knows where this Hoover team is going. It took only half of the first quarter to see they are on a different level than their opponent. The Knights lead is 16 by the time the third quarter ends. They open the fourth with a flurry of made shots that take the lead up to 23. The starters take a curtain call with three minutes left on the clock.

When the buzzer sounds the players celebrate on the court together. Having experienced this a year ago, it's a different feeling. The feat is still satisfying. To get where they want to be they needed to pass this level. Mack and Monty are overjoyed with the result tonight. Bentley and Zo held Maple Falls's leading scorer to seven points. Sasha owned the paint on both sides of the court, and their second leading scorer was bottled up by a tag team effort from Hayley and Krista. The Knights played dominating defense and were flowing on offense. It was the most complete game they have played all year. A few TV stations are present to record clips for their sports segment for the ten o'clock news. Being interviewed, Monty beams over his team qualifying for state. "It was our best performance so far. The kids turned the intensity up an extra notch. They did everything we asked them to do and a little more."

The bus is rowdy all the way home. Once they arrive, the team rushes into the Hoover gymnasium with the state-qualifying banner in their hands. They celebrate with their classmates and fans for a bit before heading downtown to cruise the loop and go wild, basking in the excitement of making the state tournament. They enjoy the moment while knowing they need to keep focused on the real prize. The state tournament starts next week, and they need to be ready to shoot for their high score if they want to finish as the only team standing.

CHAPTER 26

Monday is the best Monday of the whole school year. Hands down. Classes are a breeze. The players enjoy walking around school knowing where they are going. Before practice, they are too excited to contain themselves. They talk to each other about the weekend they had and about the adventure ahead. Who is bringing what. Who received what. Sasha is sporting brand-new shoes or "boats" are what her teammate's call them. They are the same fresh kicks Bentley and Zo have. When they go out to warm up, her teammates ask her to try to touch the rim to see if the shoes are magical like Zo and Bentley claim them to be. They are. The two JV players who are not going to shave their legs as long as they keep winning lower their knee-high socks to show off shaved H's on both legs. Their teammates plead with them to keep wearing their knee-high socks. Miss Easton walks into the gym with their state tournament T-shirts and gets swarmed. The girls feel the shirts in their hands, looking at the words and the graphics. Booster puts one on over her practice jersey right away. It's so big it looks like a dress. Everyone talks nonstop over each other. The team is on cloud nine. M&M force the girls to reign in their emotions long enough to get some productive practice time in. After Monty blows the whistle, the group slides into their normal routine. It's nothing strenuous, and the coaches mostly talk about their first-round opponent, Carson West, pumping into the players tendencies and habits they saw watching game film over the weekend.

The girls light up again after practice ends. Laney from the *Hoover Times* is here to conduct interviews. Today has a feel like no other. It's similar to when the girls were excited for Christmas break. Different though because after Christmas they got to return to each other and basketball. They will never come back to this. When they walk into school a week from today, there will be no more basketball practice. Track practice sure, but that isn't something that grabs a hold of their heart, demands commitment, and then sparks something none of them can explain. The girls are only thinking about the state tournament. The end isn't even being considered because the best part remains. The off-the-charts anticipation for their trip to Des Moines shows through the spirit of bliss that is hovering around the team. Even the ones who don't love this game, like their teammates, feel all the feelings.

Krista has never been one who loved basketball. She never got caught up in any sports. She wasn't one to take any of it seriously, and her coaches didn't like her too much for that. Or for always talking way too loudly and taking plays off. So when Laney asks Krista what she's gonna miss the most about playing basketball, at first she scoffs, like there is nothing she'll miss, as if she is out for the team simply because it's something to do. Nothing more. Krista's face changes when she realizes her time with this team is running out. This group didn't choose each other, but in choosing basketball they got something they never knew could happen. A family of sorts. Realizing this is what she is walking away from—family—Krista looks at Laney and says, "I'm going to miss that." She motions over to where a few of her teammates are. They are messing around, smiles on their faces, poking fun at each other. Laughing. There's not a basketball in sight. This game they play together means nothing, and it means everything. Krista walks away holding back tears.

Team. Basketball. Sometimes it turns into family.

~

In the locker room after practice the festive vibe continues. Bentley is beyond hyper preparing for their trip to state. "Dude, my mom got me new slides and a sick hoodie." She opens her bag and flashes Krista a peek at her new items.

Krista glances at them and gives her an approving nod. She is busy putting new shoestrings in her shoes. Her parents nixed her plea for getting new kicks for state. Bright red shoelaces will have to do.

Bentley snaps her fingers and announces loudly: "Oh and did you all hear Jim's Bakery is sending doughnuts and Pizza Barn is hooking us up with pizza for the bus ride down to state tomorrow?"

"No shit?" Krista responds loudly with her eyebrows raised, more impressed with this news than anything else.

"Krista Rae Hansen!" Miss Easton shouts.

"Huh?"

"Mouth!"

"Oh," Krista responds. "Seriously? I'm eighteen, yo."

"Well, you're still in high school, yo, so watch your mouth."

"Yeah there's a thirteen-year-old present," Sasha says.

Booster springs up and declares, "I'm fourteen!"

"Relax, we believe you, and enjoy this, Miss E." Krista smiles. "You guys are going to miss my mouth around here next year."

"No you're going to miss us," Booster says.

"Unlikely. I'll be partying my face off in a sorority while you'll be running up and downs and tripping over your shoelaces."

"I don't think they have sororities at ECC."

Everyone laughs, and Booster's face lights up.

"Sheesh, I hope you don't end up at Elmwood Community College," Bentley says. She reaches down putting a hand on Krista's shoulder and asks in a hushed voice, even though everyone can still hear her: "You're not going there, are you?"

Krista keeps her head down working her laces. "No."

It's silent for a few beats.

"Let's see if she actually graduates first," Booster says.

Krista flicks her off without looking up.

"Oh gosh," Sasha says. "Can you imagine Krista staying in high school and being a senior a few more years?"

Zo laughs. "She keeps getting held back and becomes the first twenty-one-year-old senior basketball player."

"Hey, maybe I'll be good by then."

Bentley giggles. "After games she whips out a twelve-pack. I'm twenty-one, yo!"

Laughter fills the room. Even Miss Easton can't help but chuckle.

Ellie puts her hand in the air to gain everyone's attention. "Hey, if she's here when she's twenty-one, she and Booster will be seniors together."

"Oh no thanks!" Booster yells.

Jemma steps out of the office. "This sounds like a conversation my sixth graders would have. Can you knuckleheads stop chattering nonsense and get your asses out of here so Miss Easton and I can go home?"

"Mouth!" Krista snaps her fingers and points at Miss Easton.

Miss Easton gives both of them a playful look of disdain. The girls stay and keep messing around. They don't want to leave. Maybe they do realize they won't be coming back to this. Or maybe they know where they are going is a place that requires a strong bond so you don't break easily, and they are squeezing everything out of the last time they will ever gather together in that locker room again.

๛

The team reconvenes at Hayley's house later that night for dinner. A bunch of the parents drop off homemade food. It's a feast. The players are appreciative because they know this was work. Happy work. There is something special about making it to the state tournament. It creates a magical feel in the air, and it covers the whole town. The girls take time to open up all the cards the first graders at the elementary school made for them. They smile, laugh, and adore the creations.

A bunch of them are still hanging out in Hayley's basement when the message comes into the team's group chat from Krista at 9:08 p.m.: *All clear! Come alone. Bring the scotcheroos;) enter through the back door.*

Everyone knew it meant Krista succeeded. She bragged about talking her boss into allowing her squad to use the joint. A few of the players were hesitant. Krista's place of work is part consignment store, part bar. On one side you can shop for vintage clothes, and on the other side you can have a glass of wine. A small town is maybe the only place this concept can be pulled off or at least radiant the charm this spot does.

Clusters of two and three knock on the back entrance of the shop. Krista opens the door waving them in like she is hosting an underground party that's top secret. It isn't underground, but the players want to keep it a secret. It shouldn't be a problem. A Monday night in Hoover at this time of night finds only two cars on Main Street.

After another knock, Krista opens the door and her smile fades. She looks at the ground and takes a step back. Krista's boss walks through the door and raises her eyebrows. The sides of her mouth turn upward. She knows an explanation will be entertaining. "What's going on, Krista?"

"Nothing much."

Krista worked here last summer and still works some Saturdays. She adores her boss. Krista clears her throat.

"I knew it was strange you popped your head in here earlier for no real reason. I had a strong feeling you were up to something. I heard a lot of whispering and laughing."

"Okay, well—" Krista stops to start over. She knows she has to tell her the truth. She smiles and says, "So we just like—" Krista bites her lip.

Her boss stops her. "Okay, Krista. You know at night the boutique side closes and only the bar side is open. What did you come here expecting? Did you really think you and your team could help yourself to beverages? Because I am not even letting you guys have pop."

Krista drops her tensed-up shoulders and looks at her boss with disappointment. "No. Of course not. We didn't come here for *that*."

"Then what *did* you come here for?"

Krista blushes. "We came here for your sound system."

What nobody understands about this team and their loud music is that it calms them down. The music pumping loud relaxes them. It gets them ready for when they take the floor. They start the night feeling loose. Even if some players find it hard to keep in this state, they always have that moment to refer to. The players know from last year they won't be able to play their music loud down at state, which defeats the point. The walls at state must be much thinner than the walls at Hoover High because they were told to shut off the loud music within minutes of turning it on last year. The players know the whole pregame setting before state is completely different from what they are used to. Not only will they be without their loud music but they won't have a pregame activity provided by Jemma and Miss Easton to participate in. The logistics don't allow it. So tonight, before they have a send-off pep rally at school tomorrow, they want a private one. Full of their loud music to set the tone.

Krista's boss shakes her head with a smirk, then gives her a warm smile and tells her she has thirty minutes. Krista gets the party started. It really is a great sound system. Better than the small speaker they use in the locker room. The boss stays and serves the girls water. Booster brought the scotcheroos along with her mom because she couldn't convince her this was an innocent meetup. Her mom and Krista's boss serve the girls water and divvy up the chocolate Rice Krispie treats. The girls talk and laugh together while their music blares. They dare Booster to eat six of the scotcheroos, and she does it. Ashlyn has to give her twenty dollars. Krista plays the part of the DJ, and one last time they jam. Forty-five minutes in, Krista's boss kills the music and flips the lights on and off. Bentley breaks the group down and they yell, "State" on three. The girls go out the front entrance and walk down the middle of Main Street. A few run over to give the ice cream shop's door a tug to see if it was left open, fully prepared to grab a bucket of ice cream and leave Booster's twenty on the counter with a heartfelt note. No dice on the door so they walk and talk loudly, making their way to the movie theater. When they get there they start working on poses like they are trying to decide what their album cover should be. They call Booster's mom who stayed behind to help clean up and ask her to come to the theater so she can take a team picture of them in front of the marquee that displays the words: "On to State!" Tomorrow it's go time. Nothing is finished. They haven't accomplished their goal. Last year they were happy just to be going to state. To be one of the teams. This year, they want to be *the* team.

CHAPTER 27

At the state tournament, the Hoover Knights are known. Be it from the way they wear their uniforms, to their flashy shoes, to their unconventional play and unapologetic attitude; Hoover is recognizable. A group of eighth graders from a town located on the opposite side of the state from where Hoover lies traveled to Des Moines today not wanting to miss a chance to watch the Knights in person. They were gathered together last year and witnessed Hoover make their inaugural state tournament appearance. They have been looking forward to this day since the tournament ended last season. The junior high girls had never seen girls' basketball players play that way before. Sitting courtside tonight, a few of them wear basketball shoes with their favorite Knights player's names written on them. The girls will say in a few years when they are playing high school basketball themselves: "We grew up watching those Hoover girls play."

Yesterday afternoon when the pep rally concluded in Hoover's gymnasium, the team boarded the bus with everything they had and headed south to the capital of Iowa to find out if it would be enough. Tabbed to play in the last game of the day, with the tip-off set at 8:30 p.m., the Knights had a grueling day of waiting for the chance to see. With the time finally here, they take a ravenous us-against-everyone attitude onto the court for the late-night jump ball. Red and black dominate the arena, making Carson West's crowd look diminished. Right out of the gate, Hoover makes a statement and gives their faithful fans a reason to party. The Knights score the first ten points of the game. Carson West is struck by nerves, the noise, and Hoover's speed. The Knights run, run, and run some more. Everything goes right for Hoover. Their inside game is crushing, and their defense is suffocating. They are fast breaking at will, and the Hoover crowd, who drove four hours here and won't arrive back to their homes until the middle of the night, is loving it. Sasha is running the floor and being rewarded. M&M know that for them to win a title Sasha's imprint needs to be ingrained into every game, and tonight she is firing on all cylinders.

It's a Hoover thrashing early; at the end of the first quarter it's 27–7. The girls can't help but flash smiles on their way to the sideline. Mack and Monty warn them to stay sharp. The two coaches keep their gaze stern. The girls know they are smiling inside. Their play is too crisp and dominating for them not to be. Monty implores them not to let their foot off the gas. The players stay serious in the huddle, and when they go back on the court they return to their playful nature. Bentley jumps into the passing lane stealing the ball and creating another fast break opportunity. She throws a dart over to Zo on the right, and she sends a no-look pass right back to her. Bentley strides to the middle of the lane with a hop in her gait, stops, pivots, and lofts the ball up high for Sasha who is trailing the break. Sasha plucks it out of the sky before it comes down around the outreached hands of a few Carson West defenders and takes the ball up for two more effortless points. She sends a point and a smile Bentley's way, then hustles back down the court to defend the lane while Hoover's student section is sent into mayhem. They bounce up and down in a unified rhythm. The team and the crowd are in a flow. A confident and joyous one.

This game never becomes competitive. Hoover blows out their first round opponent 67–39. The second half of the game sees the reserves for Hoover take the stage to get memorable minutes on the "big" court they were all in shock over. Mack and Monty emerge in the locker room after the game and start dousing the players with water. They let the players bounce up and down around them. They break out their Hoover chant. After Mack wipes off his face with a towel, he settles the team down by putting his hand up in the air and saying, "Great win! However, this isn't it. This isn't what we came here for. We came to win the last game."

"Job's not even close to being done, ladies," Monty bellows, over the excited commotion that Mack's words stirred up. "Enjoy this tonight. Tomorrow we go right back to work."

When M&M exit the room, the players jump around again. Bentley blares their music. Miss E is quick to turn it down to a respectable level.

She doesn't want to draw more attention to the team. Hoover is already being watched closely. The headband Zo wore to start the game was against a rule, and during a break in the first quarter she was instructed to remove it or she would have to sit out. After the game ended, Mack was pulled aside by one of the head honchos and given an earful about the style of his team's uniforms. He was asked to change them. Mack responded by saying, "We're not going to do that; that's how our uniforms are." Today's state newspaper included a blurb about Hoover that had nothing to do with their play. Instead, it was about their tendency to challenge authority; the defiant youngsters are refusing to shave their legs! The team seems to be the cause of drama down here. The Knights don't mind because there is zero drama within, and if everybody else wants to say this or that about them, so be it. They know who they are and what they are here to accomplish. What everyone thinks of them outside their circle is of no interest to them. They are single-minded, only focused on their mission: their dream of winning it all.

After the girls get changed and everyone is done with their postgame obligations, the team makes their way to a designated area where they get to meet with their family and fans. It's late by the time the Knights board the bus to make the trek back to their hotel on the outskirts of the city. The girls, to the astonishment of Miss Easton and Jemma, persuade the coaches to let them walk to the big bridge over the river before they leave. With the clock getting closer to a new day and a chill in the air, the Hoover girls' basketball team gets back off the bus and makes their way to the bridge. They look out at the city lights twinkling brightly and feel like rockstars. They snap some team pictures that will serve as a memento of the night they were let loose on Carson West, marking their return to state.

Back at the hotel, the coaches say their good nights and instruct the players to go to bed. The girls are too wound up to sleep. They gather together in the upperclassman's room and watch the replay of their game on TV. They laugh and talk over each other. They rewind Hayley's monster block on a girl that is at least six inches taller than her. They slow-mo Ellie's charge she took on their opponent's best player. They watch the entire game, adding their own commentary, what they were thinking when this happened, and that. They can't stop smiling when they watch all the fast breaks and their rabid fans celebrating. They give the JV girls a good-natured ribbing over their play, which was shaky at first because of the nerves. They rewind Booster dribbling off her foot and do the same to watch her make a great assist to Ashlyn that results in an unconventional three-point play. The girls are still amazed that M&M actually came into the locker room with water blazing after the game. They talk about that and how cool it was to take a late-night stroll to the bridge. The last team up in the city is absorbing the new memories they just made, making the most of the moment and owning the night.

Chapter 28

The bus is scheduled to depart the hotel at 10:00 a.m. for practice. It sounded like plenty of time to sleep in yesterday when the players viewed the itinerary. When you go to sleep at three in the morning, that departure time comes quickly. Miss Easton makes the rounds plenty early to make sure everyone has risen. The players are groggy and slow moving. Miss Easton knows they stayed up late watching their game. She also knows kids are resilient, and this is a once-in-a-lifetime opportunity that many kids in this state will never get a chance to experience. The players should relish it. Miss Easton puts a spring in their step when she announces she is walking next door to the coffee shop and whoever wants a free drink should follow her. It's like an ant brigade departing the hotel. Every player is a taker. The three employees manning the shop do a double-take watching an entire basketball team file in. One by one each girl contemplates how to make the most of a free order. Booster sneaks in five cake pops to go along with her hot chocolate and stuffs them into her jacket. The girls sit in the shop and shoot the breeze drinking their breakfast, waiting for the last possible minute to board the bus.

Practice at a local gym is intense from the start. The coaches don't want any hangover from last night and take them through drills at game speed. After the team is warmed up, the first string goes over their top plays against the JV team. Next, the coaches put them through game situations. The first one is a full-court press. The starters have no problem beating it, so Mack sends in the two remaining subs along with Gordy and Jemma to make it crowded. The competitive juices start flowing. It gets feisty as the starters have to battle nine people instead of five. Bentley gets snippy going through a maze of defenders who have been given the green light to be physical. You can see the starters are getting riled up and

159

are raising their level of play because this turned into more than a regular practice. They are being challenged and are rising to accept it. Sasha keeps cool when she gets four defenders assigned to her once they bring the ball into the front court. It's another day at the office for her. She's not able to do much and whips it over to Hayley who doesn't hesitate and drills a three-pointer. The starters celebrate, knowing how much work that was. They go again. Zo attempts to get the ball past half court while being hounded by Booster and Ashlyn. She stutter-steps then crosses the ball over, and Booster lunges for it. Nose meets forehead, and that pauses the action. A flow of blood comes pouring out of Booster's nose. Zo rubs her head to inspect any damage. She's fine. The coaches call for the team to head to the other end of the court while Booster is attended to by Miss Easton and Jemma. M&M change it up and go over half-court game situations. Ellie and Krista get locked up going for a rebound and tempers flare. It's serious until Mack blows his whistle and yells: "Knock it off, you two, or you'll both be sitting next to me tomorrow." Krista and Ellie hug it out. The players like that practice isn't a cakewalk. The coaches keep the intense session short and sweet then go back to the hotel to watch game film of tomorrow's opponent.

Piling into the conference room, everyone giggles when Booster enters with cotton hanging out of her nose and a big bag of ice in her hands.

"Yeah, real funny," she says. "Thanks for asking how I feel. I'm not in any pain or anything." She looks Zo's way. "You broke my nose, Jones."

Zo cringes. "Sorry."

"That was the most blood I have ever seen in my life," Ashlyn says, staring at Booster. "There was so much blood. Like a river!"

"Oh Booster, it's good for you." Krista pats her back as she passes her to find a seat. "Now you got a story."

"Yeah about how hard of a head Zoey Jones has and that she fouled me so I wouldn't pick her precious pocket and take her butt to school."

Bentley laughs at Booster's bravado.

Zo smiles. "You're lucky I only broke your nose and not your ankles. You reached in, dawg."

"Ha! Whatever. I'll need a rematch to show you."

Ellie giggles. "What you need are pain pills and a mask for tomorrow's game."

"I don't know if they can get her one made that fast," Hayley says. "Doesn't it have to be fitted?"

"Extra, extra small," Bentley teases.

"Ha." Booster puts the ice pack up to her nose, and it covers most of her face.

"We can just get her a kid's Halloween mask and call it good," Krista says.

Mack and Monty bring order to the room, declaring they need everyone's undivided attention. For the next hour they watch game film of their next opponent, Andover Park. Mack doesn't waste time telling them "AP" is tough and tall. "If we don't play well, we'll get stomped." The girls are all ears. They know the drill. They take it in and will use it as motivation when they step on the court tomorrow. When Monty dismisses the team, he tells them how important of a game this is. None of them needed to be reminded. The way in which practice went this morning and after hearing Monty's obvious sentiment, the message the coaches want to instill is this: your win yesterday doesn't mean jack. The demeanor of the girls indicates they feel the same way. Mack, Monty, and Gordy plan on watching game film of Andover Park for the rest of the afternoon to collect more information. The players are instructed to meet back in the conference room at 7:00 p.m. that night to go over an updated scouting report. Monty promises it will be brief. Their goal is to make the players feel prepared going up against a team they have never faced before without overwhelming them with information. The team gets dismissed.

Out in the hallway Krista calls out to Jemma: "Yo, Jems!"

Jemma stops and waits for her to catch up. "What's up?"

Krista puts her arm around Jemma's shoulder, and they start walking along with everyone else. "Get us out of here. Please! For the love of all things good in this world, you have to help us leave this place."

Sasha groans. "We have like six hours until our film session. They can't possibly think we can stay cooped up in this hotel again after being confined to this place *all* day yesterday. There is only so much hacky sack and cards a girl can play."

"No kidding," Ashlyn says. "Hey, we should go watch Chesapeake play."

Both Chesapeake and Mason Valley qualified for the state tournament in their respective classes. Mason Valley lost on Monday in the first round. Chesapeake plays in the second round today after winning their first-round matchup by a big margin.

"Yeah, hard pass," Krista says. "I'd rather do something else."

"Anything," Bentley says. "Just get us out of here."

"You guys are too funny." Jemma giggles. "Okay, what are your suggestions?"

Zo perks up. "How about the trampoline park?"

"Or an axe-throwing place!" Bentley snaps her fingers. "Upgrade from hammers to axes. You like that?"

Jemma laughs. "You think I'm a miracle worker? That won't happen."

"Come on, Jems," Krista says. "It could be our little secret, along with Bert the bus driver. He won't spill the beans; me and him are like this." Krista wraps her middle finger around her pointer finger.

"Miss E," Jemma says. "You want to take this one?"

Miss Easton smiles. "Ladies, I do agree. I think we all could benefit from leaving this place for an extended amount of time. However, it has to be a low-key choice. You guys play bright and early tomorrow. So it has to be low energy, and you know it has to be away from where the state tournament is being held. Come up with something easy and light, and we'll go to bat for you."

"What about the mall?" Hayley suggests.

"Yes!" Ashlyn pumps her fist.

"That would work," says Miss Easton.

Some of the girls aren't enthused with this idea, but somewhere is better than nowhere, and they all rush to get ready to leave. Miss Easton informs Monty, Mack, and Gordy they are taking the kids to the mall. They think it's a great idea with one stipulation: take their wives with them. They have been wanting to escape the hotel too. The coaches will have peace and quiet the rest of the day while they scout tomorrow's opponent.

The girls are ecstatic to be getting out of their hotel. Miss Easton reminds them to act like they have been out of Hoover before when she lets them loose on the mall. A group of players including Bentley, Zo, and Sasha hit the food court then bee line it to the movie theater to see a show, smuggling in fast food under their oversized sweatshirts. Ashlyn and Hayley take off with a few of their JV teammates with a shopping list of items they hope they can score. They buy a bunch of clothing and try on prom dresses for fun. Tonight after the team goes through their scouting session, the girls who shopped will show off their haul with a fashion show. Monty's wife scores some Hawaiian-themed outfits for him. When he walks in to show off his new threads, he gets the biggest cheers of all.

Out of the movie with time to kill, the players do a lap and get recognized. It's hard to miss them with their Hoover hoodies on and the height of Sasha. One group that is excited to run into them is another high school team that came down to Des Moines for the week to watch all the games. They tell the Hoover players they will be there to cheer them on tomorrow and hope they win it all. The girls pass by some people from Hoover who are surprised to see them out and about, knowing that Mack does his best to keep the players secluded. A fourth-grade boy is among them and is shopping for the shoes Bentley, Zo, and Sasha wear. He's hoping to find a pair so he can wear them tomorrow. The girls pose with the group before continuing on.

At 6:00 p.m., the players board the bus radiating a glow of teenage euphoria. Today was fun. Everything about this whole experience has been special. When everyone is accounted for, Jemma leans out of her seat and works on getting the attention of the entire bus. When it's quiet, she announces the score of Chesapeake's second-round game. They lost. The Hoover players are hit with a genuine reaction of surprise and a hint of disappointment. The mighty Chesapeake Saints have fallen. They are going home. There is no happiness over hearing their rival's season is over. It's a harsh reminder that the same thing can happen to them tomorrow. It could all be over. After several minutes of calmness, the bus goes back to that euphoric state because hearing Chesapeake lost reminds them they are the only team left in their conference. They still have an opportunity to win a state championship. Their time is now with their ending unwritten.

CHAPTER 29

Sasha wipes the sleep from her eyes and lunges up the bus steps. Bentley follows her eating a peanut butter and jelly sandwich her mom dropped off earlier to the razz of her teammates. Krista appears on the bus a moment later holding a large coffee down by her side. Concealing the drink is her top priority until she gets past the coaches in the front-row seats. Once she slides by M&M, she raises the cup showing it off to her teammates. More than a few flash her jealous looks, wishing they would have thought of that. Having a game start at ten thirty in the morning is odd and foreign. The one bright side is avoiding the agony of another day long wait for a late night tip-off.

The bus sputters then jerks forward, and the team is on their way to play game number two. Winner goes to the championship. Ashlyn braids Hayley's hair; besides that there is no other movement. Most girls have their headphones on. After some miles go by of riding in silence, Zo leans out of her back-row seat and raises her soft voice, "It's game morning, baby! Let's start looking for waffles."

There is a muted reaction of disagreement from her teammates. Zo has been up for hours and hopes everyone will follow her lead when she starts their Hoover chant. Nobody joins in.

"Let's go look for waffles in like an hour," Krista says without looking back at Zo. "Calm yourself."

"Come on! We're playing to get to the championship. Who cares if it's early. Hungry dogs run faster!"

This gets a more lively reaction. It's not so much what Zo said but how she said it. The mood shifts. Bentley lights up. "AP isn't going to know what hit them. Let's be ready right off the bus!"

Ellie leans up out of her seat and straightens her posture. "Let's get hyped up then!"

"All right." Krista chugs the rest of her coffee in dramatic fashion. She stands and crushes the cup between her palms. It doesn't quite do the job so she lets the cup fall to the floor then stomps on it. "Let's freaking go!"

The players start shouting the Hoover chant. After that gets played out, Booster stands in the middle of the aisle and starts singing the song they all sang before eighth-grade games. Everyone joins her. The authority figures in the front—Monty and Mack in their suits, Gordy in his jeans and polo—can't help but smile. For their first-round game they had the task of trying to get the girls to save all their energetic enthusiasm until 8:30 p.m. It wasn't easy to keep them calm when they were wound up to play by noon. The team keeps their pep rally going until the doors swing open at the entrance of the auditorium and they burst off the bus feeling loose.

The Knights bring a "lay it all out, let the chips fall where they may" attitude with them when they take the court. Going into action as part of a team that shares the same desire, the Knights look like kids who get to play on their favorite playground waiting only for the prompt of *ready, set, go*. They still have plenty of nerves; they just aren't swirling out of control. They *get* to play in this game. They are excited for their chance on this stage. Living in a small town there is nowhere for them to run. Everything is always just the way it is, and there is little in their control. But this, being in this auditorium with a large crowd gathered to cheer for or against them, this makes them feel powerful. Something important is in their hands.

Even at this early hour, the atmosphere in the building is similar to the Knights' first-round contest. An electric vibe is in the air. The Hoover crowd showed up right when the doors opened along with a few new fans of the team. The Hoover faithful are proud of this and a little protective; we loved them first. They embrace the new additions when they see Andover Park's massive and spirited crowd filling up the seats.

At center court, Hoover's starting five welcome a worthy team to engage in battle with and look their opponent in the eye with respect. Let's ball; may the best team win. Sasha is able to control the tip-off and taps the ball over to Bentley. She takes a few dribbles and gets the ball jabbed out of her hands by an Andover Park player that snuck up on her from behind. The crowd noise is already playing a factor; Bentley couldn't hear her approaching or her teammates trying to warn her. With a score to settle, Bentley catches up to the girl and hounds her every step of the way on her pursuit to the hoop. Getting an up-close feel of what Hoover's pressure defense is like the player gets near the baseline and dribbles the ball off her foot. After crossing half court, Bentley gets the ball to Zo who can't wait to see if she can give her crowd the first shot of dopamine and unleashes a three-pointer at first touch. The shot misses the mark. In rushed fashion, Andover Park races down the court to their basket. Their point guard manages to slip by Zo and Bentley, and with a glimpse of daylight appearing, she releases an off-balanced shot. Sasha leaps up to take the rebound away from everyone, and Hoover sprints off to try to get a fast break going. Andover Park sprints with them and prevents a transition basket.

The pace and the noise of this start is intense. Andover Park's whole cheering section is standing with their arms locked together. They sway back and forth, releasing a loud humming sound. It drowns out Hoover's crowd. Zo tries another three-pointer and misses. The Hoover players swarm the Andover Park player who garners the rebound, causing her to be called for a traveling violation. The Knights once again get the ball back with an opportunity to be the first team to score. Zo receives the ball on the wing. She gets her taller defender in the air with a shot fake and drives the baseline. She shoots a jumper, and it bounces off the side of the rim. Andover Park goes back on offense, while Hoover resumes its harassing defense. The Knights are giving Andover Park no other choice but to rush things. They look timid and uncertain trying to play offense. Sasha blocks a shot in the lane, and it's a race to see who can recover the ball on the baseline. Bentley's pressure causes the AP player who gets to it first to panic and fumble the ball out of bounds. It's evident Andover Park is not used to this kind of pressure defense. Mack always tells people the way his team plays defense is worth the price of admission. This morning that defense is showing out and backing up their coach's words.

The first quarter continues to play out in this hurried dance between the two teams. Andover Park's tall players with long limbs are forcing Hoover to take tough shots, and Hoover is preventing Andover Park from even getting a shot off. So far, only Zo and Bentley have field goal attempts, and they are zero for six. The middle of the lane is congested. Zo passes the ball into Sasha anyway. Happy to get a touch even with all the numerous bodies hanging out in the lane with her, Sasha fakes one way and turns to square up for a shot. Her attempt bounces off the rim too, and away AP goes hoping they can be the team that wins the first to score face off. It's not to be. Hoover forces yet another turnover with Andover Park failing again to get a shot off. Hoover gets set up in their half-court motion offense. Zo catches a crisp pass from Bentley in rhythm and lets fly another three-pointer with a tall AP player laying out her body to contest it. This time, Zo's shot is all net, and Hoover's crowd can finally be heard as they go into a frenzy over the lid coming off the hoop. Feeling good about striking first, the Knights go back to defending in their suffocating style. Sasha and Krista surround an Andover Park player who catches a pass near the basket on the baseline. Krista pokes at the ball; the player manages to hold on to it and gets a shot off only to have Sasha bat it right back down in her face. Surprised, the player gets a grip on the ball and passes it out of the lane as fast as she can. Andover Park swings it around trying to keep possession. A pass to a streaking cutter gets an AP player free in the paint until Sasha appears; the girl gets an altered shot past Sasha's outstretched hand. The ball clanks off the backboard. Zo jumps to secure the weak side rebound and takes off running down the court determined to attack the rim. AP's athletic forward meets her at the hoop and blocks her layup attempt. With one hand Zo is able to propel the ball back into play before falling out of bounds with it. The ball lands at the free-throw line, Bentley grabs it off the bounce, and charges to the hoop going up for a tough layup surrounded by Andover Park red. The ball drops through the hoop making it 5–0 Hoover.

Andover Park races down, desperate to get some points on the board. After playing keep away with Hoover's guards, they are able to get an entry pass into their post who turns to shoot. Sasha swats it away with force sending the ball straight into Bentley's hands, and everyone pivots to run the other way. Bentley rushes down the court and stutter-steps by one girl at the three-point line, then has one setup ready to take a charge. Bentley goes up for the layup and they collide, both falling to the ground. The refs let the game play on, and Andover Park rebounds the miss. They throw an outlet pass with hopes of trying to get a fast break going. Zo nearly picks the ball off but can't hold onto it and falls to the ground trying to. The ball splices around the floor causing a fight for it. Krista hustles after the ball, diving on the ground to grab it. The ball gets ripped out of her hands, and it ricochets off the leg of an AP player rolling past the half-court line right to Hayley. Mack and Monty both rise up out of their seats and fan their hands down, wanting the craziness to be brought down a notch.

Hayley exhales then walks the ball back across half court and gets it to Bentley. The Knights take a moment to regroup. They walk to their positions before they start to work the ball around. Nobody guards Zo when she catches the ball on the left wing more than a foot outside the three-point line so she takes a shot. The ball bounces off the rim, and Bentley grabs the long rebound and takes it to the hoop for a short shot that swishes through the net. Points aren't easy to come by in this contest, and the seven-to-zero Hoover lead feels monumental. Andover Park's student section is still standing but long gone is the synchronized humming and swaying. They have no reason to make any noise. Andover Park calls a time-out. The clock shows 3:56 left in the first quarter. Everyone in the building uses the break to catch their breath.

The Hoover coaches are pleased they are executing their game plan to perfection, which is simple: be us. Play the same way that got us here. Let Andover Park change for us. Mack and Monty's message in the huddle is to maintain their aggressiveness. Shots may not be falling but don't change what you're doing. Don't stop swinging big, and keep bringing the defensive pressure.

Andover Park comes out of the time-out with urgency. Their point guard makes a move and gets to the top of the lane to take a shot. It looks open until Hayley hustles to meet her and blocks the shot. A late whistle sends their point guard to the free-throw line, and Andover Park finally gets on the scoreboard making one of two foul shots. Bentley brings the ball up the court to the return of the humming sound coming from Andover Park's crowd that refuses to sit down. Andover Park came out of their time-out in a two-three zone. They want to stop Hoover from scoring their points near the basket and force them to have to make outside shots. After trading a pair of scoreless possessions, Zo gets the ball on the wing and immediately sneaks a pass between two defenders into Sasha who shoots a short shot up and off the glass for two points. On defense, Hoover adds to their tally and Bentley records another steal. There is no chance for a fast break, and once past half court Bentley waits for her teammates to get in position. She surveys the defense then penetrates the lane getting the defenders at the top of the zone's attention before she flips a no-look pass behind her to Zo who catches and shoots a three ball; it swishes through the net making it a 12–1 Hoover lead.

On defense, it's Hayley who strips the ball this time. The whistle rings out, and she's called for her second foul. The bench doesn't agree. It looked like a clean pick; even so they stay quiet, letting the Hoover fans be the ones to express their frustration. Sasha deflects the pass coming in from out of bounds and Hoover chalks up another take away. Andover Park has yet to get comfortable on the offensive end and work hard on what has prevented Hoover from breaking this game open: their transition defense. They get back fast enough, taking away the chance at a fastbreak forcing the Knights set up in their half-court offense. Sasha sets a screen for Zo to curl around her past the three-point line. The space gives her enough time to catch and shoot another three. The ball hits the back of the rim and bounces straight up in the air. It comes right back down in the hoop catching nothing but net. With that lucky bounce Hoover goes up 15–1 and you can feel Andover Park's spirit deflate. The Knights have scored a quick eight points since AP called timeout and switched defensive strategies.

Andover Park swings the ball around looking like nobody wants it in their hands. The ball makes it back to the top of the key, and their point guard throws up a three-pointer that swishes in. Andover Park's crowd erupts at the sign of life. With Zo getting warm, Andover Park assigns one defender to Zo making it a box and one defense with the two lower defenders paying close attention to Sasha. Bentley opts to keep the ball and drives into the sea of red. She makes it all the way to the low block where an Andover Park player attempts to take a charge and falls down, knocking over her own player in the process. Bentley flips the ball up to Sasha who is now free of one less defender. She keeps the ball raised high and makes another shot off the glass taking their lead up to 17–4.

Andover Park's shot selection continues to be an issue. Hoover is doing a great job of disrupting their entire flow on offense. Krista rebounds a missed jumper and outlets it to Zo. Andover Park again rushes back to defend the hoop giving Zo the easy decision to pull up and take a twenty-five foot heat check from the top of the key. Zo follows her shot knowing it's short; she catches it in stride then glides right down the lane for a finger roll. The crazy first quarter comes to an end twenty seconds later with Andover Park attempting and failing to beat the buzzer. Hoover is winning 19–4.

The Knights have found a rhythm on offense, they are controlling the pace and driving Andover Park mad with their defense. In the huddle, Monty preaches to the group to maintain their level of play. He knows his players respond better when games are close and when they have a lead they have a tendency to get lackadaisical. He stresses that this is the state tournament; prepare for Andover Park to get back in this game. The starters bob their heads. They know from how hard they had to work for those seventeen points in the opening quarter that this game is far from over.

The second quarter finds Andover Park desperate to turn the tide. They come out in attack mode. Their aggressiveness gets rewarded, and the cover finally comes off their basket. On the bench, Hoover's coaches are more nervous having a lead. Andover Park has nothing to lose, and every time they score they are gaining momentum. Hoover starts getting called for what Mack thinks are ticky-tack fouls. Knowing he can't jeopardize getting worked up, he holds his tongue. Hayley picks up her third foul, and both Zo and Sasha have two. Playing from behind, Andover Park creates momentum and gets back in the game scoring twenty-three points in the second quarter to Hoover's eighteen. The Knights take a 35–27 lead into the half.

In the locker room, Mack and Monty point out the need to stick to their game plan and return to that intense level of defense they started the game with. They never like it when their team gives their opponent hope. Andover Park's crowd is back in this game. The coaches show trust in their players though, knowing they thrive in these pressure situations. The girls don't have to be reminded of what they are playing for. When the third quarter begins, the Knights waste little time and squash the momentum Andover Park worked hard to generate. Zo scorches them with another barrage of three-pointers, and Sasha goes to work controlling both sides of the paint. Hoover raises their defensive intensity, and they take the buzz out of Andover Park's crowd by making stop after stop much like they did in the first quarter. Hoover puts themselves in great position going into the fourth quarter with a 53–38 lead.

Andover Park starts rallying, knowing eight minutes is all that remains in their season if they are unable to turn things around. They switch to a full-court press on defense, and it leads to Hoover turning the ball over on consecutive possessions. Hoover goes into keep-away mode waiting for the clock to run out. Monty calls a time-out to settle his team down. If they can hang on to their lead, they will be playing for a championship. He urges them to take what the defense is giving them and not force the situation. Andover Park lays it all out to try to pull off a comeback. Halfway through the quarter with the lead slashed to nine, Sasha gets called for a fourth foul. Both crowds know if Andover Park has any kind of chance of winning they have to make their move now. Ellie comes in to relieve Sasha, and the next few minutes are mentally exhausting for Hoover as they work hard to protect the lead and cut off hope for Andover Park. Hayley closes the door for good by drilling a wide open three-pointer with 2:04 left to play. The rest of the game is Andover Park sending Hoover to the free-throw line. With game in hand, Krista goes up to block a shot and comes down on her opponent's foot. She bends down to assess the damage of her ankle turning over. There is a fight over the loose blocked ball. Ellie comes away with it and is fouled. The buzzer sounds a few seconds after she shoots her free throws.

In straightforward fashion, the Knights took care of business this morning. The score indicates they won by ten points when in fact it never seemed that close. Hoover had the upper hand from the start and never let go. They shake hands with their opponent and give hugs to one another. In the locker room, they keep it low key sharing fist bumps and chatter about "one more." All those seen and unseen hours come down to one day. One game. Their mood is far different now than it was when they skipped in here full of chants and unbridled joy. They are focusing on the magnitude of where they find themselves. Can we be champions for one day?

Krista sits with her head in her hands shaken up. Her teammates pat her on the back and offer encouragement. It was a good sign she was able to walk off the floor on her own. Jemma sets an ice pack down next to Krista. She kneels down to examine her ankle and reassures her there isn't much swelling. It appears she only tweaked it. Krista doesn't move, keeping her head down in her hands. Having never sustained any kind of injury before, Krista doesn't see any silver lining and fears the worst. Using whispered voices players check in with Ellie to see if she will be prepared to start if Krista can't play. Ellie is sick over the thought of Krista coming all this way and not getting to finish what she started. She really hopes Krista will be good to go tomorrow night. Krista lets out a piercing scream, causing her teammates to jump. She grabs one of her shoes, winds up, and whips it as hard as she can against the wall. She sits back down and puts her head back in her hands.

Miss Easton approaches her. "You need to stop that right now! If you want to play tomorrow night you have to start preparing mentally." Miss Easton pauses to let her have a moment. "It's okay that you are showing emotion. But you've expressed it; now it's time to get over it. There isn't time to dwell; the championship is thirty hours away. So let me know right now, Krista, if you're serious about wanting to play tomorrow night. If you're not, respect your teammates and keep your outbursts to yourself!"

Krista stays silent. Her teammates stand frozen in place because Miss Easton's voice has taken command of the room. All of them are waiting to see where this goes and pleading internally for Krista not to erupt on Miss E. After an uncomfortable amount of time has passed, Krista pulls her hands away from her head and looks up with tears in her eyes. "I want to play more than anything." She wipes at her eyes and sniffles.

Miss Easton nods. "Then start believing you will and I'll do everything in my power to help make that happen. Now, get that foot elevated and ice it."

With the suspense over, Bentley starts clapping and everyone laughs, then joins in. Krista lowers herself to the floor and props her foot up. Booster helps her out and positions the ice where it needs to be. Krista keeps telling her teammates she's sorry and assures them she's not going to sit out tomorrow night. Later today, Miss Easton will call the front desk asking them to give her a wake-up call at the top of every hour starting at midnight. They will think it's a prank and won't believe her until she goes down to the front desk in person to make the request. Miss Easton will go into Krista's room to administer treatment to her injured ankle every hour tonight believing if that kid gets to be out on the court tomorrow night with her teammates, the lack of sleep will all be worth it.

Hoover's play is the topic of chatter after the game. Their style gets called big city, playground basketball. Talking to news outlets, the opposing coach calls them "flamboyant" and says, "They freestyle the whole game. It's like they're playing streetball."

Outside their locker room, the Hoover coaches are informed of what is being said about their team. Mack laughs and a big smile washes over his face. "You can call us whatever you want. Tomorrow I hope the whole state has to call us champions."

CHAPTER 30

Almost from day one you knew this team had a date with destiny locked into their future. The time would arrive when everything would be on the line. The work, the longing, the suffering, the excitement, the dream—all of it would come down to a few moments. In the dark of the night, with light snow flurries floating around their bus, the Hoover High school girls' basketball team is off to meet their fate. It's the date they wanted. Right here. Right now. Tip-off for the championship game is under two hours away. They did it. They made it back.

To the players, winning tonight is the only thing that matters. It's been their sole focus for a year. Will a loss tonight really mean the season is a wash to the players and everyone else who went through this journey with them? Coach Gordy Williams thinks about this question as he sits on the bus during the long ride to the auditorium. Gordy is thrilled to be a part of this team no matter how the season ends. Win or lose, it can't erase what this team has done or what this team has meant to the town of Hoover. They have captured the imagination of the youth. They introduced many of them to what having a dream is. Showing them you can fall short of that dream, get right back up to double down on your dream, and declare it lives on after wiping away tears. They have given the people of Hoover something to feel good about. These things can't be taken away no matter what the scoreboard says at the end of the evening. Even so, Gordy sure hopes this team will end up as winners tonight. Become champions. He coached every single one of them. Always for the love of the game. During the season where he coached that eighth-grade team that was special, he stepped into a drill to show the girls how he wanted it to look. Gordy made a hard cut, there was a loud pop, and he went to the ground. He was hurt but there was no way he was going to shortchange the girls. There was a lot of practice left, and he didn't even pause it. Ellie will never forget watching him crawl across the gym floor continuing to conduct practice. The next day he was on crutches. His Achilles tendon was torn. This mindset rubbed off on his players. Never quit. Play until the end. Give everything you have.

Sitting behind Gordy is Jemma and Miss Easton. They also have their minds on what the night holds and what the results will mean. Both are anxious with one being a little more anxious than the other. They have shared in the experience of coaching their respective teams and in witnessing every step of the way along the path the varsity team has paved. Jemma bites her nails, and Miss Easton looks at the bright side. She brings up the quote by Amelia Earhart that hangs on the bulletin board in Jemma's classroom as consolation if the game doesn't fall in Hoover's favor. In whispered tones, they talk about believing the Knights will be holding up the championship trophy. Because, why not them? They have seen these girls be resilient all year. If it doesn't happen for them and they are on the losing end, they know the disappointment will be great. The two coaches hope that if that's the case, the team will feel the same way they will; the adventure in itself was worthwhile.

In his front-row seat, Coach Monty is thinking about everything that is on the line tonight too. It has been one hell of a year for him. Difficult, brutal, and exhausting have been words thrown around in his head all season long. Magical too. Even beautiful at times. Rewarding and worth it. Monty starts to think fate is orchestrating this path they are on. It has to be. No way this team went through what they went through and came together like they did only to be crushed with another championship loss. Monty feels pressure because he isn't sure he believes in fate. So as the bus is hurtling toward their destiny or whatever you want to call it, Monty is going to make himself prepare for an alternate scenario, one only the coaches on this bus are giving any thought to right now. Because he knows the outcome of a game doesn't always favor the best team or reward the best effort or take into consideration past heartbreaks. So Monty sits, preparing himself for the worst. As the head coach he feels he needs to. It's part of the job. Still, he feels good, the players' confidence—the way they seem to flow and be in tune with each other—calms him. It's almost like they know something nobody else does. That they can't lose. There is an effortless poise they began walking around with ever since the regular season ended. Monty wouldn't bet against this team, and he would choose those girls against anyone in the state.

Mack sits in his seat across from Monty beaming with pride. If you don't know him you wouldn't think it was pride. His firm lips and hard glare make him look ultra serious. Even more than usual because he is a ball of excited nerves. He is living his dream. The season started with him in a hospital bed with an uncertain future. Mack is not going to take this for granted. He is calmer than he was before. He needed to bring it down a level, and he obliged because he wasn't going to miss another moment of this. Especially not the end. Not when everyone sacrificed and worked so hard to run it back and take what they felt was theirs for the taking. The Knights are right where Mack envisioned them being with the only thing left to do is to play thirty-two minutes of basketball. Like Monty, Mack wouldn't bet against his troops. The confidence he sees oozing off them sends chills through his body. Tonight is the fun part. They get to be a part of something special. On the bus he reflects over the past season. He remembers lying in the hospital bed the night before his surgery and thinking he would give anything to be healthy enough to return to the team. He thinks of the nights he couldn't help himself and slipped into the gym sitting up in the rafters. While in pain physically and emotionally, he watched his team go on without him. Tonight he gets to coach for a state championship. He isn't a spectator. Mack made it back into the arena. There is nothing more he could ask for.

When the players board the bus tonight they huddle up closer to each other than they ever have before. They talk and laugh, sharing a part of themselves that nobody else gets to see. They go silent when the bus sputters to a start. They stay quiet until they can sense the destination is near. Bentley gets Krista's attention by plucking her in the back of the head with an empty water bottle. "Start our jam." Krista smiles from getting picked to do the honor. She belts out the first line of "Red & Black," the song Bentley and Zo made up on the long bus ride down to Des Moines. The rest of the girls join in and sing the lyrics. It took all week for every member of the team to get it memorized, and earlier in the day when they took a lap around the hotel to waste time, they finally jelled. When they add claps and stomps, the bus feels like it's bouncing.

M&M look at each other across the aisle in their front seats and nod. The slight smiles that radiate off them indicate they approve of the girls behaving in this way; they are being themselves, a good sign.

Everything comes down to one night, one game, one chance. Only a win will be acceptable. This is the standard they set for themselves. When the bus pulls into the parking lot, everything is still undetermined. What will the night hold? Nobody knows. The team wouldn't mind staying in this moment for a while, to keep cherishing being a team that is playing for a championship, a team who still has its hopes and dreams alive.

The players and coaches walk off the bus looking confident. This is where they want to be. They have zero doubts this year about whether they belong. The team silently walks through the underbelly of the arena into their locker room looking like a team that is expecting to engage in a fight. The faces of Bentley, Sasha, and Zo show a seriousness reserved for such a moment. The underclassmen are hyper and nervous as they start to get ready. They are bracing for what to expect when they run out on the floor. To the three girls who started in the championship game a year ago and got beat handily, this is personal. The loss bound them together and they made themselves accountable that day. The pressure of the time arriving makes them focus, and they look intensely locked in on getting the job done. When out of the speaker their song starts playing at a low volume, the last one they play before the coaches come in, most players start to bounce around, not them. When it comes to the part in the song where the beat goes crazy and the team collides into each other for the finale, Zo and Sasha dart up to start jumping along with their teammates. It's go time. Zo calls out for Bentley to join. Bentley looks up from having her head in her hands in a startled way and begins nodding her head, then rocking her body back and forth. With the rest of her teammates looking her way, Bentley leaps up and jumps into them with force. When the song ends, the players bring their arms around each other and form a huddle. They sway back and forth.

"This is it, guys," Bentley yells. "Only one team will be left standing, and it's going to be us. Let's bring it!"

"We go balls to the wall!" Krista yells.

They let out piercing screams.

"Together on three!" Bentley shouts. "One, two, three!"

The coaches enter a few moments later. There are no smiles offered, only last-minute instructions and of course sayings the girls heard the coaches repeat all year. The consistent theme from Coach Mack since his return has been: "Leave it all on the floor." He knows how precious this game is after it was abruptly taken away from him. The thoughts of wishing he had said or done this or that loomed large while he waited to get back to the team. No longer. He has learned you can't have regrets. Give your all the only way you know how, and be satisfied with the results. Coach Monty's most-used phrase is: "How you do one thing is how you do everything."

Monty looks around at the players and says, "You have been doing the little things and the big things this season that led you to this title game. Go out and play the way that got you here."

The girls always faced what was right in front of them bravely. It wasn't always pretty and it sure wasn't textbook, but they always owned it; they put themselves out there. If they were to look back over this season and the one before, they would see they consistently did things the same way—with work, sacrifice, resilience and a belief in each other. They built themselves up for this moment.

After both coaches say their piece, the team makes their way onto the court. Running out on that floor with the bright lights in their face is like no other experience. It isn't normal playing in front of thousands of people with the stakes being so high and having the game broadcast on television across the state. The girls on the team who are new to this experience can't get over how many people are assembled here to watch them play.

When the scripted introductions, the handshakes, and the buildup to the main event are completed, and when at last the wait is over, Sasha steps into the center circle ready for the jump ball. She closes her eyes and thinks about how slow and fast a year has passed to put her right back in the middle of this court again. Everything is different. She's different. Tonight she feels comfortable and confident. Sure of herself and her team. She's prepared. Ready. To her left is Bentley who has her fists together and alternates blowing deep breathes into each one. Maybe she will always feel like she has to fight for herself and her people, but she knows this is the final brawl alongside this pack of girls that have been hers to protect since she was fourteen. A look of determination and anger is on her face because *almost* isn't going to be the word people will use to describe her team. Across from Bentley stands Zo. She has a serious look on her face. Inside, she is bursting with joy, thrilled to be where she always wants to be—the place where she was set free: the basketball court. Zo glances around, looking at the big stage they get to play on, and sees a blank canvas. Krista is to Zo's left. She whispers a thank you to the basketball gods and Miss Easton for being able to play tonight. This team has been nothing to her. A lie she told herself for the times when she didn't get any of the glory and for the time when it would all be over. The truth is this team means so much to her. She needed to play in this game. Had to. For herself and her teammates. Krista stands tall ready to give herself for the goal. Straight behind Sasha, near the three-point line, is Hayley. At times this season she played like she was trying to keep her head above water. But the fact is she turned herself into a valuable part of the team by getting better and using the traits that gained the respect of her teammates: hard work and selflessness. Here they are. One last time together on a court in the state's capital. Thirty-two minutes to win a state championship.

The ref enters the center circle and officially starts the title contest between the Hoover Knights and the Marion Bulldogs. Sasha reaches the jump ball first and tips it back. Hayley secures the ball and finds Bentley. Feeling the adrenaline pumping off the charts and hearing the crowd noise, Bentley wastes no time and drives right down the middle of the lane. She throws a pass that deflects off a defender then hits Krista's fingertips before going out of bounds. The crowd noise halts, and every player heads toward the opposite end of the court. Marion moves the ball quickly on their offensive possession and scores the first points of the game. The intensity from the get-go is high. Marion face-guards Zo. After her barrage of threes in the second-round game, they are not going to give her a chance to scorch them. Zo's shoulders drop, realizing their game plan is to have her shadowed by a defender whose sole purpose is to not to let her even touch the ball. The player guarding Zo is Marion's best guard—a first team all-stater who according to Monty's scouting report is a strong, scrappy, and tenacious defender.

With Zo being bottled up, Bentley keeps the ball again and drives the lane. She is able to get by her girl and hits Sasha right in the hands.

Sasha scores Hoover's first two points off the glass. The Bulldogs hurry right back down the court. Their center shoots from close range. The ball glides through the hoop. Bentley pushes the ball. Off a screen Zo gets open. She is so eager to prove she can't be contained and instantly unleashes a deep three. It misses and clanks off the rim. The Bulldogs run the floor, and Krista fouls their center going up for a fast break layup.

The first quarter unfolds in a frenetic pace that pleases both sides. Neither team is shooting a high percentage, and both teams are showing great intensity on defense. It's a low-scoring contest with the Knights leading 17–15 at the end of the quarter.

"Pace, pace, pace. Let's keep playing fast, ladies," Mack says. "Turn defense into offense, and we can get some fast break points."

"Krista and Sasha," barks Monty. "Offensive rebounds. This is where the game can be won. Work the boards."

Zo, frustrated by her lack of getting to touch the ball, bounces her knees up and down. Marion is being physical with her, bumping and bodying her as much as they can. Zo isn't feeling so free on the court right now.

"On offense," Mack says, raising his voice over the noise of the crowd. "Bentley, keep attacking the lane. They are determined to keep the ball away from Zo. Don't force the ball her way. They are daring someone other than her to beat us. Let's stick it in their face. Hayley, they are leaving you wide open. Take the shot. Make them pay."

"The best girl is the open girl," adds Monty.

In the second quarter, the score stays close. With Zo being denied, it becomes a chess match inside. The Knights' offense is Bentley keeping the ball in her hands and fighting to get into the lane to dump the ball off to Sasha who is holding court, getting pushed around, and absorbing the blows. Sasha is carrying their offense and is the game's leading scorer with twelve points.

On an offensive possession, Bentley patiently waits for Zo to find a way to lose her defender. Bentley hits her in the hands through a tight window. Zo darts to the basket, changes directions in the air when a post defender appears, and flings up a wild shot that nearly goes in. Zo is the only player whose misses can generate as many astonished gasps as her makes. The Knights hustle back to defend the house, junior-high style, like Gordy taught them. Hayley is the only one who slaps the ground. They all dig in and get more aggressive. Krista rises with her girl and blocks her shot coming down with the ball in her hands. She gets the same crowd reaction as Zo's miss and hides a smile by biting her lip when she heaves an outlet pass to Hayley who manages to get the ball up ahead to Zo, barely whizzing it past her defender. Zo, excited to feel the ball in her hands and believing these rare touches must be fate giving her a gift, slings up another three-pointer. This time she gets nothing but air and hears the crowd chant, "Air ball" all the way back down the court. Zo doesn't react. Even so, she and the Hoover crowd have to be wondering where the magic went from the last game.

On the other end of the floor, Krista makes a hustle play leaving her girl to get in the passing lane. She deflects the ball before it can land in the hands of a Bulldogs player, and Hayley scoops it up. Every Knight player pivots and races back toward their basket, knowing it's a perfect chance for transition points. Hayley throws the ball up ahead to Zo who is already past half court with her defender closing in. It's enough daylight for Zo to make a frantic dash to the basket. With another defender trying to slow her down, Zo doesn't think about the air ball or anything else. She stops on a dime, crosses the ball over, then glides up between two Bulldogs smoothly finger-rolling the ball into the hoop.

On defense, Hoover is doing a good job of pestering the Marion guards, making it hard for them to get off outside shots. What they are allowing is entry passes into their post players. Sasha and Krista are working their tails off down low trying to contain the Bulldogs' quick post players. The matchup between the two teams is evenly poised, and it's apparent to the crowd that it could be anyone's game.

The score is tied up when Krista gets the ball stripped from her and Marion charges down the floor. Bentley races down and shuts off a drive to the basket. The feisty guard, the one assigned to guard Zo, gets her team set up to run a play. She takes a running start and attacks the lane, knocking herself into Bentley then dropping the ball off to her slender center who performs an up-and-under move getting Krista to hack her arm in the process. Krista put her hands to her face, disgusted that she let herself get burned. It's foul number two on her. There is no movement for a substitution from the bench. Mack and Monty are going to stay with their starters until there is no other choice. Marion starts bringing heavy pressure to Hoover's post players on defense, knowing if they can get them in foul trouble they can put themselves at an advantage. With Zo being denied the ball, the Knights can't run their normal plays. It's up to Bentley to try and make something happen. Marion is doing a good job of hounding her too with up-close pressure, and while she has five assists she only has four points, missing a lot of shots around the basket that she would normally make. Marion's half-court defense is the best Hoover has faced all year. They are keeping Bentley and Zo contained while letting Hayley roam freely. They show no concern when she gets the ball. They stay off her, daring her to be the one to beat them. Hayley knows she has to step up and musters up the courage to brave the elements. She takes off dribbling to the middle after receiving the ball on the wing. Getting deep into the lane, Hayley lofts the ball over Marion's towering center and it lands in the outstretched hands of Sasha. She puts it right off the glass and in. On the next possession, the Bulldogs once again leave Hayley on the wing, baiting her to make an outside shot. Hayley hesitates and then lets go a three-pointer that is way off the mark. Marion takes the long rebound and is able to turn it into a fast break layup. Back down on Hoover's side, Bentley has no choice but to pass the ball to Hayley again who is alone and the only open option. She dribbles inside the three-point line, and when there is no movement by any defender to close the gap, she shoots the ball. It floats through the hoop. The Hoover fans and the coaches on the bench exhale. They hope the made basket sparks Hayley into getting more aggressive. It does. She strips her girl on defense when she attempts to drive past her to the basket. The Knights players light up and start a fast break. Sasha sprints like she never has before and gets rewarded with a slick pass from Zo. The Hoover crowd loves seeing their team get a chance to do what they do best. A minute later the horn sounds, putting a pause into the championship game and sending both teams into the locker room to recharge.

"I didn't know you could run that fast, Sasha," Monty says, walking near her in the tunnel. "You were lightning."

Sasha points down. "It's the shoes, Coach."

Monty laughs and shakes his head. Those darn shoes. To him they look like shoes that came straight from the moon.

The coaches wait outside the locker room to let the girls have some time to themselves to unwind. They discuss tweaks they need to make. The team is facing a high turnover count and getting edged out in the rebound battle. Marion's defensive game plan is affecting the Knights, and their shooting woes are alarming. Zo, their leading scorer, has a season low of four points. The coaches are even more concerned about the intensity of the battle. Will the girls be able to refrain from getting frustrated and turning emotional if this comes down to the wire? With a championship on the line, can they stay focused when the team they are facing is absorbing all their punches and giving them blows right back? The Knights usually play with emotion but rarely get emotional. Tonight they are having their buttons pushed by a team that is giving them a taste of their own medicine.

Inside the locker room the girls are on edge. They know they are in a fight like they haven't been in before. Marion is as close to them as any team they have ever gone up against. The way they are playing has their attention.

"Sash," Krista yells.

Sasha looks up from having her head in her towel.

"I'm going to show a double-team to #42." Krista stands and shakes her arms and legs out.

"Yes," replies Sasha with raised eyebrows. "She doesn't like pressure at all."

Krista nods then sits down again and takes a long pull of water.

"How's your ankle, Krista?" Ellie asks.

"Not great, but not bad. I'm good."

"Yo, my girl is about to get a smack down," Bentley calls out, making it sound like a warning to her teammates. She is pacing around the locker room like she's a security guard on duty. "She's going to meet my elbow real quick."

"I could tell you were about to lose it on her," Sasha says. "Keep your cool."

Bentley gives her a pleading look. "She keeps yanking on my jersey. I swear if she does it again…" Bentley balls up both fists.

"At least your guard isn't inches from your face," Zo says. "Mine literally, like, gets her face right in front of mine and follows my every move."

"She looks like your synchronized dance partner," Booster says, "who's possessed."

"She's on me like a rat on a Cheeto." Zo puts her head back on the locker behind her and folds her arms. Zo's natural state is free flowing, no rules, no limits. The Marion Bulldogs have her in a cage. She's discouraged and has yet to accept what the defense is doing. She gets up and joins Bentley in bobbing around the room patrolling the perimeter. Bentley is being tested tonight too; they are running her ragged. Despite the duo's struggles, this is a high-intensity game that is fun to be a part of. Nothing in this game is coming easy, and the two of them like the challenge. The competitive spirit of their opponent is similar to their own, and their reaction is to bring it. They are locked in a battle, and the winner gets all the glory. This is what they play for. They pace and wait for a chance to get back out on the floor.

The coaches walk in, and the players who are up and moving around are ordered to find a seat. Everything they have done this season comes down to the final sixteen minutes between those lines. The coaches look at this team of kids who don't know much about the world yet and hope they can administer some motivation to get them to the finish line victorious. The coaches do know that on that basketball court they are willing to do anything for one another. They go over strategies and adjustments with calmness. The players are anxious to get back out on the floor to be able to put their emotion and energy into action. All of them are standing up by the time Mack and Monty stop talking. They break the huddle with a fierce "together" yell and march back out to the court to go play the second half of a game that, right now, means absolutely everything to them.

CHAPTER 31

The third quarter starts with Marion swishing in a three-point basket. They come out with a rapid burst of enthusiasm and gain the lead. Hoover doesn't have a response to their haymaker. Halfway through the third quarter the Bulldogs are maintaining their momentum. Zo remains ice cold from outside, missing two three-pointers she was able to fire off before her defender could get a hand on the ball. Monty calls a time-out when Marion makes two free throws to go up ten.

With the game trending toward getting away from Hoover, Mack, who has been letting Monty take the lead in the huddle, tosses his clipboard down at the players' feet in frustration and kneels down in front of them. "When in the world did you guys decide you can stop playing tough?" Mack's eyes scan each starter. "They came out to win a title this quarter, and you guys are standing around watching them do it. You're giving them too much room to shoot and giving them too much confidence. Now get up in their shorts and let's go!" Mack pauses then stands up. He put his hands on his hips.

"He's right," Monty says, glancing from player to player. "We have to be more aggressive, ladies. We need to go back to what we've been successful with. They haven't been able to stop Sasha when we get her the ball. Make better entry passes. Krista, they are leaving you open to double Sasha. Go up strong when you get the ball. And Hayley, you have to be more assertive. You stick a couple shots and they will have to play you differently."

The five starters walk onto the court close together. Zo shoves a soft forearm into Sasha's side. "Time to feast, girl. They can't hold you down."

Sasha nods. "Just throw it up high; I'll go get it."

Zo, Bentley, Hayley, and Krista give confident nods to Sasha; her play has been carrying them all night.

Krista sticks her pointer finger out and shakes it. "We turn it around now!"

A snarl comes across Bentley's face as she brings the ball up the court and prepares for the pressure she will be met with. When her defender rushes her she jukes, jives, and drives into the lane. She flips the ball up to the backboard getting off a tough shot that bounces off the rim. Krista is in excellent position for the rebound and takes it up strong for an easy basket. Back on the other end of the court, the Hoover guards get in their shorts like Mack asked them too. The ref blows his whistle calling a foul on Bentley for hand-checking. Both Mack and Bentley spin in frustration hearing the ruling then clap their hands together.

Bentley doesn't let up—it isn't in her nature—and she applies the same pressure, forcing her girl to get rid of the ball. The errant pass gets tipped by Hayley, who grabs the ball and flips it ahead of Bentley who is off to the races. Bentley catches it in stride and elevates for a layup. With the make, the Knights' faithful and anxious crowd come alive with an encouraging roar. The Knights are in comeback mode and they go to work, scoring in a flurry to catch up. Sasha is able to make back-to-back buckets, and then with all the attention on her during the next possession, she throws the ball to a wide-open Hayley on the wing who fires and connects, making a jump shot just inside the three-point line.

Hoover's defense is working hard, and the Bulldogs start to cool off from the outside. The Knights push the ball on offense, hurrying to score and get back in the game. Zo, who is still being face-guarded and denied the ball, manages to grab a long rebound and attacks the rim, throwing up a circus shot that goes in, to the amazement of the crowd. Hoover's fans get to their feet. The Knights have shaken off their sluggish start to the quarter and have come back with a vengeance. They make another stop on defense, and when the buzzer sounds moments later to end the third quarter, the ten-to-zero run Hoover just went on brings the score to 48–48.

In the huddle, the girls catch their breath and brace for the final eight minutes of their season. The coaches do their best to keep their composure. Time is running out. They are locked in a stalemate. One team punches and the other counterpunches. Both teams are laying it all out. Monty stresses defensive stops in the huddle and pleads with them to be ready for another Marion run. The girls are calm in the huddle.

Krista's ankle aches. She ties her shoe tighter. Sasha looks irate, but really she is just focused. She's been phenomenal all night leading the way offensively for Hoover even while being double-teamed. Hayley bops her head up and down. She has gained confidence throughout the game and is determined not to be one of the reasons they lose. When they break the huddle, Hayley asks Gordy if he has any of that magic gum on him. He does and quickly unwraps a piece.

With only six points on the night, Zo hopes Marion will drop their coverage and play her normal. Marion isn't taking any chances, and Zo's shadow meets her at half court. After receiving the inbounds pass, Bentley pauses a moment to scope out Marion's defense. She gives her trademark "I dare you" look to their point guard and starts to run Hoover's offense.

Marion has been playing tough defense tonight. The only exception is inside where they haven't been able to stop Sasha once she gets the ball in her hands. Adding to her double—double of nineteen points and fifteen rebounds—Sasha skies up to grab an overthrown entry pass from Hayley, and with her back to the basket, she performs a fake to her right and goes left to the hoop to score. On defense, Marion sets screens for their two guards, and Hayley gets called for a foul trying to bust through it. On the inbounds play, Krista gets charged with a foul defending a ball screen, sending Marion into a one-and-one bonus. Monty and Mack worry about fouls piling up. They can't afford to lose a starter.

Marion gains the lead, and as the quarter progresses they are the team that is showing more fire power in this heated back-and-forth battle. They are wearing Hoover down with their physical defense, and on offense they are being aggressive. Marion's center scores and gets fouled. She makes the free throw, putting them up seven with three and half minutes left. Monty shakes his head on the sideline. He stands up and calls out for Bentley to run a play. With the amount of gravity Zo is creating on the perimeter, they run a play to get the ball inside to their post players. The possession results in a turnover from a Marion defender deflecting a forced pass to a cutting Krista. Marion scores on their end to go up nine. With time running out Hoover needs points. They can't afford for their offense to stall any longer. Zo gets free off a screen on the wing and drives the ball to the hoop, putting up a contested shot that bounces off the rim. Marion secures the rebound.

Hoover goes down to the opposite end of the court and does what they do when they need to change the momentum. They commit to defense. Hayley deflects a pass into the post. Sasha fights off everyone to get possession of the ball then whips a long baseball pass to Bentley who is already near the Hoover three-point line; she takes it straight to the hoop for a layup. That gives Hoover a spark, and they start rallying by going into a full-court press. Marion is out of sorts and throws the ball away trying to get it into the front court. Hoover works the ball around, and Bentley is able to drive and dish it to Sasha. She fights for positioning and elevates to put the ball off the glass and in to cut Marion's lead to five.

Marion gets the ball past Hoover's full-court pressure and plays keep-away, wanting to take as much time off the clock as possible. Monty jumps up and calls a time-out. He wipes his sweaty palms on his suit pants and starts clapping. The time on the scoreboard keeps ticking off with the score and momentum not on Hoover's side. One minute and forty-seven seconds is all the time they have. With how difficult Marion is making it to get good shots off, the five-point deficit looms large. The coaches kneel in front of starters, and their teammates form a cocoon around them. Monty goes over strategies. Marion has the ball, and Hoover needs it back. It's up to their defense to get a stop. The coaches talk about fouling to stop the clock, knowing Marion will run the clock down if they don't. The intensity is thick in the huddle, yet they all know what they are facing isn't real adversity. It's opportunity. When it's time for the players to go back out on the court, Mack holds up his hand and says, "It's simple. How do you want to end your season? The choice is yours."

"And you have to make it now," Monty adds.

The coaches didn't phrase it like this, but in reality what they really are asking them is "how do you want to be remembered?" There is less than two minutes left in their season. The players don't discuss it. Their minds were made up a long time ago. They walk on the court talking about one thing: they don't want to foul, they want to get the ball back. With their "we're coming for you" swagger, they match up with Marion to guard the inbounds pass that is happening in front of Marion's bench. Marion's point guard jabs at Bentley then throws up her right hand, indicating she wants the pass to come to her. With her left arm she holds Bentley at bay. Her teammate throws in a bounce pass for her to go get, and Bentley slashes in front, betting that she can beat her to it. Bentley wins. The Marion player swats at Bentley's hand attempting to stop her from getting control of the ball. It's too late. Bentley streaks off down the court and gets up an uncontested layup before anyone can catch up to her. When the ball goes up in the air and raindrops through the nylon, the auditorium noise goes to the highest decibel level of the night. Down three, the Knights hustle and get set up to administer their full-court press. Marion manages to get the ball in and Zo bumps into the girl going in for a steal, resulting in a quick whistle. Marion's guard makes two free throws putting them up five again. On offense, Hoover works the ball around and gets it to Sasha in the lane. She makes a move and gets called for a traveling violation. The girls don't show any reaction. They lay on their press with all they have and right away are able to force a Marion turnover. With the ball back under their basket, Zo throws a lob into Sasha on the inbounds. Having to reach back to save it from going over her head, Sasha gets a firm grip on it and squares up. Her point-blank bank shot goes in and sends Hoover's crowd back into a frenzy. Again, Hoover has cut Marion's lead to three.

A minute and five seconds shows on the clock. Hoover sets up with aggression ready to execute the press again. The pressure and their attitude is rattling their opponent. The inbounds pass goes over everyone's head, and Bentley races to reach it then drives straight to the basket. A Marion player steps in front of her trying to cause a charging foul. The noise is so loud from the crowd that Bentley doesn't hear the whistle and keeps proceeding to the basket going up for a layup. A Marion player reaches up to grab the ball and Bentley out of the air. Bentley takes exception to the force she uses and turns to confront the player. Zo steps in and swings Bentley around in the other direction walking her into Hayley, Sasha, and Krista. They calm Bentley down and show faith in each other; this is their game to win. The whistle was for a blocking foul on Marion, and the Knights get the ball under their hoop down three points with a lot of time left on the clock.

Marion calls a time-out. The Hoover players go to the bench hyped up. The coaches do their best to show calmness. It's hard. They have to yell to be heard over the noise and commotion surrounding them. Down three points, they call for their out-of-bounds play that gets Zo the ball on the wing for a chance at a three-pointer. When they break the huddle, Monty and Mack both have remorse. They agree they should have called for the previous inbounds play that got Sasha the ball in front of the hoop. She's the one with the hot hand; Zo hasn't made any of her three-point attempts. With the crowd noise booming and the players getting into their positions, the coaches know it's too late to change the play. The ref hands Zo the ball with fifty-nine seconds left in the game. She brings the ball high over her head to get it over the outstretched arms of her defender who is crowding the out-of-bounds line. Zo lobs it up to Sasha on the wing who is pushed closer to the three-point line than what the play calls for. Sasha's defender gets a hand on the ball and it's tipped in the air going even farther away from the basket. Sasha uses her athleticism and strength to control the ball. Zo steps inbounds, and her defender uses her forearm to make immediate contact. Zo goes toward Sasha and gets the handoff, running her defender right into Sasha who has angled her body to enforce a screen. Zo sees her girl trying to go under the screen to meet her on the other side. Zo shows like she is going to go that way, then takes a side step to the right and launches up a three-pointer. It hangs in the air in slow motion. The ball splashes right through the net, tying the game! Zo and the Hoover fans jump up in the air. Zo races to get in position for the full-court press. She can't stop her momentum and runs right smack into Marion's point guard. The clock stops, and Marion gets a chance to take the lead back at the free-throw line. The whole crowd is into this enthralling ending, and there is a loud buzz in the air. The attendees who aren't on a particular side appreciate the competitive nature of this game.

The Marion guard makes the first free throw in the one and one bonus. The ball bounces off the rim on her second attempt. Krista rebounds the ball and Hoover comes down the court looking to take the lead for the first time this quarter. Once she has the ball in the front court Bentley gets it poked away from her with a reach in from behind. Marion recovers, and their crowd goes wild over the takeaway. Forty-six seconds are on the clock. Bentley, Zo, and Hayley try to set a trap for their guards before they can cross half court. Marion is able to make it across and clings to a one-point lead. They play a game of keep-away with Hoover who is desperately trying to get the ball back. The clock goes all the way down to twenty-four seconds before it's stopped for a foul charged to Hayley with the reach in. It's a good foul; valuable seconds were draining off the clock. Hoover is still alive, even if Marion makes both free throws.

Still in the one-and-one bonus, the Marion player takes an extended amount of time as she prepares to shoot the free throw. The ball comes off her fingers with force, and it ping-pongs around the rim before it falls off the right side of the basket. Sasha jumps up, tipping part of the ball in the air, and Bentley skies to grab it. There are twenty-one seconds left. Down by one point, the Hoover players go down the court with confidence and great purpose; they have what they always wanted, a chance to win it. Bentley brings the ball into the front court and passes it to Zo on the right wing. Zo dances back and forth seeing if she can shake her defender. She's got nothing, and whips a cross-court pass over to a wide-open Hayley. Marion has been playing Hayley loosely all night. Since time is dwindling down and Marion needs just one stop to win a championship, a defender closes out on her. Hayley, on instinct, dribbles to the middle of the lane with her defender all over her. She jump stops, then sends up a pass to Sasha who flashed open. Sasha has to jump to catch the ball around multiple arms and bodies. She comes down with it under the hoop. Twelve seconds left. Sasha doesn't have an angle to take the ball up. Eleven seconds left. She takes two dribbles to get in better position. Nine seconds left. Sasha turns the best she can with two players on her and attempts a shot. One of the Marion defenders leaps up and swings her arm down to prevent the ball from going up to the hoop. A whistle rings out. The force from the strike sends Sasha to the ground. She's slow to get up and puts her hands on her knees. Zo bends down to meet her and throws an arm around her. "You got this." Eight and a half seconds is all the time that remains for everything. Sasha stands up and stretches out her right knee, then makes her way to the free-throw line. Her teammates line up for the free throws and don't say a word to her. Sasha bends her right knee and stretches it out again. The whistle blows. Marion calls their last time-out to try to ice Sasha.

Gathered together at the bench, Monty makes sure Sasha knows he believes she will make the foul shots then goes over hypothetical scenarios. This is it. Everything comes down to right now. They break the huddle with a meaningful "together" yell. The players get lined up for the free throws again. Sasha's teammates feel good with her on the free-throw line with two chances to tie the game or go up one. Even so, none of them can watch her go through with it. The fate of their entire dream is in her hands. They keep their heads down. Sasha spins the ball with her fingertips then dribbles two times, bends her knees low, and shoots her shot. The ball floats in the air... Her teammates peek at the last possible moment to see the ball go through the basket. They release animated emotion, pumping fists at the game being tied. Sasha stays neutral knowing nothing is finished and gets ready for her second foul shot. She goes through the exact same routine and releases the ball. This one is money too; Hoover has a one point lead! With only eight and a half seconds left on the clock, Marion gets the ball in bounds and scurries down the court with the Knights defending the frantic movements with determination. It's a mad dash with the seconds disappearing. Marion's guard throws the ball overhead to her teammate waiting just inside the three-point line for a chance to heave up a shot to win it. Swooping in at the last moment is Bentley who deflects the ball, changing its course. She rushes to get her hands on it, then holds the ball tightly up against her heart, not letting go for anything. The buzzer rings out. The Hoover Knights are state champions! The players run and fling themselves in the air at each other. All of the coaches—Miss Easton, Gordy, Jemma, Monty, and even Mack who had his mended heart tested multiple times tonight—leap in the air. They congratulate each other with hugs. The players skip around exuberantly, hugging, hollering, then diving in the center circle of the court. They get corralled to the side to shake hands with their opponent. It's all respect between the teams. Marion gave everything they had. Sasha offers hugs to the ones who have tears in their eyes. She remembers all too well how coming up short feels. Marion is presented with their runner-up trophy and accepts it with class.

When Hoover gets called out to claim their championship trophy, it's Bentley, Zo, and Sasha who lead the way. Without needing to form a pact or make a promise, or for that matter utter any words to each other, the three of them decided after losing in the title game last season they were going to win a championship. That loss bound them together, and they held each other accountable. It wasn't just a goal, a wish, or a dream to them. It was happening, and they knew they had to be undeniable.

Bentley, with a do-whatever-it-takes attitude, Zo, with her no-fear shots, and Sasha, the center of the team, both figuratively and literally. The three of them grew up together on the court, and now they were hoisting up a state championship trophy.

The three of them shined with the game on the line, yet they didn't do it alone. Their teammates rose up along with them and were at their best. Krista became the reliable teammate who gutted out every possession. Tonight was no different. She needed to do the little things—the dirty work—and she did just that. Hayley stepped up, making key contributions and made the perfect decision on the last play of the game. Neither one of them cowered from the big moments. Ellie was the only sub who saw the floor tonight, relieving Krista for a few minutes in the first half. The bench players would have liked to play more but showed no jealousy or ego. They bought in. You can see it by their faces, the happiness they have for one another as they celebrate together. The Hoover players took responsibility for the success or failure of the team. That's what they were doing after the losses to Chesapeake and on the night of the ring of fire too. They were taking responsibility for everything, their play, their effort, their mistakes, and how the rest of their season would unfold. In doing so, they put the weight all on their shoulders, making sure there would be zero excuses and no second-guessing. Win or lose they were going to hold themselves responsible for the outcome. That's what allowed them to be confident when they found themselves down with time running out.

Hoover departs the court right after the trophy ceremony because there are two more teams ready to vie for a state title in a different class. A microphone and a camera are thrown in Mack's face after he steps off the court.

"It was a total team effort," Mack shouts over the noise. "It was a tough, gritty game, and these girls were somehow able to tap into some extra energy at the end to pull off a win!" Mack gets asked another question and cuts off the reporter: "Go ask the head coach that question." Mack points over to Monty who is still making his way off the court. "Our team was never without a head coach when I was out. I'm extremely happy I was able to make it back and be here." Mack tells the reporters he is feeling great right now. The only issue is his voice; he's losing it. He excuses himself and goes to hug his family.

Monty's face is flushed. "Wow, what a feeling!" He is congratulated by Laney and a slew of other reporters, then gets asked how his team managed to keep their composure and walk away with the championship. "Honestly, I'm going to have to watch the tape. Those last few minutes and then the last few seconds are a blur. It seemed like the longest seconds of my life. I'm not even sure how it played out. We somehow came away with the ball before the buzzer." Laney tells him it was Bentley who made the game-ending steal. Monty beams. "Not surprised one bit it was her. By golly. Unbelievable. Zo was zero for everything, and she hit that three. Then Sasha drains both her free throws to win it. Remarkable. You know Krista played through a bum ankle, and Hayley was scrappy all night. The team stuck together and never quit. All year long they kept working toward this. They needed to elevate their game to win a championship, and that's a lot of pressure. I don't know what else to say."

Another reporter asks about his team's unconventional style. Monty chuckles. "We play a little differently, don't we? I think it shows you don't have to be a certain way to win. You can be who you are and still have success. It's not always easy for me to watch, and we may not be the best team down here, but we may just be the most determined. Sometimes I really think having faith and determination is more important than anything else, and those kids sure did believe."

The players are punch drunk. They spray water on each other and sing "We Are the Champions" in the locker room. Sasha hugs her teammates, taking them airborne. Laney tries to conduct some interviews in the midst of the party. She asks Bentley about being down with under two minutes left and the coaches along with everyone in the crowd calling for them to foul to get the ball back.

"Well," Bentley says, a half smile and half snarl highlighting her face. "We didn't want to foul; we wanted the ball back."

And about her steal that ended the game, she says, "That's my job to mix it up on defense and make something happen."

Zo is asked about the pressure of playing from behind during the fourth quarter and her made three-pointer that tied the game. "We never doubted or panicked. We believed and kept playing. I wasn't hitting my shots, but I have a shooter's mentality, always believing the next one will go in."

Asked what she was thinking before she shot her free throws, Sasha smiles. "Laney, I tried not to think. I just tried to relax. I'm not the best free-throw shooter, but I knew my teammates had confidence in me. Our dream was a championship, and I wasn't going to let them down."

"We the champs!" Krista screams and pours water on Sasha's face. "Just write that, Laney. We the champs!"

Hayley, the youngest, tells Laney about the huddle where the coaches challenged them to make a choice about how they wanted their season to end. "We chose to win," Hayley says, smiling.

Bentley ends her interview with Laney saying, "It's been my dream to win a state championship. To go out my senior year winning it all is super special. I don't want it to end though. I wish we could keep playing. I'm really going to miss hanging out with my friends and just balling."

This team always played like what they had was too good to be true. That somebody could yell cut at any moment and the ball would be taken away from them. They never even thought that time would eventually bring it to an end. When you're going through it, you don't consider it won't exist anymore. Completing the journey becomes the sad part because you love it so much when you're living it. Then it's over. In the end, you could say winning the state championship wasn't really their dream. Their dream was the journey. The chance to chase an epic goal and go through it together. That's why their locker room was almost always joyful. They were celebrating a little bit along the way.

Tonight this team gets to be winners, heroes, and in the moment before they go off to become who they are going to be, they will celebrate together one last time. When they make it back to their hotel, they will go straight to the pool where Mack, Monty, and Gordy will stand at the edge to toast their title team before sailing into the water. The players will jump in after them. They will play and pull in family and friends who gather to celebrate with them. When they arrive back in Hoover tomorrow, the gymnasium will be packed for a welcome home rally. They will be announced in the dark with strobe lights from the drama department lighting up the court. The players will feel like champions. Time will bring everything back to normal in their lives and in their town. The feelings will fade without being forgotten. The players will soon realize that winning a state championship doesn't change your life like they thought it might, and what you're left with is a collection of memories, from all the big moments and the little ones in between.

AUTHOR'S NOTE

While this is a work of fiction, it's inspired by my days of playing high school basketball with my teammates at Sibley-Ocheyedan. Abbi Schutte Wych, Londa Dreesen Brunette, and Amie Hartwig Elser, spending time recalling our greatest hits is something I always cherish. Thanks for reminding me how we rolled back then. There is a little bit of every teammate I played with in this book. It was a joy taking the court with all of you. To get some of you back, all these years later, as friends, means the most. I never intended to base the coaches in my stories off my real life ones, but when I started writing, I couldn't help but think of all of them. During their time together they won two state championships, including one during the six-on-six era. Thank you for the time and commitment you made to our team. I appreciate that you let us make mistakes and grow. Henry Eekhoff, you pushed us to be our best and supported our need to wear baggy shorts. Much love! Vint Bellows, you showed so much patience with our playful ways. Thank you for your humility, easygoingness, and guidance. Marty Wallace, you believed in me, and I'm forever grateful. I appreciate the passion you brought to the court. Lori "Frau" Westhoff, thank you for caring so deeply about all of us. My aunt Julie is no longer with us. If she were, I would tell her how thankful I am that she was there. It wouldn't have been the same without her. Lori Wiser-Dyas, I had no desire to write a sequel, and you were the first to encourage me to do so. I appreciate the advice and your support. Karla Berning Crichton, thanks for your friendship and for bringing the laughs. To the members of the 2023 Sibley-Ocheyedan girls' basketball team, you were living some of this while I was writing. Thanks for sharing your state tournament experience with me and for inspiring me to lace up my high-tops again. Your footprints are in this book. To the people of Sibley, Ocheyedan, and Northwest Iowa, thank you for your support way back when and today. Big ups to my entire family, I love you all. Ireland, you are my favorite dream come true! Gerhard, you let me dream freely, thank you for this and for knowing without ever being told that buying me fresh kicks and throwback jerseys is the way to my heart.

www.ingramcontent.com/pod-product-compliance
Lightning Source LLC
Chambersburg PA
CBHW022151240626
47153CB00007B/2609